FAKE DATING THE DRAGON
MOTHAM CITY MONSTERS
BOOK FOUR

LILITH STONE

FEATHERS & STONE PUBLISHING

Copyright © 2024 by Lilith Stone

All rights reserved.

No part of this book may be reproduced in any form or by any electronic or mechanical means, including information storage and retrieval systems, without written permission from the author, except for the use of brief quotations in a book review.

This is a work of fiction. Names, characters, places, and incidents are products of the author's imagination or are used fictitiously. Any resemblance to actual events, locales, organizations, or persons, living or dead, is entirely coincidental.

Digital ISBN: 978-0-6486484-1-3

Print ISBN: 978-0-6486484-2-0

Editor: Vanessa Lanaway, Red Dot Scribble

Cover design: Mariah Sinclair Cover Designs, https://www.mariahsinclairdesign.com/

Map illustration: Sarah Waites, Illustrated Page Design.

READER SENSITIVITY WARNING

While Fake Dating The Dragon is a sweet and cozy monster romance, with a Happy Ever After guaranteed, please proceed with caution if you are sensitive to the following topics:-

Death of parents and resultant grief, anxiety issues, attempted sexual assault (not by main character), mild violence.

Please also be aware this is a high heat human/non-human romance with explicit on page sex and non-human sex organs. It also contains frequent cussing.

Now that's out of the way, please enjoy Ethan and Minerva's journey into love…

PROLOGUE

"What do you mean they've turned down our proposal?" Ethan felt the scales bristling all the way down his neck as he stared at his team around the boardroom table. "We've spent *months* on this. We've done the full environmental study, the plan for rehabilitation of surrounding areas. There was *nothing* we hadn't considered."

Ethan's chief project officer, Troy, a frill-necked lizard, looked uncomfortable as he shuffled the papers in front of him.

"There's a stumbling block."

"What kind of stumbling block?"

"The—erm—the fact that Blade Wing Air is fully dragon owned."

"Oh, for fuck's sake! We've been transparent about that from the get-go. It was all fine at the last meeting we had with them."

Troy's long forked tongue flicked nervously around his lips. "Yes, but then they made a policy change."

Ethan raked his claws over the scales on his head. "What? When?" His steely gaze swept the assembled team. No one answered him. "Why are you only just telling me this now?"

"We've only just heard ourselves," Ebony, his publicist, explained. "The Tween Council of Towns have moved the goalposts. Which means we'll need to go back and tweak a few things."

"Tweak?"

Ebony wouldn't meet his eyes, lowering her beak over her papers.

"Just spell it out, guys. I really don't have time to beat about the bush," Ethan growled.

"Okay." Ebony fluttered her wings, which she only did when she was at her most uncomfortable. She was usually unflappable, as you'd expect from a raven. "Basically, if you had a human partner, the Council of Towns would look more favorably on the proposal."

This was ridiculous. Ethan shoved back his chair and stood up. "I am not going to enter into a business partnership with a human. Period."

An ominous silence descended on the room.

"We're not talking about a *business* partnership." Troy's neck frill fluffed out and changed to a dark red. And still, not one of the assembled staff would meet Ethan's eyes.

Finally, Ebony said, "The new rules specify that any monster applying to buy human lands must have a *committed personal relationship* with a human…"

A puff of smoke curled out of Ethan's right nostril. "Are you saying I have to magic up a human love interest?"

Troy rubbed his pointed chin. "In a nutshell, yes."

"And exactly how am I supposed to do that in a month?"

Ebony piped up, "Well, obviously we've considered the options, dating apps and the like, but—"

Ethan rolled his eyes. "We don't have fucking time for that."

"Exactly. So we did some further research."

"And…? Just spit it out."

"There is one service in Motham City that might be able to help," Ebony said, tapping her pen against her beak.

Ethan curled his fists. Why did this deal suddenly seem like it was jinxed? "Details on my desk in five minutes," he snarled as he stormed toward the door, "or all your asses are on fire."

CHAPTER 1

When the little brass bell outside the bookshop tinkled, Min was kneeling behind the desk sorting through a box of books. She poked her head over the counter to see a woman enter wearing the most beautiful iridescent blue coat, her white hair styled in an elegant French plait.

Min jumped to her feet. "Can I help you?"

"I'm looking for the business section," the woman said.

"Anything in particular?"

"Contract law."

"Third row to the left," Min said. "Call me if you need anything."

"I most certainly will." The woman gave her a charming smile before making her way briskly down the rows of books.

That coat is like a peacock, Min thought as she went back to sorting books. She was soon engrossed. The box was from a centaur's house clearance. She noted down the titles on a pad of paper: *Before the Great War*, *A History of Forest Dwellers*, and *Hoof Power: Run Better, Run Faster*. She guessed that one was for the likes of minotaurs, centaurs, and fauns.

The bell tinkled again. Another customer. Two on a

Monday morning was a rare occurrence. Min got to her feet, smiling and pushing her glasses up her nose.

Her heart sank.

It wasn't a customer at all.

It was Quentin Jordak.

His appearance usually spelled a rent rise, which meant parting with money she didn't have. "Hello, Quentin," she said stiffly.

His pale gray eyes skimmed down her body, pausing a fraction too long on the swell of her breasts. Min pulled her cardigan tightly around herself.

"Hello Minerva." He always addressed her by her full name. Even though he was probably only a couple of years older than her, Quentin was one of those guys who seemed old before his time. Tween high-breed humans were like that. A little bit stuffy, and somewhat boring. And even though Min ostensibly came from a high-breed family herself, her upbringing had been anything but.

She really had nothing in common with high breeds.

She took a deep breath and planted her hands on the desk. "What can I do for you, Quentin?"

Quentin adjusted his blue silk tie with slender white fingers. "I need to discuss some changes regarding your lease."

Min stifled a sigh. "Let me guess. Another rent hike?"

"Not exactly," Quentin said. "Your lease is getting close to its renewal date."

Min tried not to look surprised. "I thought there was another year before that was due."

"There was. But the terms have changed." Quentin brought out a paper from his official-looking briefcase and handed it across the counter. As she took it, his fingers slid over hers, and lingered a moment longer than necessary.

Quickly, Min withdrew her hand. It wasn't the first time she'd sensed Quentin had less than professional intentions toward her. The lingering looks he cast over her body, the way he would lick his lips as his eyes strayed to her breasts — it made her uncomfortable.

She usually wore jeans and baggy t-shirts. Unfortunately, today's tee had shrunk in the wash and her breasts tugged at the tight material. If she'd known he was going to turn up she would have found something baggier to wear.

Like a sack.

Focus, Min.

She stared down at the piece of paper in her hands. There was a lot of legal jargon she had no hope of understanding, but the address on the top of the document was unmistakably the right one: the Westerly Bookshop, Lot 305 Motham Perimeter Road. Below that were the words "Lease Termination."

Min's eyes widened. "Perhaps you could explain this to me in more detail."

Quentin smirked. "Of course. Shall we go into your office?"

Min's chest tightened. Sure, she needed to understand this, but no way did she want to be alone with Quentin. "There's a customer in the shop at present. Let's sit in the nook."

Quentin nodded. When she circled the desk, his eyes did a once-over of her body. Her jeans weren't even tight fitting, but that look made her feel like she was parading around in her underwear.

Min stifled a little shudder as she led the way.

The reading nook was nestled into the front of the shop, in the curve of the bay window, where it always caught the warmth of the sun. Gingerbread, Min's cat, was asleep on one of the comfy wing-backed chairs. He opened a lazy yellow eye, fixed it on Quentin, and immediately all the hairs on the back of his neck bristled. With a small hiss, he got up, jumped off the chair and stalked off.

Min guessed Gingerbread didn't like Quentin either.

Once they were both seated, she looked over the paperwork again, trying not to let her panic show. "Why is the lease terminating?" she said finally.

Quentin gave a little shrug. "I guess with the death of your father last year, the Council felt..." He hesitated.

"What? That I couldn't run the shop on my own?"

"Not at all. Just that this was an opportune time to put the property on the market."

Min's eyes widened behind her glasses. "The market. You mean sell it?"

Quentin fidgeted. "You are, of course, welcome—encouraged, even—to put in a bid. And you have a month to consider whether you want to."

"A month?" she parroted. It was all she could say with the numb disbelief pervading her body.

"I'm sure with you being the last of the Westwind family, your offer will be looked on favorably. But we do have to be fair and competitive." Quentin sat back in the chair, steepling his fingers. "The lands close to Motham are much more sought after than when your father first signed this lease, Minerva. You could say it's prime real estate these days."

She gave a bitter little laugh at that. "I never thought I'd hear someone from Tween say the Motham Perimeter was prime real estate."

He shook his head. "Personally," he glanced out the window, "I wouldn't call it that in a million years, but..."

Min followed his gaze. Past the pretty garden of the shop, the rubble of Motham's city wall was clearly visible from here. The big boulders had been left where they fell more than a decade ago, forming a gaping hole between monster and human worlds. The part of the city behind the rubble was now imaginatively called The Hole In The Wall District, a conglomeration of shops and offices, a few modern high-rises, but mostly a hotch-potch of monster architecture. It was the spot where humans and monsters now traded openly, and the hole had certainly made the bookshop more accessible to monster customers in recent years. Even so, it wasn't a profitable enterprise. Far from it.

Min tried to gather her scattered thoughts. She'd always envisaged growing old here, becoming an eccentric spinster with Gingerbread and a string of other cats for company. But now... what?

She'd be homeless in a month, unless she could come up with the finances. Her father's bookshop and everything he'd worked for would be gone.

"I'm sorry, Minerva," Quentin said, sounding more smug than sorry. "Please believe me, I did fight for you to have extra time to work this out. But the Council were adamant. They don't want to tie up the land for any longer."

"I see." Min tried to stop her hands from trembling. She wanted to tear the document into shreds, scream, chase Quentin out of the shop like a mad banshee, but of course she wouldn't.

She wouldn't let this smug high-breed human know he'd got to her, even though her heart was about to crack into pieces. Because the Westerly Bookshop was much more than a business. It was her home. She'd been born here and lived above the shop with her father since her mom died when she was a baby. She'd played here, studied here, worked here all her life.

Following her father's tragic death in a car accident last year, Min had assuaged her grief by pouring more love into The Westerly. Refining the shop's set-up, with clearer categories, giving it a lick of new paint and spending time in the garden, making it as pretty as she could, imagining her dad looking over her. She'd had only Gingerbread for company, and her friend Bonnie, a gorgon, who helped out in the shop from time to time.

Sensing Quentin's gaze boring into her, she tried to keep her face expressionless as her mind whirred. She had a dwindling trust fund from the Westwind family, which helped keep the shop afloat, and topped up the rent, because the Westerly didn't make anything resembling a profit. Her father had died almost penniless, having spent what was left of his inheritance on maintaining the shop and donating money to monster causes.

Face it Min, you are flat broke.

Quentin's words jerked her out of her thoughts. "I'm sure your offer would be looked upon favorably by the Council."

"Even though my father tarnished the family name?"

He smirked. "Nothing could tarnish the Westwind name, Minerva."

Was she supposed to be grateful that Tween folks tolerated her father's eccentric ways because of the supposedly heroic deeds of her ancestor?

Pull yourself together, Min. "Thank you, Quentin. I will go over the paperwork and get back to you, very shortly." She stood, desperate for him to leave so she could process all this. Alone.

Or at least, she would be after the woman in the peacock coat left.

Quentin's gaze roamed from her hips to her waist and then her breasts, before finally reaching her face. His tongue flicked over his lips and his pale eyes gleamed.

As he got up, he took a step toward her. "If there's anything I can do to help, just call me, Minerva."

Min smiled tightly and stepped back. "Thank you, Quentin, I'll bear that in mind. Now, I must get back to work, I have a customer who may need assistance."

Turning on her heels, she moved briskly toward the desk and slipped behind it. She waved with false cheer as Quentin strolled to the door.

After he'd gone, Min leaned against the counter, feeling dizzy. How did you deal with being told that you were going to lose your livelihood and your home, all in the space of ten minutes?

Her gaze swept helplessly around the cozy little shop, taking in the floor-to-ceiling shelves crammed full of books, the crooked beamed ceiling, the windows set deep into the ancient Malilbar stone walls with their leaded glass panes.

There was no denying it: the Westerly Bookshop was a strange and unique place.

It stood completely alone, a three-story ramshackle building on the road that connected the human towns to Motham City. Not much grew around here except gorse bushes and heather. But somehow when they'd first arrived here, Min's parents had managed to cultivate a garden around the shop, a little oasis in this barren land. As for the building itself, it was rumored to date back to The Great War. The story went that it was set up as a hospital by an entrepreneurial mage to remove monster curses from humans before returning them home to the towns of Tween and Twill.

Yes, altogether a very odd place to set up shop—*any* shop, let alone a bookshop that sold mostly books written by and for monsters.

But then, her father had always been a maverick.

A rule breaker, one who was fascinated by monster history and literature and determined to help monsters gain an education.

Except now it seemed his legacy would be gone. A great big lump formed in Min's throat, and tears pricked her eyelids.

The sudden thud of books on the counter made her swallow back her tears.

She looked up to see the beautiful white-haired woman standing beside a pile of books.

Min took a deep breath and forced a smile. "You found what you needed?"

"I did indeed, thank you."

Min busied herself tallying the price, wrapping the books in brown paper, and tying the parcel with string. Just for something to say, she asked, "Are you a lawyer?"

"No. But my line of work requires a good knowledge of the law."

"What do you do?" Min asked. At least focusing on another person would help her to get her emotions under control.

"I'm a business consultant. A procurer of sorts."

"That sounds painful." Min let out a brittle laugh and winced. The quirky Westwind sense of humor often came out at inopportune moments.

The woman replied, "On the contrary, it's very rewarding." Then she leaned across the counter toward Min. "I couldn't help overhearing your conversation with the gentleman earlier. He's a Tween Council of Towns official, yes?"

Min's eyes flew to her companion's bright green ones. Was she human? She looked it, and yet... there was something about her radiant skin, the prisms of light that sparked from her eyes. The pure white of her hair, and that amazing coat.

"I got the sense," the woman said quietly, "that the terms of sale were not to your liking." Min's mouth fell open. How could she possibly know?

"I—oh, no, I never said that."

"You didn't need to my dear, your energy went all wobbly." The woman smiled kindly. "If I may make so bold, I am in the perfect position to assist you."

Min stiffened. "Thank you, but I was taught never to borrow money."

The woman laughed gently. "I don't lend money, my dear, but I do put people in touch with benefactors."

Min focused on the parcel of books, knotting the string with care.

Snapping open her sparkly purse, the woman withdrew a business card and handed it across the counter.

Min took it and read

Adina Thrimble
Midas Touch Partnerships

The peacock-blue lettering sparkled, just like Adina's coat.

"What exactly do Midas Touch Partnerships do?" Min tried to sound casual, putting the card down on the desk and handing over the books.

Adina looked admiringly at the parcel. "Beautifully wrapped," she murmured. "I assist humans and monsters to form mutually beneficial business arrangements. You need to find a lot of money fast, am I right? Money that you don't have."

"I—oh—" Min faltered.

Adina's eyes sparkled like emeralds. "Perhaps you will let me explain? Shall we sit for a moment?"

What have I got to lose?

For the second time that morning, Min found herself taking a visitor into the nook. The woman sat in the chair opposite Min and placed her parcel of books on the floor next to her. Suddenly, Gingerbread appeared as if from nowhere, and jumped straight onto her lap.

Adina laughed softly as she stroked the cat's thick pelt.

"What's his name?"

"Gingerbread."

"He's a discerning feline," Adina murmured as Gingerbread started to turbo purr.

Min blinked behind her glasses. Gingerbread was usually wary of strangers. He was also a very good judge of character. A little seed of hope lodged in her chest. Maybe this beautiful woman could be trusted after all. "Please tell me more."

"You may be aware that it is not easy for monsters to develop business interests outside of Motham," Adina said.

Min nodded. It was something her father had always advocated for. As a supporter of monsters, he had believed they should be able to trade openly outside the city walls. It was no mistake that he'd set up the Westerly Bookshop on the edge of Motham, in a bid to help monsters read more, study more, and understand their rights.

Adina continued. "There was a rather unfortunate event a while back—hushed up—where a vampire was allowed to buy land without the proper checks and balances put in place. It all ended very unpleasantly. Since then, the Council of Towns have been far more cautious about selling land to monsters. But here's the rub, my dear. They need monsters' money. They are desperately short of coin. So they've come up with a solution: if a monster has a human partner, they will be allowed to buy land in the Valley."

Min had heard of such a case, quite recently in fact, involving an orc and a realtor in Motham. They'd bought up an island off the coast. She'd read about their wedding only recently in *Motham Monthly*.

"Currently I have a very wealthy client on my books, looking to partner with a human." Adina said.

Min frowned. "How do you mean, 'partner?'"

"Form a business alliance."

"You're saying they'd want to buy the bookshop? I really don't think—" The Westerly ran at a shocking loss. No monster in their right mind would invest in it.

"It's not the bookshop they want, my dear. It's your name. Despite your father's *eccentricities*, shall we say, the Westwind name still carries clout."

Min guessed that was true. During The Great War two hundred years ago, Colonel Westwind had brought the monsters to their knees. He'd orchestrated the building of the wall around Motham, imprisoned them all inside and hoped they'd fight each other to the death. While of course, that hadn't happened, the name Westwind was still revered among high-breed humans.

Still, she struggled to see the logic. "How would my name benefit them?"

"If you were in a... relationship with said monster, then their application to buy land to the north of Motham would be looked on favorably."

Min's spine stiffened. "So you're proposing a—a *personal* relationship?"

"Only on paper."

"But still, a relationship..."

"A *fake* relationship."

"How long for?" Min's voice went up an octave.

"A month, two at the very most. Just long enough to get the deal through the Council. After that, you can take the money and run. With the sum my client is prepared to pay, you'll be able to buy this little patch of land and have plenty spare to keep it running."

Min couldn't help but perk up. Adina was right, this had the potential to solve all her problems. She looked at Gingerbread, happily curled up on Adina's lap. It almost felt like serendipity.

Still, her cautious nature knew there was more to consider. "May I ask... who is this... monster?"

"A very successful business owner with a large enterprise in Motham. I would prefer to say nothing more in case word spreads—not that I don't trust you, my dear, but walls have ears. I will courier you the details later today."

"Could you at least tell me his species?" It wasn't that she had any prejudices—Min mixed with all kinds of monsters here in the shop. But still, it would be good to know.

"He's dragon."

A dragon. Min felt her pulse speed up. She'd had a fascination with dragon kind since childhood. Something bubbled up inside her whenever she found a book on them. Which didn't happen often — books on dragons were the rarest kind. "I see. And when will you require a decision?"

"By tomorrow. Or I will have to consider other options for my client."

Min sighed. Her morning so far had been full of shocking revelations — and ultimatums.

She nodded. "I will await the paperwork then. And let you know by tomorrow."

"Thank you. You will not be disappointed if you choose to accept." Adina looked down and gave a rueful smile at the cat, still curled up on her lap. "He's asleep."

"I'm so sorry. He's never done this before."

"It's not a problem. I adore cats," Adina said. "But you may wish to remove him. Gently."

With a little smile, Min bent over and scooped Gingerbread off Adina's lap. Giving a small mewl of complaint, he nestled limp as a baby against her shoulder.

Anyone would think this woman was a cat-whisperer. Or maybe her beautiful peacock coat was like catnip.

Adina stood and, picking up her bundle of books and her glittery purse, sashayed toward the door.

"Lovely little bookshop." She glanced around before she left. "It would be such a shame to lose it."

CHAPTER 2

The wailing sound echoed down the stairwell of the Blade mansion as Ethan strode through the front door. He braced himself.

Mother was having another of her turns. And he'd just had the worst fucking day at the office.

But as the eldest of the two Blade sons, the only responsible, sensible one at that, it was his job to calm her down.

Grimacing, he shoved his fists into his pockets as he made his way up the ornate staircase, taking the steps two at a time, then strode down the corridor to her room.

She lay limply on the bed, in her fancy clothes—why she wore so much lace, he had no idea; it was highly flammable—one silver stiletto kicked off, panting and breathing billows of smoke. When she wailed again, a little puff of fire licked out of one nostril.

Gods, she'd set the bed cover on fire if she went on like this.

"Mom, sshh, all the staff will hear you."

"I don't care. Oh, Ethan." Her features crumpled. "It didn't work."

He tried not to roll his eyes. Honestly, he tried to be

caring, sympathetic, he really did, but his mom's "turns" had gone on for as long as he could remember, and had gotten worse since their father died. She leaned on him, relied on him to fill his father's shoes. Sometimes it wore a bit thin.

But he did his best. He goddamn ran the whole of Blade Wing Air, had major plans to extend, to build a new airport, just as Dad has planned to, but sometimes the burden on his shoulders felt too much.

"Mom, you're hyperventilating." He sat down gingerly on the bed and handed her a heatproof handkerchief. "Here, use this, at least it won't ignite," he said. "Now, let's practice your breathing exercise, shall we?"

As if she hadn't heard him, she grabbed his arm, her claws digging in, and big tears pooled in her golden eyes. "They promised the treatment would make me shift. But I lay there and lay there and still... I'm *this*." She swept a hand down her body with a grimace of despair.

"Mom, you're beautiful," Ethan countered.

"I'm a twilight dragon, Ethan," she snapped. "I can't transform, I can't take human form."

"You have *some* human parts, Mom."

"Yes, my farcical body has human legs and arms, and then I have a tail and... scales, and I keep setting fire to furnishings at social gatherings if I get too animated. It's so embarrassing."

A puff of smoke swirled out of one of Ethan's nostrils. "See, Mom? I suffer the same problem."

"Of course you do, you're my son!" Cressida wailed. "And... and my eyelids..." She burst into paroxysms of tears, sobbing into the heatproof handkerchief.

Ethan sought to find the right words. "It's just a matter of perspective, Mom. Your eyes are beautiful." He gentled. His mother *was* beautiful. She was just... dragon. A non-shifting dragon. And you couldn't get away from that fact.

None of them could.

It was said that centuries ago, dragons could shift with ease, from dragon into human form. But something had gone wrong before The Great War. Maybe dragons exhausted their shifting capacity while fighting the humans. Maybe a malicious spell had been cast by a mage. Whatever the cause, their shifting had weakened and finally ground to a halt, leaving dragons in a kind of limbo state. Not fully dragon, but not able to take on human form either.

Stuck. With dragon skin and scales, smaller wings than the original dragons and a forked tail. They had legs and arms like humans, a curved spine like a human, but then there were those small scales running up and down their vertebra, remnants of their dragon heritage.

They had hands and feet very similar to humans, but with sharp claws on their fingers and toes.

And eyelids that blinked sideways.

And nostrils that breathed fire.

Modern dragons were a bit of a mishmash, to be honest.

But other species had gotten used to them this way.

Except humans. Humans found them kind of... off-putting. Scary even.

And that was a major stumbling block. Being stuck in half-shift mode had limited their capacity for success as a species. Twilight dragons, they'd been nicknamed. Some of their kind had fallen into petty theft, living in dens on the tip and in the Wasteland to the north of the city with loot they'd pilfered on night flights.

Thankfully, that had not been the Blade family's fate. They'd poured their skills and intelligence into aviation. Powering the skies.

The Blade clan dragons had helped Atholrose Motham— their mothman leader after The Great War—to build Motham City. Later, Ethan's grandfather had invented the first airplanes. His father took that further, adding hover crafts and building the airport in the east quarter of Motham, and now—

well, Ethan liked to think the Blades ruled the skies like kraken ruled the seas.

And they'd made money. Copious amounts of money. His father had capitalized on the changes happening in Motham these past few decades, grabbed the opportunities.

But then he'd died, four years ago in a freak accident.

The love of Mom's life. Gone.

Cressida had never been emotionally stable. She was beautiful, vivacious, and charming, but also very highly strung, an offspring from the only other well-to-do clan of dragons in Motham, the Delawares. She'd borne her husband only two dragonlings, distraught that she'd laid eggs instead of birthing her children like a mammal. She'd never let her sons forget how few of her eggs had resulted in hatchlings, telling them how she'd nurtured them, sat on those eggs at risk of her pelvic girdle collapsing. Breastfed them until they were a few years old.

Dad had shielded the two Blade boys from her anxious nature. But as the eldest of her sons, it was Ethan's job to look after her now that their father was dead.

So he sat down on the edge of the bed, took her hand, and held it, and waited, trying not to let his own anxiety peak. That was the problem. He had some of Mom's issues. He tried to keep it under wraps, but at times like this he could feel his breathing growing fast and shallow. Had to fight the urge to set things alight, just to ease the tension inside his chest.

Ye gods, as head of an aviation corporation, you couldn't do that.

Mom was hiccupping now, her tears and swirls of smoke slowing. "Do you know how much I paid for that therapy, Ethan?" she whispered.

"Mom, it's okay, don't worry about the money, it's just… I wish you'd stop putting your faith in quackery."

"They promised results," Cressida whispered hoarsely.

"Lots of folks promise lots of things, Mom. Promising is the easy part. It's delivering that's hard."

Gods, didn't he know that? Just like his issue now with the human Council of Towns. How easily they'd dragged the rug from under him, showing no regard for how long he'd been working on those airport plans. He patted her hand, smoothed the green skin, soft and warm. That was something dragons seemed to have inherited from their shifting past: blood that was warm, and soft skin. People didn't often realize this about dragon skin. Even their scales were surprisingly soft to the touch.

Until a dragon got riled or angry. Then they hardened.

But right now, Mom was limp and tired, and her skin was like velvet. He kept patting her hand rhythmically until he sensed her breathing slowing.

"I have some news to cheer you up," he said, and she eyed him hopefully.

Ethan took a deep breath. He hated lying to her, but he hated her being unhappy more.

"I'm seeing a human." Gods, he hadn't even met her yet. Adina had simply mentioned that she'd found him a suitable match.

Cressida sat upright, all her scales spiking. "As in, dating?"

He gulped, then nodded, wishing he hadn't brought it up.

"Oh, my oh my oh my. Ethan. Truly. You're dating a human?" He nodded again, and she clasped her hands to her ample chest. "Oh, my goddess, there's hope for our race. Oh, Ethan, you realize if... if..."

"Mom, stop jumping the gun please. It's very early days. But if our relationship does progress, then... we will have a lot better chance of fulfilling Dad's dream to build the new airport on human lands."

"And reviving shifting again. With your hatchlings."

Ethan cringed inwardly. "Mom, that is just hearsay—rumor. Let's stay with the facts, shall we?"

Yeah, the fact you are lying through your fangs.

By now Cressida was bouncing on the bed. "Oh darling, I am so happy for you. I must meet her—very soon, I hope? Let me plan a party. Dinner? Whatever. Oh, my green goddess I am so excited. Is she pretty?"

Ethan couldn't say, because he had no freakin' idea. Nor did he really care. His mother's superficiality as far as pretty things went was so dragon. He'd escaped the worst of it. He didn't hoard, didn't get taken in by glitter and glitz. He had a small box of precious things in his study, but his only piece of bling was an antique, jewel-encrusted dragon egg that his parents had given him on his twenty-first birthday.

But for the sake of a quiet life, he hoped this human was at least passable looking.

"Well, it's early days, but the chemistry between us is..." *May the good gods forgive him.* "Is definitely strong.'

"Oh darling. If you have half the love your father and I had..."

"Yes—well." Ethan smirked tightly and stood, trying to close the gate on his mom's enthusiasm. "I will keep you informed."

His mother sprawled back on the pillows, hugging herself, a huge smile showing off her pearly white fangs. "Darling boy, you have made your mama so happy. Now, I must rest. I'm exhausted."

Just at that moment a pounding bass beat started up somewhere in the house and his mother's whole body went rigid. She let out a plaintive whine. "Oh goodness, Beau's playing that awful rap music again. Please tell him to stop, it gives me such a headache."

Ethan sighed. "Yes, Mother."

"And Ethan, ask Mrs Green to send up one of my special

soothing teas. And a fruit scone. No, make that two, with lashings of butter and strawberry jam."

"Yes, Mother."

Stalking out of the room, he made his way down the corridor toward the sound of the music. By the time he got to the door it was literally vibrating in its frame.

He knocked.

There was no answer. Ethan pounded harder and then after another moment, exasperated, he shoved the door open with his shoulder.

Striding over to the flashing electronic bar on the wall, he turned down the music and looked around for Beau in the messy den. He finally located him posturing in front of the mirror in a leather jacket.

And—Gods be damned, he was *fucking smoking*.

"Put that thing out." Ethan went and yanked the cigarette out of his brother's mouth. "You breathe enough fire as it is, you don't need to add this shit into the mix."

Beau raised a lazy eyebrow. Eleven years younger than Ethan, he was ridiculously cool and good looking, the kind of cool Ethan secretly envied—admired, even, though he'd never tell Beau that. Gods forbid the kid's head should swell even bigger.

"You'll mess up your lungs."

Beau gave him a glare out of bright golden eyes, just like their mom's. "I don't give a fuck about my lungs."

He strolled over and took another cigarette from the pack on his dresser. With an angry growl, Ethan grabbed the pack and shredded them in his claws, then dropped them in the bin.

"You want to add to your mother's anxiety? Selfish little shit."

Beau shot two sharp flames at him, and the heat licked onto Ethan's neck. It was tempting to respond in kind, but he held back. They didn't need to get into a fight; he'd ruined more than a few of his designer shirts that way in the past.

Besides, he was more than a decade older. He knew better.

He stepped back. "I repeat, you're making Mom's anxiety worse."

"Dad dying did that. I'm not wearing that guilt shit. You do it well enough for both of us." Beau picked up a wire brush from the dresser and passed it over his scales.

"Where are you going?"

"Out."

"Where?"

"Just somewhere."

"Haven't you got classes tomorrow?"

"Yeah, so? I perform better with a hangover."

Ethan let out an exasperated growl. "Be back before eleven. And if you buy any more cigarettes, I'll install smoke detectors."

Beau guffawed loudly at that. "Bro, stop trying to play Dad. You'll never fill his shoes. You're too fucking tame."

Ethan balled his fists at his sides, tempted to rip his little brother a new one.

"I've got better things to do with my life than toe the Blade line," Beau sneered, and with that he flung open the balcony windows, jumped onto the balustrade and took off, his wings soaring and his tail snapping behind him.

Ethan gritted his teeth and swore under his breath. His brother was a thorn in his side, always had been. The pretty dragonling his mother adored. The handsome bad boy who was allowed to get away with anything, while he, Ethan, was the sensible one. No, damn it, he wasn't tame, but he did have a deep sense of duty. He was ordered, meticulous, cautious in his dealings.

He'd done okay.

Until now. Suddenly his father's dreams to expand the aviation business past Motham's boundaries, had stalled dramatically.

Simply, it seemed, because Ethan was a dragon.

Maybe if he could shift, take on human form... *shut up, you're sounding just like Mom.*

He pulled himself together. Glanced in the mirror and straightened his spine. He was good-looking enough, not the bad boy cute of his brother, but presentable in his own way. He had a good strong body, his eyes were striking, his bone structure strong. He'd had girlfriends—plenty. There was always a queue for dragon dick, let's be honest.

But never, ever a human.

Truth was, he hadn't even tried to date one. Because humans wouldn't consider a dragon for their mate, particularly one who couldn't shift. There was too much blood under the bridge between dragons and humans even if it wasn't fully understood, or even spoken about in recent times.

But now, everything—fucking *everything*: his mom's happiness, his self-respect, fulfilling his duty to his dad—all rested on him having a human girlfriend.

Fake human girlfriend, he reminded himself.

As Ethan closed the door on his brother's debauched den and strode toward his own apartment on the other side of the house, he sure hoped that Adina Thrimble could deliver.

CHAPTER 3

"A package for Miss Minerva Westwind. I was told to deliver it straight into her hands." The courier, a troll by the look of his stocky build, even though he still had his bike helmet on, stood at the counter eyeing her closely.

"I am Minerva Westwind," Min replied.

"ID please."

"Sure, of course."

Adina was clearly taking this whole process very seriously. Min ducked behind the counter and took out her purse, then showed her ID card.

The troll grunted. "Sign here."

She signed the paper he handed her and in return, he handed over the thick envelope.

As he turned to leave, he glanced down the rows of bookshelves that stretched toward the back of the shop. "Got a career section?"

"Absolutely. You're a troll, aren't you?"

"Yep."

"There's a whole shelf devoted to trolls. Why don't you have a browse?"

He grunted again. "Can't, too many deliveries. But I'll come back another day maybe."

"Please do."

His taciturn face brightened behind his visor, big yellow troll teeth and tufts of coarse red beard visible as he flashed her a grin. "Cool."

"And thank you," she said. "For delivering this."

He responded with another grunt. She knew most monster kind didn't take compliments well, but it was important to always *acknowledge* them. Monsters had spent too long being vilified by humans. Her father had taught her to always go out of her way to make them feel comfortable in the shop. Monsters being allowed to openly read books was something that had only really come about since the Hole In The Wall happened. Before that, they would open the Westerly under cover of darkness to allow monsters to visit in secret.

She watched the troll speed off toward Motham on his bike, then she went and locked the doors, put the *back in five minutes* sign up and went to her office at the back of the shop. With shaking fingers, she ripped open the envelope and took out the file.

A very swish folder met her eyes.

The first thing she noticed was the name on the front, and the photograph, neatly framed as if in a cameo, with gold filigree around it. Very posh and professional.

PRIVATE AND CONFIDENTIAL
Introducing Mr Ethan Blade

Oh. Gosh—she'd heard of this guy, hadn't she? Of course she had. Everyone with money in Motham used Blade Wing hover cabs. Then there was Blade Wing light air for short jaunts and Blade Wing jets for longer trips across the mountain (not that she'd ever been, of course). Min peered closer at the photo.

He had a lean strong jaw, neat horns sprouting from the sides of his skull, piercing blue wide-set eyes and a broad brow. His head was covered in neat scales, and he was smiling, showing off a line of perfect white fangs. And going by what she could see of him—it was only a head and shoulders photo—he was of a broad build, with just a hint of his neatly furled wings showing behind his back.

She turned the page and read his profile:

Ethan is Managing Director of Blade Wing Air. The company services all aviation needs in Motham, owns Motham airport, and the police and militia aircraft. He has plans to extend his operations outside of Motham City and thus needs to partner with an eligible human in order to purchase lands in human territory.

Personal history: Single. Ethan's father died four years ago. Since then, Ethan has been heading up the company. He currently resides in the family home in the salubrious area of Motham Hill with his mother and younger brother.

Mr Blade's interests include keeping fit, reading and playing the piano.

He describes himself as serious, hard-working, something of a workaholic, conscientious, honest, and family-minded. He likes to look after his health and believes he has a good sense of humor once he is comfortable in a person's company. Due to his single status, there are no complication or impediments.

Min's eyes scanned lower and then widened.

. . .

Mr Blade will offer the following terms.

1–2 months of an intimate relationship—on paper only—which will involve the following:

Mixing publicly at events and one-on-one dinners.

Interviews with media as required.

Being photographed together, and these pictures being shared with media outlets as required.

A committed relationship must look authentic to the public, and particularly the Tween Council of Towns and the Land Department, thus some small shows of public affection are expected and will be agreed upon between both parties.

Finally, her gaze scanned to the financial incentive and her eyes nearly fell out of her head.

The proposed sum was for a period of one month, to be renewed at the same monthly or pro-rata rate.

Three hundred thousand Motham dollars.

Three hundred thousand Motham dollars! For a month of fake dating a dragon. The bookshop here, the land around it, that would surely be worth no more than half of that at the most, leaving her with a hefty sum to continue running the shop. To upgrade it, even.

Min sat blinking at the page until the numbers jiggled in front of her eyes.

Could she do this?

Could she pretend to be in love with a dragon?

She'd never had to pretend anything in her life. But then... with a dragon... maybe it wouldn't be so difficult. After all, she'd always been fascinated by dragon kind, even though there was so little written about them. "It's perplexing," her father had told her once, "that I can't find a more comprehensive history of dragons. A pity, really, because rumor suggests a closely intertwined relationship with humans in the distant past."

Now she picked up one of the only two books she owned on dragons, which she'd read and re-read since Adina's visit. It was titled *Dragons Since the Great War: A Brief History.*

She turned the pages. As history books went, this one was sketchy, authored by a human, not a dragon, but it did have nice illustrations. She'd studied it often enough, but re-reading it now, it suddenly seemed far more pertinent.

While early dragon/human relationships were believed to be harmonious, with shifter dragons fighting alongside humans to ward off aggressive ogre hordes, it is understood that a souring of relations occurred in the lead-up to The Great War. Shifting powers in dragons faded, and eventually they froze into their current dragon form.

There is no adequate explanation for why dragon kind lost their ability to shift. Or why they now retain mixed human/dragon characteristics. Certainly, dragons became more wary of humans in the tumultuous period leading up to The Great War, and it is rumored that as punishment, humans got powerful mages to cast spells on dragon kind to weaken their shifting powers.

Unfortunately, no texts have survived to support or refute these stories.

Min sighed. If her father hadn't found any more books on dragon history, they probably no longer existed.

She returned to reading.

Modern day dragons: Two strains of dragons now live in Motham: the ferals and the aviators.

The ferals are a smaller, wily, gray-green species with sharp claws. There is believed to have been cross-breeding with other lizard species that accounts for their different characteristics.

The second strain, the Motham aviators, are broad and well-built with strongly humanoid characteristics to their frame, including their legs, arms and torso. They retain the scales and facial features of dragons. This species is directly descended from two dragon clans, the Blades and the Delawares. Bartholomew Blade helped Atholrose Motham establish the city of Motham. These two families share minimal DNA with the ferals. To this day they are considered to be decent, upstanding citizens of Motham City.

Min snapped the book shut and put it aside. There was no point trying to fathom human/dragon relationships in the past. It was the here and now she had to focus on.

She was relieved to read that the aviation dragons were deemed to be hard-working and successful dragons. They were respected in Motham. And clearly, wealthy. And one of them was willing to pay her handsomely for a month of the Westwind name.

Min looked at the sum again. She blinked and shoved her glasses up her nose with a shaky finger.

It was a crazily large amount. Almost too good to be true.

With a plaintive meow, Gingerbread jumped onto her lap.

Min stroked the cat's ears absently. "What do you think, Ginge? Should I do this?"

The cat nudged her hand with his snout, purring loudly.

Min glanced down at him with a smile. "So, you approve?"

Another nudge with his furry chin. Then he dabbed his paw on her cell phone. Min decided to take that as a good omen.

"Well, Gingerbread," she said as she brought up Adina's number, "seems like I'm about to fake date a dragon."

CHAPTER 4

Two days later, Min found herself seated in the reception of Midas Touch Partnerships. It had the most amazing décor; everything shimmered. The chairs shimmered, the chandeliers shimmered, even the coffee table magazines had a pearlescent glow to their covers. A plant in the corner twinkled as if covered in fairy lights—except, as far as Min could see, there were no lights adorning it.

Did that mean the leaves themselves were sparkly? She made a mental note to find out what kind of plant it was.

Once she had given her name to the receptionist, she'd grabbed a magazine off the pile on the occasional table and sat, feeling quite drab in her neat gray dress with its princess collar and her plain black pumps. She had on her mom's pearls and frankly, felt like she was completely out of place.

Up until her father's death, Min's sheltered life hadn't worried her that much. She'd been quite happy immersed in the books, helping Dad in the shop and tending her garden. As for dating, well… Min hadn't met anyone she'd wanted to date in the human world.

But now—since yesterday, to be precise—that fact niggled at her somewhat. From his profile it was clear Ethan Blade was worldly, and handsome. He must have dated plenty of species. How would she measure up, with no experience of the game at all?

There was one other small issue related to her dismal lack of experience.

The fact that she was a virgin.

Min fidgeted, starting to feel hot in her woolen dress.

Truth was, she wasn't averse to the idea of dating. It was just... frankly humans had never appealed to her. The few guys she'd met were all like Quentin, pale and uninteresting. Maybe it was being home-schooled by her father, raised among customers who were, in the main, monsters. She'd gotten used to seeing all kinds of species in the shop, and that had become her yardstick. She found their horns and tails, hooves and beaks, so much more interesting than humans. A young griffin had asked her out once, and she'd nearly accepted. But she'd been too shy, and missed her chance. No matter, she lived inside her books anyway. Her stash of monster romances kept her going.

So no, she had no desire whatsoever to date a human male.

But yes, if she was honest, fantasies of dating a monster... even, dare she say it, a *dragon*, had crossed her mind quite often, especially when in bed at night, under the covers with a racy monster romance.

The silver clock on the wall suddenly shot out a small blue bird that chirped the hour, all eleven of them. Min nearly jumped out of her skin.

"Annoying, isn't it?" The receptionist laughed. "Pity me, I have to listen to that thing seven times a day, five days a week. Drives me insane."

The girl was clearly fairy or elf. She had the cutest pointed ears, pierced with different colored gems all around the edges, and she was wearing a sparkly little outfit that perfectly fitted in with the decor.

"We're just waiting on Mr Blade and then Adina will be with you." The girl smiled sweetly.

"No problem," Min replied, and buried her nose in an article on how to use highlighter to make your cheeks appear thinner. Clearly it was aimed at goblin and orc kind by the photos.

A moment later there was a sudden blast of hot air as the outer door flung wide.

And then... in strode Ethan Blade.

His photo didn't do him justice, Min realized as her jaw nearly dropped to the floor.

He was tall, wearing the snappiest blue-gray suit, his wings furled tightly into his broad shoulders and his scales spruced off his forehead. His ice-blue eyes held a look of determination, and his nostrils flared, letting the tiniest billow of smoke escape. A rather pleasant cedar wood scent wafted around the room.

He strode over to the desk and, flashing a smile that showed a row of sharp white fangs, said in a deep, gravelly voice, "I'm here for an eleven o'clock with Adina."

"Certainly, Mr Blade. I will let her know you're both here."

"Both?" He swung around and Min found herself pinned by the most intense stare she'd ever experienced. His lips tightened, covering those impressive fangs, and the tiny scales along the bridge of his nose ruffled then flattened. His neat green horns twitched. "Ah, you must be Miss Westwind."

"H-hello there—" Min squeaked, aware she was probably blushing. She lifted her hand and gave him a little wave. His brows lifted, his mouth opened as if to speak and then, thankfully, Adina wafted out of the door to their right.

"Wonderful to see you both, please accompany me into my office."

As Min jumped up, the magazine slid off her lap onto the floor. With one swift move the dragon deftly picked it up and placed it on the coffee table. As he turned, she noticed his tail, smooth and green with a pointed tip. The way it snapped back against his lean hips sent a pleasurable little tingle right down her spine.

"Thank you," she mumbled. He didn't answer, just inclined his head, and then as Adina stood back for them to enter her office he also stood back, allowing Min to walk in first.

Min registered another little hum of pleasure.

Good manners. Tick.

You're not really dating him, Min.

No, but if I have to spend lots of time around him, good manners will obviously help.

When they were all seated, Adina beamed at them both from across her desk.

"Time for formal introductions. Mr Ethan Blade, meet Miss Minerva Westwind."

Min imagined it was like the olden days when you were matched off with a suitor of your parents' choice. She hesitated, uncertain what the next move was, but then he reached out and extended his hand. She glanced at it to see that apart from being green, it was quite human in shape, with a hint of claws at the tips that retracted immediately.

She didn't hesitate; she slid her hand into his, and met his eyes steadily this time. They were long and narrow, set deep and slightly to the side of his angular bone structure. His irises were the sharpest, brightest blue, his pupils dark narrow obliques.

She'd always thought dragons had golden eyes, not this polar ice blue that did weird things to her heart rate. And then he blinked.

Good goddess, his eyelids flicked sideways. It took all her manners not to let out a little squeak of surprise.

"A pleasure to meet you properly, Miss Westwind," he rumbled in his sexy baritone.

"And you, Mr Blade."

A tutting sound came from Adina. "I haven't heard many lovebirds calling each other by their surnames. Let's start again."

For a second, Min felt his fingers tighten around hers, and a tingle went up her arm this time as she registered his hands were cool but not cold, his grip strong and firm.

He pulled back now, and his long mouth quirked sideways in a rueful grin. "Of course. Hello, Minerva."

"You can call me Min, most people do."

"I'm Ethan," he responded. "No short version. Just plain Ethan."

Plain, he certainly was not. You'd have to say he was extremely handsome. Those razor-sharp cheekbones, mimicked by the flare of his nostrils and the slant of those piercing eyes. Her gaze strayed briefly to his crisp pale blue shirt and darker blue tie. Impeccable.

He plays the piano. He likes to read. Min breathed more easily, remembering his profile. They would have books in common, at least. And she loved listening to music. Maybe he would play for her.

When Ethan let go of her hand, they both turned to face Adina. It felt to Min like they were school children being briefed for an exam. "You have both received the paperwork, so will have some idea of each other's personalities and interests. Now is your chance to find out more about each other, in person. Since you have agreed to spend a month, maybe longer, pretending you are... in an intimate arrangement, I'd like you to feel free to sit and ask each other the necessary questions." Adina tinkled a laugh, as though the whole business delighted her. "I'm going to leave you alone for a half hour, to chat, and then we will meet again to discuss the practicalities."

Ethan muttered something in a growly voice and Min detected that tiny puff of smoke from his nostril again.

Did that happen when he was nervous? she wondered.

"I have put together a list of topics to get the ball rolling. Use them as prompts if you like." Adina handed them each a sheet.

There was an embarrassing silence while they both read through the questions.

What is your favorite food/beverage?

What is your morning routine?

Favorite hobby?

Best way to relax?

How do you show affection?"

What do you wear to bed?

Now that last one would make her blush if he asked her.

Adina stood up and swept around the desk. "If you're ready, I'll take you into the meeting room."

They were ushered into an attractive room with a French door into a small garden. "It's a lovely day, would you like to sit outside?" Adina asked.

Min looked at Ethan, who raised a brow. "Your call."

"That would be lovely, thank you."

When they were alone, Ethan cleared his throat. "Perhaps we'll leave Adina's questions for last," he said, folding his piece of paper in half, then again. Min noted that his hands shook slightly, and a rush of sympathy filled her chest.

He *was* nervous.

Clearing his throat, he glanced at her. "So, you own the Westerly Bookshop?"

"You know it?" She was certain she'd remember him if he'd ever been there.

"I haven't been there personally, but I've heard good things about it. The Westerly is really quite an icon nowadays."

"That's good to know. It's only been the past few years that monsters have more openly frequented the shop."

"Yes. Well, we wouldn't have been discussing this…

arrangement, a few years back," he said. "It would have been considered ludicrous for me to be dating a human, let alone a Westwind. That's a very influential name in the human world."

"It's a double-edged sword." His intense blue eyes encouraged her to continue. "My father was always ashamed of our name, and I second that. Colonel Westwind, he… he was no hero as far as monsters were concerned. You'd know, obviously, about his…"

"His role in The Great War? Yes. Though we only studied that period briefly at school."

"I guess it's something Motham residents would rather forget." She hung her head a little. "Nowadays, I hope our name has redeemed itself through the bookshop. My father studied monster history at university, and of course he was totally sympathetic to monster causes. He was something of an embarrassment to his family, and for a while they disowned him, but with Dad being an only child, they relented in the end, and made up before my grandparents died."

"I noted in your profile that your parents are deceased, your father only last year, I understand," he said softly.

She nodded, feeling tears prick her eyelids.

"I'm sorry for your loss. That's something we have in common. I lost my father in recent years."

"Yes, my commiserations also," Min said softly.

"Do you mind me asking what happened—to your father? It seems important I should know."

Min gulped. It was still hard to talk about. "He was killed on one of his book-hunting jaunts into Motham. He'd gone to the Wasteland—which was really foolish—on a tip-off about an exciting find, and on his way home his vehicle was hit by a weremonkey in a stolen car."

"I'm so… sorry." He really did sound it.

"And your father?" she said, swallowing the lump in her throat. "H-how did he pass?"

"Also a sad accident. In aviation. The wings fell off a prototype and he didn't have time to eject. The irony is that if he hadn't been strapped into the vessel, he could have flown to safety. Innovation, eh? Not always a good thing." His mouth tightened. "Mother has never recovered; she's still grieving."

"You must miss him too."

"Yes. But I had to take over the business straight away, and all the projects he had in the pipeline—one of which, his biggest dream, was to build an airport on human-owned lands. I guess my way of grieving is to try and bring his dream to fruition. It helps me make sense of him dying, I guess."

"Finding new meaning after someone we love dies, that's important," Min said.

There was a moment's silence. From under her lashes, she watched his knuckles paling as he clasped his fingers tightly together in his lap.

"And you... how do you find meaning in life, Min?" Min's gaze rose to his face to find those intelligent eyes trained on her.

"Ah—" She gave a little shrug. "Like you, continuing my father's dream, the bookshop, building on where it is now, so it can reach more monster species, help them to get an education and just, you know, learn to love reading. When I'm sad, I lose myself in make-believe worlds... and the garden, of course, I spend time tending that. The soil needs a lot of work with the Westerly being in the middle of a sandy plain."

"What do you read?"

"Novels, biographies, anything that passes through the shop, really. I've learnt a lot about monsters that way."

"Ah, yes," he said softly.

"And your interests... You play the piano, right?"

He looked away now, embarrassed, she thought. "I hesitated over whether to put that down."

"Why?"

"Oh, you know... It's just a hobby." He shrugged. "But it gives me pleasure."

"Doing things for pleasure is just as important as achieving things, don't you think?" Min said.

She saw his tail, which had been coiled around the chair leg, flick, just the end of it, and felt a little flip low in her belly that she couldn't explain.

He laughed a little huskily. "Well, this got very deep, very quickly. We haven't even got to Adina's set questions."

"No. I guess we should, then."

They both stared at their respective papers. She peeped up over her glasses to see him chewing his lip and frowning, the scales on his forehead ruffling up and down in a cute, boyish way.

He must have felt her eyes on him because he looked up and their gazes caught again. Min blushed, noting his color also shifting and shimmering. *Was that the equivalent of a dragon blush?* she wondered.

"Er, well, we've mentioned hobbies so erm... Yeah, what's your favorite food?" he asked.

"I'm vegetarian. I'm very partial to avocado on toast. With poached eggs on top."

"Same. A breakfast favorite of mine. Though I do add bacon."

"Well, there we are," Min breezed. "That covers breakfast then."

She tried not to think about what happened *before* breakfast.

"Sure. Do you drink coffee or tea in the morning?"

"Tea. Coffee gives me the jitters."

"I have a strong short black. Sets me up for the day."

Min nodded and then, to her utter dismay, blurted, "And, er—just to address what I wear in bed, it's pajamas with unicorns on them."

His brows shot up. "Right." Then his lips twitched. "That is not so surprising."

"Really. Why?" She cocked her head. She felt almost... flirtatious. *Just getting into role,* she told herself.

"There's something... I don't know, almost innocent about you."

"Is that a polite way of telling me unicorn pajamas are childish?"

"No, not at all." He looked suddenly alarmed. "On the contrary, it's... charming."

"Right." Min took a deep breath and squeezed the paper tight in her fingertips. This was feeling very personal. But not unpleasantly so. In fact, she was finding Ethan remarkably easy to talk to. She read the next question. Morning routine. Imagined him pulling off the bed cover and padding to the bathroom... *naked.*

"So um, how do *you* start the day." It came out almost a squeak.

"I shower. Dress. Drink my first coffee. Then I play the piano. I find it focuses my mind."

Unbidden now, Min imagined him seating himself at the piano, arranging his tail behind him as though it was the tails of a dress coat and laying those long fingers on the keys.

As if reading her thoughts, he said, "I hope my appearance," he swept a green hand down his body, "is not off-putting to you."

Min shook her head vigorously. "Not at all." Goddess, far from it, it would seem, after her little fantasy about him at the piano.

She felt telltale heat climbing her cheeks again, knowing how easily her pale skin gave away her emotions.

She scanned down the question: How do you show affection? She had absolutely no idea how to even begin to address that.

But thankfully before there was any need to say anything else, in walked Adina.

"How did your tête-à-tête go?" She beamed at them.

"Very well thank you," Min said primly. "I mean, I think so…" She glanced at Ethan, who nodded with a smirk. "Like a house on fire," he said, then palmed his forehead.

Min couldn't help a giggle. Glancing at her, his face suddenly relaxed, and he chuckled. "Er… maybe not the best phrase to use."

"Well, you clearly share the same sense of humor. Which is a big plus in these kinds of arrangements," Adina said.

They both nodded, still smirking—like two naughty school kids, Min decided.

She wondered if they'd passed their exam.

"Well then, Min and Ethan, if you feel ready, let's go back to my office, and sign those papers."

CHAPTER 5

Ethan's PA, Sonia, poked her head round the door of his office. "Minerva Westwind has arrived."

Ethan felt his scales tighten. "Right."

"Shall I go fetch her from reception?"

He stood up abruptly, sending his coffee cup flying. "No, I'll go down and greet her myself."

"And I'll clear that up." Sonia smirked.

Ethan couldn't help casting a glance at himself in the mirrored wall panel in the elevator. He'd made sure he'd looked his best this morning—trimmed the tiny scales around his jaw, spruced back the ones on his head with Iron Hold, the special hair gel for dragons.

Now he adjusted his tie, did up one button of his suit jacket, then blinked. Gods, he hoped his dragon blink wouldn't be too hard for her to take on a daily basis.

This is a business arrangement. It doesn't matter what she thinks of your blink, mate.

He tightened his lips.

Thank the gods Min had agreed to the liaison, because he really didn't want to work his way through a whole list of possible humans. When his copy of their signed agreement had landed on his desk, he'd immediately got his PA to arrange a meeting to discuss the finer details. Adina had been right; Min was perfect, and the Westwind name... well, that was a major asset. Now he just had to make it work. Correction, they *both* had to make it work. She needed his money. He needed her name. Win-win.

And no doubt about it, she would be pleasant to have around for a month...

He felt his heart lurch at the possibility that the airport deal might get delayed, meaning she'd have to date him for longer.

And then what? When they split...

Ethan felt his chest squeeze.

Mom would nosedive. He'd be picking up the pieces for months.

His mom thought this was real. Finally, a romance between a dragon and a human. If she realized he was only doing it so he could pull off his father's legacy, she'd be gutted.

She was putting all her eggs into this particular basket, desperately hoping that they would have offspring with shifting capabilities—which was nonsensical, and not grounded in science at all.

And then, of course, there was another worry. Would Min be able to keep up the façade for as long as needed?

Would this serious young human be able to pull off the illusion of being madly in love with him?

Their first meeting had been remarkably pleasant. She had been so easy to chat to. So yes, he thought it could work.

He raised his chin, admiring the long, lean line of his jaw, his spruced scales. Dad would be proud of him.

Then his claws furled inside his shoes.

Damn it, he had to control this habit. He went through the soles of way too many good shoes doing this.

But the displacement activities were necessary, otherwise

he'd huff smoke, and the occasional inappropriate flame. He held out his hands in front of him, checked the shakiness in his fingers. Tugged down his jacket and straightened the lapels as the elevator jerked to a stop and the doors pinged open.

And with that, he strode out into the foyer.

A zing of pleasure travelled down his scales as Min stood to greet him.

He hadn't set eyes on her since their meeting at Adina's a week ago, and despite regularly reading through her profile and studying the photo of her on the front of the file, he'd kind of forgotten her energy.

All the pent-up anxiety inside him suddenly receded, and the heat in his chest cooled.

Everything about her was soft. The way her hair curled in thick copper waves around her shoulders, the ivory glow of her skin, and full soft lips. And her chocolate brown eyes were thoughtful and intelligent behind her glasses.

She was wearing a beige-colored dress with a dark brown jacket. She seemed to favor muted colors, he noticed. Already he was imagining her in something more vibrant, some sparkling things around her neck and in her ears. The dragon way.

But really, the modest pearls peeping at her ears and the string around her neck, well, they suited her.

"Hello Ethan." She smiled softly, shyly, as she walked toward him. He wondered whether he should shake her hand again. She'd looked at his hands that time in Adina's office, with—what? Not horror, but maybe surprised curiosity. Which wasn't unusual when folks touched dragon skin. They expected it to be cold, hard, rough.

This was one of the most interesting thing about twilight dragons, the softness of their skin. Ethan's arms, chest, neck, belly, the skin there was golden, smooth to the touch, rippling over his well-toned muscles.

It was one of the few features of his body he really liked.

But enough of these thoughts. Time for business.

He smiled. "Hello again, Min. Welcome to the Blade Wing Building. My office is on the twenty-fifth floor. Please follow me."

As the elevator doors slid closed, Ethan was painfully aware of them being alone together. Her perfume was delectable, sweet and floral—like her. As he stood against the rail, his tail accidentally flicked out and touched her hip. He apologized profusely and reeled the damn thing back close to his body.

"No problem," she murmured.

And then, to hide his embarrassment, he found himself talking about the weather. The *weather*. Couldn't he come up with something more interesting than that? He racked his brains for something to say that wouldn't bore the hind legs off her. *She only has one set, idiot, she's human*. And they were very nice legs indeed—at least what he'd seen of them.

Ethan pulled himself into line.

It was not appropriate to find this human remotely attractive. Except the truth was, he'd always been secretly attracted to human women. He'd never had the confidence—or, he guessed, the opportunity—to consider dating a human before. Which was probably why this particular human was doing weird things to his pulse rate.

It's fake dating remember, Blade.

Once they reached his office he watched as she gazed around in awe. He had to concede it was pretty magnificent. His chest puffed up with pride.

"This building is incredible," she gasped.

"Yes, my father built it. It took me a while to feel I should legitimately be sitting at this desk."

"Do you now?"

"Mostly. Though there are still days when I doubt myself." Why was he telling her this? He didn't discuss his insecurities with anyone. Next, he'd be blabbing about his anxiety issues.

Quickly he changed the subject. "Can I order you a tea? Your morning drink, right?"

A soft smile curved her full lips. "You remembered."

Of course he remembered. He'd kept reliving everything about their first meeting. He felt a frisson of pleasure as her face lit up and deep dimples appeared in both cheeks. Sure, those heavy rimmed glasses made her look studious, but behind them her eyes were soft and large, her lips full and... the only word that came to mind was *inviting*. He found himself imagining kissing them, and his tail jerked.

Holy dragon's balls! *Do not think of her that way.*

Ethan strode behind the desk, ostensibly to rearrange some papers, but to be honest it was to give his libido time to take a hike.

He couldn't afford to stuff this up with misplaced lust.

Especially since everything about Min did not in any way encourage such feelings. She was modestly dressed, appeared to be wearing no make-up and her vibe was totally professional. Except... hadn't he caught a spark of a fun sense of humor that first time they'd talked.

The unicorn PJs, remember?

No, don't.

He found the notes his team had drawn up.

"Please, sit." He indicated one of the chairs with a wave, staying firmly behind his desk. He needed more time to drag his body into line.

Min sank down and placed her purse neatly beside her. Finally, it felt safe to stride around the desk. Seating himself opposite her on one of the leather couches, he casually crossed his legs. "Firstly, I want to say I am honored that you've accepted my proposal," Understatement. He'd had this weird desire to fly in circles and whoop. "And I wanted to meet this morning to work out the terms of the arrangement in more detail, just the two of us." He passed her a copy of the paperwork.

"Of course. Yes."

"I trust you haven't spoken about this to anyone."

"Absolutely not. I understand the importance of this appearing... real between us."

"Great. Fantastic." He heard himself laugh, a little too heartily. Where was all this effusive nonsense coming from? He was, for the most part, almost taciturn. Ask his team. But with Min he felt like he wanted to smile, laugh, banter even. He cleared his throat.

"I also wanted to clarify the payment terms: a down payment now, a payment halfway through, and the final payment at the end of your contract."

She frowned as she glanced at the paperwork. "It looks like you've added more to the original sum cited?"

"A bonus, yes, if this leads to a successful outcome for Blade Wing Air. Which it will, of course."

"That's very generous, particularly on top of what you've already offered."

He met her gaze steadily. "This needs to work, Min, for both parties."

"I agree."

"And since you will be uprooting your life to live with me for the duration—"

"Sorry, what?" She blinked at him from behind her glasses.

Dismay pleated his browbone. "Didn't you receive an email about that from Ebony?"

"Ebony? Who's Ebony? No—I—don't think so."

"Ebony is my publicist."

She shook her head, her own frown deepening, "I don't recall..."

Damn it, he was going to kill that raven. She'd just got

engaged to her centaur boyfriend and had gone completely feather-brained of late.

But even so. She'd told him she'd get the information to Min before they met.

"To be honest, I don't look at my emails as often as I should. So she probably has sent it," Min mumbled.

Flaming gods. This was a potential fuck-up. His fingertips started to tap out the first chord of his favorite Mopin nocturne on his leg. He saw her gaze flick to his hand and stopped abruptly, furling in his claws. Sometimes when he was agitated it was either tap out a tune or have a rogue flame escape from his nostrils. The first was more socially acceptable.

"The authorities will be checking to ensure we are a… bona fide couple. Obviously, anyone can put that down on paper. They will want evidence that we are living together." He paused. "Also, I would prefer you didn't work in the bookshop for the duration of our arrangement. I will need your total focus and attention on dating me—I mean, pretending to date me."

"Right, yes, I understand."

"Will you be able to arrange cover? I will pay for that also, of course."

She nodded. "I am sure that won't be a problem." An embarrassing silence followed, until thankfully, his PA brought in the drinks. Ethan curled his hand into a fist, resisting the urge to tap.

"Will that be all?"

"That's all, thank you Sonia."

As the door closed behind Sonia, Min asked, "Does living in your home mean… we will be sharing a room?"

She was peering over the top of her glasses at him, biting on her lower lip. Her eyes were darker, wider, more beautiful above the rims, and the way her lip pillowed softly under her teeth was... rather too pleasing. Again, the kissing image came to mind. Again, he had to punch his libido into oblivion.

"You will have your own room. Rest assured, you will have absolute privacy."

She nodded, but her features were tight.

Maybe she didn't want to be in such close proximity to a dragon. Maybe even being in a nearby room would be bothersome for her. Did she think he breathed fire at night, or burnt down doors to ravish humans? "Min, I really don't want you to be uncomfortable about any of this. But the issue is..." He dragged in a deep breath before continuing. "A high-breed human like you, dating a dragon, even a rich dragon, may be hard for the Council of Towns to believe unless there is evidence that..." He ground to an embarrassed halt.

She sat staring at her hands clasped in her lap.

"I'm getting the sense you're not happy with this..."

"It's not that. It's just..."

He stared at her, trying to read her expression. Her cheeks were flushed bright pink, and she adjusted her glasses on her nose with fluttering fingers.

When she looked up, her blush had intensified. "It's just... I've never dated anyone, let alone lived with a guy. So I—I guess you may have to advise me on how this all works."

A wave of shock traversed his spine, along with something else in the mix, something he wasn't prepared to unpack. "You've never dated? At all? Not even a human?"

"No, I—I—I guess no one ever swept me off my feet." She gave a nervous little laugh.

"I see." Heck. This was disconcerting. She'd never dated. Did that mean... that she was a virgin? Ethan shifted position.

She looked over at him, head cocked. "I surmise that *you* have dated. I mean, you seem like a guy who..." her voice trailed off. "Who is worldly-wise."

"Yes, I've dated." He cleared his throat. "But I'll be honest, never a human."

"Okay. Well, I guess we'll both have to learn the ropes as we go, won't we."

"Indeed." Ethan snapped his eyes away from her mouth. "There will be public events, photo shoots and the like. Obviously, we will have to, um, look like we're genuinely dating, and of course I will ask permission to touch you, but I may have to put my arm around you, hold your hand." He quickly aborted an image of winding his tail around her waist and pulling her close.

He really must not let his tail get involved.

Staring miserably at his shoes, he watched the leather tighten as his claws curled inside them.

"Don't worry, I'm a fast learner." She smiled brightly at him as she picked up her teacup from the coffee table. "So, when should I move in?"

～

This weekend!

He'd pretty much grunted the words at the ground—she'd had to ask him to repeat them.

Already Min's brain was scrabbling to work out the logistics. Today was Wednesday. That would give her just three days to get organized, pack, work out who would run the shop and look after Gingerbread.

Min hoped her glasses hid the rising panic in her eyes.

This was going to be a roller-coaster, that was now obvious. She was going to have to be seen out with him, holding hands and goddess knew what else—in public. Go to events, and dinners out and… and… living in the same house, maybe she'd bump into him in the bathroom. Wearing only a towel.

Her pulse sped up.

Eek. She'd never seen a human guy naked, let alone a dragon. When she told him she'd never dated, she guessed by the stunned look on his face that he'd surmised she was a virgin.

To be nearly twenty-five and still a virgin. Not the best credentials for the job.

But then, it wasn't relevant to the job, was it?

Min gathered her scattered wits as he asked her, "Does that give you enough time?"

"Oh, yes," she said brightly. "I have a friend who helps out in the shop from time to time, and I'm sure she'll be happy to do so for a month. She needs the money, she's hoping to go to college."

He frowned. "I'm afraid she can't know that this is a fake arrangement."

She heard herself laugh. "No problem. I'll make something up. I don't think she'd buy that I've fallen madly in love with you. She knows me too well."

She thought he looked slightly crestfallen. "Sure. I get it."

"I didn't mean because you're a dragon, I just meant, you know, it's out of character for me to fall in love. Period." Oh dear, now she'd probably offended him. "I guess I could tell her I'm going on an internship. With your company, to learn to manage the business side of the bookshop better. And then… if she… hears, we could say we had a whirlwind romance. Ha, a Westwind in a whirlwind." Min winced at her awful attempt at a joke.

He laughed, a warm, genuine laugh.

But then he sighed. "If it's any consolation, I will be doing the same and … unfortunately, my mother… you'll have to deal with her rampant excitement."

"Excitement?"

"Yeah, at me dating a human. It's been her wish for a long time."

Min grimaced. "I guess she won't be happy when it ends then."

"You're right. I'm not looking forward to the fallout. But that's my problem to deal with when you're gone."

Min twisted her hands in her laps. "So um, how *does* our relationship end?"

Another rueful, rather attractive smile tugged at one side of his mouth. "You'll dump me."

"Oh dear, that's not very nice of me."

"Min, you must understand, I couldn't possibly dump you. It would look bad to the authorities." He barked a laugh. "And my mom would never speak to me again."

Min arched her brows. "Does she think it's time you were married off, Ethan?"

"Yes, I believe so." He seemed to stiffen, and she decided to drop that subject. Even so she couldn't help wondering what other relationships he'd had.

"I hope I'm a good enough actress," she mused.

"Just keep thinking of the end goal," he said, sipping his coffee.

"I've been telling myself that, whenever I worry I've…"

His brow quirked. "Made a mistake?"

"Oh no, I didn't mean that." Min scrubbed two fingertips over her tight forehead. She seemed to be saying everything wrong. "It's just, I've never really done anything that demanded I be remotely, shall we say, adventurous. It was just me and Dad for many years. I was even home-schooled—it was too far to attend school in Tween every day, and I point-blank refused to go to boarding school."

Did she imagine it, or did those ice blue eyes soften?

"You must think I've led a very dull life." She sighed.

To her surprise, he threw back his head and laughed. Min found her eyes fixating on the roped muscles above his shirt collar as his throat moved. "Ah Min, what I'd give for a dull life. My mother has regular panic attacks and sets fire to her room. My brother went off the rails after Dad died and prefers to party instead of attending college, and I'm so busy with work I wouldn't notice if someone set my tail on fire. Really. A dull life sounds wonderful."

She saw a tiny puff of smoke curling out of one nostril.

"Jokes aside, Min, I will do everything in my power to make this easy on you, I promise. I am eternally grateful you've agreed to help me further my dad's dream. And... I do genuinely want to help you to keep the Westerly open." He smiled brightly, and he looked so devastatingly handsome, Min's breath caught in her throat. He truly was a gentleman. Her hunch had been correct—his scales and horns clearly hid a kind interior.

They stood now, and he walked her to the elevator. When he extended his hand she took it without hesitation. It was warmer than the first time they'd shaken hands, but just as firm. An honest handshake. "Thank you, Ethan. I appreciate the opportunity to discuss all this in more detail." She smiled up at him and bade him farewell.

It was only the second time she'd met him, but she'd come to the conclusion that Ethan Blade wasn't just a handsome dragon. He was a really nice guy, too.

CHAPTER 6

Min hated lying. She'd never had to lie to anyone about her whereabouts; never stayed out late at wild parties and had to pretend she was at the library. Never done anything she was ashamed of and had to cover up. Not that she was *ashamed* of dating a dragon. Far from it. Each meeting with Ethan had left her with a warm glow inside her. As for the little frisson she felt low in her belly when she recalled his broad shoulders, his tail, the intensity of his gaze resting on her… well, that was something best not dwelt on.

Truth be told, fake dating Ethan Blade wasn't going to be such a chore. There were worse ways to ensure her father's beloved bookshop remained open.

That didn't stop her from feeling bad about lying, though —particularly to her good friend Bonnie, who was now helping her bring her bags down the rickety staircase to the front door of the shop.

"I am so excited for you." Bonnie grinned, the snakes on her head dancing as she added Min's final bag to the pile. Bonnie lived in a government housing scheme just the other side of Motham's gates. Gorgons often had it hard in Motham due to the erratic behavior of their snakes, but Bonnie had been granted rental assistance as a minority species. They'd been firm friends for five years, since Bonnie had come to the bookshop one day looking for books on snake taming and the two girls had immediately hit it off. Bonnie had been Min's biggest support after her dad died, and it was wonderful to be able to give her work from time to time.

Bonnie had been overjoyed to be offered a whole month live-in.

"I've left a bag of kibble for Gingerbread in the cupboard in the laundry." Min said, glancing up at Bonnie's squirming curls. "When you interact with him, maybe keep your head well away from his claws. He might think your snakes are, um, something to play with."

"Oh yeah, I'll remember that."

Min glanced out the open door to see the hover limo touching down outside. "Ah, here's my ride."

"Wow!" Bonnie's eyes popped as she stared out at the sleek green vehicle. "That's a spiffy ride."

"Yeah, the company likes to pick up new interns." Min internally winced at yet another lie.

"Half your luck!" Bonnie hugged her, and Min hugged her back, gently untangling a couple of snakes from around her neck as she pulled back.

"You are going to kill it, babe," Bonnie said. "I'm so proud of you."

"Thank you, hon. I'll call in a couple of days. And feel free to phone me with any queries."

"Sure, no worries. Should be fine, I've worked here often enough. Enjoy the ride in that limo."

Min vowed she'd buy Bonnie a flight in one once this was all over.

As she opened the door, she hesitated. She'd already said goodbye to Gingerbread. Twice, in fact. Even so, she was having trouble leaving him. Dashing back inside, she found him in his usual spot in the snug and kissed the top of his head. He opened one eye a mere slit, then shut it again. Surely he wasn't miffed at her?

"You encouraged me to do this," she whispered in his ear. His tail flicked, but that was the only acknowledgement he offered.

By the time she got back to the front door, a liveried chauffeur was grabbing her bags. "Ma-am." He smiled, tapping his cap with a claw. "I'm Vincent. At your service."

Bonnie's eyebrows waggled. "I might apply for that scholarship next year."

"Um, yeah, good idea," Min said airily.

Inhaling deeply, she followed the uniformed lizard down the path. As she closed the gate, she looked back and waved to Bonnie. There was no sign of Gingerbread, of course. What else would you expect from a cat?

As Min stepped into the limo, she wondered yet again if she could really pull this off. Being away from her home, her shop, which she'd barely left in the whole of her twenty-five years.

You have to, Min. There's no other option.

Glancing around the cabin she was bedazzled by jewels. Jeweled ceiling, jeweled walls, jewels around the windows. The seats were leather, but the armrests had jewels set into them. As the doors of the capsule zapped shut she felt a little claustrophobic.

"All buckled up in there, ma'am?" Vincent asked.

"Please, just call me Min."

As they zoomed sharply upward, Min looked down at the bookshop, set in its little garden, like a doll's house in the middle of the low-lying plain. As the Westerly turned into a little dot, she pulled back her shoulders and lifted her chin.

It was high time she stepped out of her comfort zone.

Except... she'd never imagined it would be quite like this.

~

Ethan flipped a look at his watch. Gladys, his goblin stylist, was carefully clipping the scales around his scalp. She was doing a great job, but she was really taking her time. "Could you hurry this up, Gladys? I really have to get somewhere."

"That sounds like a man on a mission."

He didn't even know why he said it, but out came the words, "I've got a date."

"Woohoo, Ethan Blade, you wicked boy." Gladys tapped his shoulder lightly with the clippers, and Ethan grinned sheepishly at her in the mirror. He'd been going to Gladys at Monstrously Beautiful for years now, she really knew how to treat his scales. "This sounds like something out of the usual run of things," Gladys said.

His spinal scales tingled. Probably just nerves, he kept telling himself, even though thoughts of Min's big brown eyes blinking owlishly at him from behind those glasses and her soft lips had been pulling his attention away from work for days now.

"Do you want a quick head massage?"

It was tempting. Gladys did a great job—there was something about the way her fingertips tweaked the end of his scales—but as he glanced at his watch, he knew he had to decline. "Sadly no time," he said. If he didn't get home before Min arrived, she'd be meeting his mom or his brother first, which would not be a good start.

The last thing he needed was for her to lose her nerve and bail on him.

Once he'd paid Gladys, adding a hefty tip, he went out onto the street and called up his limo.

"We're stuck up here in a queue," Igor, his bald-headed eagle pilot, informed him.

"How come?"

"There's a concert happening, quite a few flights backed up," Igor said. "Just waiting on clearance."

Fuck. Knowing he couldn't override his own traffic safety

policy, Ethan paced up and down, flexing his claws anxiously. He could fly using his own wings, of course, but there was an agreement that free-winging should be limited to the gargoyles from Tower Security. If you saw winged monsters in the sky, it meant security. Free-winging as a dragon was only allowed in the outer suburbs. He'd been part of the planning committee that voted in favor of these guidelines, so he couldn't over-ride them.

Not that fucking Beau paid the slightest attention to the rules.

So why should you?

Heck, he had a reputation to uphold. That's why.

He was going to be late, and he was too chicken to check if Vincent had picked up Min. Every time he thought about it his heart nearly jumped into his freakin' throat and strangled him.

Why was he so nervous? Everything had been properly prepared. The room next to his had been all made up, new bed covers and feminine touches, special lotions in the bathroom he'd had put there by his valet Snibs, who he could trust not to gossip to other staff or tell his mom, who would wonder why they weren't sharing a room.

But the truth was, the idea of that rather delectable human sharing his wing of the house for a month was more than a little exciting. Sleeping, showering... gods save him. He closed his eyes, imagining her in the shower, imagining her naked, her fingers moving over her soft curves, flicking those long, burnished waves down her back.

His cocks stirred.

There he went again, getting turned on like a horny teenager. He literally couldn't recall when he'd last felt this way around a female.

He paced some more, flicking his tail—the natural response to arousal in a dragon. Reeling it in against his body, he took a deep breath, then leaned against a lamppost nonchalantly and pretended he was scrolling through his phone.

Finally, he saw his limo descending, the unmistakable flash of lights showing it was coming in to land. The traffic stopped obligingly, clearing space as Igor brought the dark green limo with its bright gold wings emblazoned on the sides onto the street.

The Blade Wing insignia always stopped traffic.

Folks waited as Ethan strode over and climbed in, and then they took off to a chorus of friendly horns. He liked that Motham folk loved his airline, that they saw him as a Motham success story.

"Sorry for the delay, sir."

"Looks like it's mayhem out there."

"Grilka Gray, the fae singer, is playing at The Pod," Igor explained. The Pod was the new arena, daringly built on the edge of the Wasteland. So far, there had been no ferals gate-crashing concerts because of the high levels of security.

"Well, you're here now, and if you exceed the air speed limit a little, I won't notice."

"No problem, sir."

They'd risen a little higher over the city now and Ethan could see it stretching out, the bright lights and winding streets of old Motham, the wall itself, and the long perimeter road that ran toward the city gates. There on the road not far from the gate, he could detect one lone lit-up building.

The Westerly Bookshop.

Surely she must be on her way by now.

Then his phone pinged.

It was his mom. His neck scales tightened as he read her message.

"Ethan, she's here! And she's totally adorable."

CHAPTER 7

"May I help you out, Ma'am?" Vincent asked, offering Min his gloved hand. She took it and stepped carefully out of the limo, then looked up at the mansion in front of them and struggled not to openly gawk.

They were on a helipad, set slightly to one side of a sweeping gravel drive. In the center of the driveway was a huge fountain, lit up to make the tumbling water look like a rainbow.

Behind it stood an imposing four-story building, made of a white marble flecked with jade. Around the grand pillared portico were what Min initially thought were colored lights, but she quickly realized they were jewels, backlit to make them glow in myriad shades that matched the fountain.

It was totally ostentatious, yes, but there was no denying it was beautiful. Like landing in fairyland.

Vincent grabbed her bags, and in seconds a buggy arrived, as if from nowhere. A friendly lizard creature tipped his cap. "At your service, ma'am."

Vincent put her luggage in the back. "I'll leave you in Bradley's capable claws," he said, and hopped back into the limo.

Goddess above, how many staff did Ethan have?

When they reached the house, the door was opened by yet another reptilian species. Was everyone here lizard-kind?

She stepped nervously through the door, and barely had time to take in the grand hallway with its wide sweeping staircase before there was a sound from above.

Min looked up to see a full-figured female dragon standing at the top of the stairs, decked out in — unsurprisingly — a lot of jewels and a billowing silk kaftan, her head wrapped in a sparkling turban. Huge gold hooped rings hung from the frilled scales around her face and her lashes were long, possibly false, above slanting golden eyes.

"Oh my, oh my, you must be Minerva." The dragon literally flew down the stairs, her wings flapping behind her. Up close, her eyes were even more striking, and as she smiled, her sharp white fangs sparkled.

"Darling girl, you're here! I'm Cressida, Ethan's mom, and I am so excited to welcome you to my humble abode." A little fireball flew out of each nostril, and she quickly put a metallic-looking handkerchief to her nose.

"Oh dear." She patted her nose with the hanky. "When I get excited, my dear... well, this is what happens. It's a family problem. Ethan has it too, but he controls it better... Anyway, you have no idea how long I've waited, how long I've wished he'd meet a... a lovely... human... and here you are! Just look at you. So pretty. I feel quite teary..." A little sobbing laugh escaped her.

So this was what Ethan had meant about his mother being desperate for him to be with a human. She was certainly wearing her heart on her sleeve.

Minerva plastered on her brightest smile. "It's lovely to meet you, Cressida. Ethan has told me so much about you."

"Not all bad, I hope?" Cressida grimaced. "One always worries what one's children will say to their partner. I'd hate to come across as the overbearing mother-in-law."

Min tried not to let her alarm show. It seemed Cressida had already earmarked her as marriage material.

Cressida held out her arms. "May I hug you? I promise I won't set your beautiful hair alight."

Before she could even answer, she was enveloped in plump green arms. A tiny puff of heat settled on her neck.

"There, you survived." Cressida drew back, smiling. "Not even singed." She swept her gaze over Min's outfit, and Min noticed a double sideways blink that did nothing to disguise her dismay.

I am totally not dressed for the occasion, Min thought, passing a nervous hand over the simple string of pearls at her neck.

"Ethan is not yet home—I think he may have been held up in the traffic. There's a concert on at that new Pod thing, and I only know that because my naughty son Beau has flown there. I daresay he'll get home in the early hours and wake us all up. Now, do you want to go to your room immediately, or shall we share a pre-dinner drink in the parlor?"

Cressida was already asking a uniformed snake girl to bring the canapes to the formal lounge, so Min figured she was expected to stay for refreshments. Cressida tucked a green hand in the crook of her arm and escorted her toward a set of big double doors on the other side of the hallway.

They entered a room furnished in rich shades of sapphire, fuchsia and emerald green.

Vases decorated with ancient dragons were displayed on elegant occasional tables, and paintings in ornate gilded frames hung on the walls. All dragons. Mostly modern dragons, Min surmised, judging by their partially human form. One in particular caught her attention. He was seated with his head held high, wearing a dark suit and his eyes were piercing blue, like Ethan's. Cressida followed her gaze.

"My late husband, Clifton," she said proudly. "He built Blade Wing Air from scratch."

Min murmured politely in response. But as Cressida walked her around the room, pointing out more Blade relatives and exquisite antiques, a sense of panic rode up her throat.

How on earth would she carry off being the partner of a wealthy dragon when in every respect she resembled a small brown sparrow? Who honestly would believe it? Least of all, the Tween Council of Towns.

She was a hair's breadth away from blurting, "I'm so sorry, but this has all been a terrible mistake," when the double doors were flung wide and there stood Ethan, silhouetted in the entrance.

Big, green, and just as handsome as she remembered—and looking decidedly thunderous.

"Sorry I'm late. The traffic was terrible," he growled as he strode over. And even though they'd discussed the fact that he would be touching her, she wasn't prepared for the way he took her hand in his and raised it to her lips.

She went a little limp, the panic draining out of her at the softness of his mouth on her skin and the warmth of his breath, with just that slight hint of delicious cedar.

When he stepped back and looked at her, his blue eyes glowed as if... as if he really *did* feel something toward her.

"Oh Ethan, darling," she heard his mother keening from somewhere behind them, "just pretend I'm not here and kiss her properly."

For a moment they stared at each other. Min's eyes widened, her pulse suddenly racing.

Ethan's expression appealed silently to her, as if asking her permission.

Knowing she needed to let him know she was okay with that, Min placed her hand against his chest, and felt his pecs tense up. His chest was... very much human, even if the skin that stretched below his open-necked shirt was definitely dragon in its gold and green hues.

Glancing up into his eyes, she gave a miniscule nod.

Gently, he placed his hand on her shoulder, then bent his head and his lips brushed hers, just on the corner of her mouth. She'd expected... what? That his long mouth would be hard and cold? Instead there was a warmth and softness to the lips that slid over hers. As he drew away the tip of a forked tongue appeared briefly, before he reeled it in, and his eyelids blinked across those mesmerizing eyes.

Something stirred deep in Min's belly, something she'd kept under wraps for so long. The certainty she'd felt when reading a monster romance, that she was not destined for a relationship with a human. It was the same feeling she'd had when a handsome monster had appeared in the shop, and her body had responded with a primal energy she couldn't quite explain.

And now... up close and personal to this handsome dragon, there it was again—the mad fluttering of her heart and the warm, syrupy sensation spreading between her thighs.

For a second her hand bunched against his chest, and she felt the tension in his muscles mimicking hers. For a second more, his body length pressed against hers, before he moved abruptly away and said, "I must not forget to say hello to you, dear mother." Striding over, he gave his mom a kiss on either cheek, while Min tried desperately to bring her heartrate under control.

"Seems like you've been making Minerva feel at home, Mom." He turned now as Cressida stared adoringly from him to Min.

"As soon as I set eyes on Minerva, I knew why you've fallen madly in love with her. Isn't she beautiful?"

Ethan's eyes glowed as he stared back at her. "She is indeed."

Min felt the color rising up her neck.

Not only was Ethan successful in business, he was also, clearly, a very good liar.

∼

He had to give it to Min, she was handling his mom admirably.

She nodded and smiled in all the right places, politely listening to his Mom's embarrassing stories of when he was a dragonling. He tried not to look at her, lest that sense he was being bewitched come over him again. It made no sense. She was quiet, pale, and studious. And her clothes were, by dragon standards, desperately dull.

But her presence made his whole body light up.

He also felt at ease in her presence. Like she didn't judge him, or have expectations of him. Like she accepted him for who he was, which was crazy, since she hardly knew him.

Her touch on his chest. The warmth of her palm through his shirt. The electricity that surged through his body at just the slightest pressure of his lips against hers. Had there been a moment there, when she'd returned the pressure, just a fraction?

He must have zoned out for a second, reliving that kiss, and when he focused in on his mother's words again, Ethan wished he hadn't.

"The Blade Wing gala ball is less than a month away." Cressida's voice was rising in excitement. "We must go shopping for a dress for you." She turned her gaze to Min, her lips turning down ever so slightly as she surveyed her. "And jewelry fit for the occasion."

Ye gods, any second she'd be dragging Min off to her cave room and trying to bedeck her in bling.

Enough was enough.

Ethan stood abruptly. "I think it's time to show you to our apartment, my... love," he said, expecting the words to feel odd rolling off his tongue. But his mind seemed to relish the sound of them. "Mother, we will dine alone tonight, it being our first night and all."

His gaze fleetingly met Min's. Behind her glasses it was hard to tell if she was relieved to get away from his mother's enthusiastic bombardment or alarmed at the idea of being alone with him.

He hoped it was the former.

Cressida flapped her wings. "Of course, darling boy. I didn't for one moment expect we'd all eat together. I am going out with Lydia and the girls tonight. And Beau is out."

Ethan rolled his eyes. "Not at the fae concert?"

"I'm afraid so. He'll be late home and probably a little the worse for wear."

"Gods save us," Ethan muttered.

Min jumped up, quickly pushing a wave of hair behind one ear, a habit he already found endearing. Her long neck, the small shell of her ear, the glimpse of her collarbone. Not overtly seductive, but for some reason his cocks stirred.

Both of them.

This was deeply disconcerting... and potentially embarrassing.

He strode toward the door and heard the tap-tap of her heels behind him.

"Ethan, wait for Minerva," his mom called after him. "So like his father, he always made me rush after him."

Ethan heard Min laugh sweetly and bid his mom a quick good night, and then her feet were once again pattering after him.

As they headed toward the elevator on the other side of the grand hallway, he consciously slowed his step so she could catch up. Sometimes when he was nervous, he'd skim along using his wings rather than his legs. This was not the time.

"Sorry about my mom," he muttered, giving her a rueful smile as they waited for the elevator. "She gets a bit overbearing when she's excited, but she'll simmer down. She wants to please; it comes from a good place."

"On the contrary, I found her very kind and welcoming."

"And you are very understanding," he said as the elevator doors opened.

Inside the small space, he was suddenly lost for words. Just him and Min, her sweet perfume and her soft human body so close was turning his brain to mush.

They stood in what felt like agonizingly awkward silence, watching the elevator display signaling the passing floors.

"You'll find I don't have the same love of ostentatious bling as my mother."

As the elevator doors finally swished open, they were confronted with his bejeweled antique dragon egg.

"Apart from that," he muttered.

"Oh," she said, stepping out and examining it. "It's so beautiful." He watched her fingers flutter above it.

"You can touch it."

"Really?"

"Sure." Reverently she smoothed her fingers over the surface. "It looks really old."

"It is. Rumor has it, it was brought from a far kingdom by one of our first. That it was stolen by a human and finally retrieved about a hundred years ago—"

She cocked her head, gazing at him. "Why was it stolen?"

"I guess when the trust was broken between dragons and humans."

She held his gaze, her dark eyes serious behind her glasses. "I have a book that alludes to that."

"Really? I'm surprised you found a book on dragons at all."

"They are certainly rare," she agreed. "My father was always trying to locate more books on dragonology for the shop, but there are hardly any around."

"That's because they were burned."

She blinked at him owlishly behind her lenses. "Sorry, w-what?"

"It's long been said that most of our books were burned to avoid humans stealing our magic. When the balance tipped from a natural symbiosis to something... shall we say, more toxic, around the time that our shifting powers weakened."

"Did humans have anything to do with that, too?"

He shrugged. "No one is exactly sure. It could just be coincidental." She clearly wanted to know more, but he wasn't prepared to go into details about the strange physical characteristics that arose from dragons' inability to shift, some of which would probably be alarming to a human female.

He drew his wings close to his shoulders. "This probably isn't the time or place for me to give you a lesson on dragons. Let me show you around instead."

She looked a little disappointed, he thought. Was she really that interested or just being polite?

As he led her around the modern open-plan living area, he couldn't help feeling proud. His apartment took up the whole floor on the north side of the house, with views over the formal gardens and past that, the rooftops and high rises of The Hole In The Wall District. He'd thoroughly modernized the space, taking out the fancy cornices and ornate chandeliers, and put in modern glass sliding doors that showcased views of the city perfectly. The whole apartment was decorated with soft, muted colors, with just a few brighter accents in pictures and cushions. No bling, which made his mother shudder on the few occasions she came up here. He had finally succumbed to her insistence that "No dragon home would be complete without chandeliers," and had purchased —at great expense—a simple modern chandelier from over the mountain ranges for the main living room.

"It's very tasteful. and it has a calming energy," Min observed.

"That was my intention," he said, feeling chuffed that she approved of his taste.

He hesitated, then decided to lead her down the corridor

and open the door to his music room. Just entering it made a warm glow bracket his heart. The honey-colored wood floorboards and exotic rugs. The dark red velvet curtains at the window, the music chest, the shelves adorned with old instruments he'd collected from the early days of Motham City, when monsters made music as they built the city together.

He glanced sideways at her to see her mouth open in a little gasp of pleasure. Watched the wonderment chase across her features. Min had so many fleeting expressions he wished he could just stare at her. Drink her in.

What was it about this human that fascinated him so much?

She glanced at him, and he said softly, "Go in, if you like." She did, and he followed her, as she went over to the piano and touched the keys. "Do you play the piano?"

She shook her head. "No. I would have loved to, but it was too far to go to Tween to take lessons. And when I was a kid, you wouldn't go into Motham for lessons, not as a human." She smiled ruefully. "I taught myself the recorder. Badly. In the end I decided to stop torturing Dad."

He couldn't help laughing, imagining her as a cute little girl, frowning as she tried to teach herself to play music.

"How long have you played piano?" she asked.

"On and off since I was a kid. It helps me with…"

"With…?"

Ah, here he went again, wanting to tell her things about his life, things he'd not confided in anyone before. "I was an anxious kid. Music soothed me, stopped me fire-breathing, which was a real problem when I was a dragonling. When dragons hyperventilate it's really hard to control the heat building. But the concentration I needed to learn the piano took my mind off my anxiety."

"Will you play for me?" she asked softly.

He laughed nervously. "Ah, no. I just tinkle really, for my own pleasure."

"This doesn't look like tinkling." She flicked through the sheet music resting on the piano. "Mopin, Hubert, Monzart. These are quite complex pieces."

"Ah well." He laughed, that stupid nervous laugh, then shrugged and made an effort to sound gruff. "Not many jobs for dragon pianists out there, so aviation it is." He strode toward the door, making it clear their discussion was over.

His dreams of being a professional musician were a thing of his youth.

And imagining Min listening to him play, applauding him once he was done? Well, that was a dream too.

And he had no time for such things.

Back to practicalities, Blade.

"I'll show you to your room," he said as she joined him. "It's next to mine; I hope that won't be a problem for you."

He nearly showed her his bedroom, with its triple king bed, but immediately thought better of it. He didn't want her to think he was hinting at anything. Even so, as they walked along the corridor back toward his suite, he had this urge, crazy as it was, to let his tail curve around her hip and tug her gently into his flank.

Gods, it seemed he was more than a little attracted to this human.

And that was awkward.

He'd have to hold himself in check.

Keep his libido under wraps.

Not that he would ever… make a move. He was the epitome of self-control and good manners.

But with his cocks hardening after just the briefest fantasy, the idea of being in close proximity to Minerva Westwind for the next month should worry him.

Except it didn't.

It made him feel happier than he'd been in years.

CHAPTER 8

Min stood gazing around her very grand and spacious bedroom. Like the rest of Ethan's apartment, it was exquisitely furnished in muted shades.

"Is it to your taste?" he asked her, his ice blue gaze unblinking. The way he stared at her probably should make her uncomfortable. After all, Quentin staring at her made her want to squirm. But this handsome dragon gazing at her didn't have that effect at all. Instead, it sent little bubbles of delight fizzing through her veins.

She nodded. "I have a very small room in the eaves of the bookshop." Her lips quirked. "I'll *just* about cope with this."

For a second his brows pleated with concern, then his face relaxed. "Ah, you tease." As if suddenly catching the double meaning, he changed the subject quickly. "Your closet." He threw open the door. "Plenty of space for your clothes." She cast a self-deprecating glance down her gray shift dress. "This is one of two dresses I own. You may have noticed I wore it to one of our meetings. I normally wear shirts and pants, or jeans and tees in the shop."

His brows quirked. "You don't like fancy clothes?"

"It's not that. I've just never had a need for them... My

life is quiet, I don't socialize much. I guess I'm your classic introvert." She smiled. "But I'm happy to wear what I'm expected to."

"We will keep it within your comfort level. My publicist, Ebony, is bringing over some suitable outfits for you to choose from. And please, if my mom ever takes you shopping —which she will no doubt insist on— don't feel you have to succumb to her taste."

Min nodded. Walking over to the window, she gazed out over Motham Hill, the palace, the sprawling city, its twinkling lights stretching out until they became hazy with the smog cloud that hung over the industrial east side. "What a view. How long have you lived here?"

"We grew up here. The house is built on the footings of the original Blade cave. It's the wine cellar now, but Dad was always adding on and building bigger and better. He'd just about finished when he died, so he never got to enjoy it fully."

"That's sad."

"It is what it is."

He stood next to her, chewing with a sharp fang on his lower lip. He looked boyish suddenly as he rubbed at the back of his neck with one hand. "You have complete privacy. The only thing that adjoins your room to mine is our balconies. I promise to make sure I am decent if I wander out there."

She was tempted—her wicked Westwind humor bubbling up again— to make a joke about naked cavorting dragons on balconies being fine with her. But she didn't want to embarrass him further. She'd already caught a few fleeting expressions that showed his discomfort. She wasn't sure how she could tell so easily. His facial set, with his high angled cheekbones and long jaw, that wide mouth full of fangs and his side-set pale blue eyes were not human at all… And yet, his expressions were so readable. There was a vulnerability to him; the way his scales ruffled on his head, and down his neck sometimes. The sudden softening in his eyes. Even the twitch of his tail gave little clues to his emotions. Her eyes lingered on it now and she saw the tip twitch.

She wondered what it would feel like to have that tail coil around her waist, folding her into his big, strong body.

Goddess, what was up with her?

This was strictly a business arrangement. She couldn't go focusing on what his tail would feel like. Hot all over now, she snapped her eyes back up to Ethan's face. The expression on his lean features was raw, almost hungry as he gazed down at her.

Then he blinked, and her little tail fantasy evaporated as he turned to go.

"I'll leave you to settle in. I have arranged a pre-dinner meeting at 7 pm with two of my staff, my publicist and my business manager. It will give us a chance to go over the diary, if that's okay with you?"

Min dragged her focus away from the heat in her cheeks and the even more disturbing warmth between her legs.

"I'll be ready," she said briskly.

At 7 pm on the dot, there was a sharp rap on her door. Min stopped unpacking her meager belongings and practically ran to open it.

Ethan stood in front of her, smiling. He'd changed into more casual clothes, and the look suited him. Polo shirt and light slacks in a green that complemented his skin. His head scales and those along his snout flicked up and he blinked. She was getting used to his blink by now—she actually liked it.

The way his clothing was adapted fascinated her; the slits in his polo shirt from which his wings sprang, and another neat slit in the back of his pants for his tail to exit, which now flicked out to the side of his lean hips. "If you're ready, we'll go to my home office. My staff are there waiting."

"Of course," Min said. "Should I bring a notepad?"

"No need. Everything will be documented, and we can add any amendments we feel are necessary."

"Okay." She trotted after him, watching that tail swish from side to side, enjoying the view of his back, the breadth of his shoulders narrowing into his waist. His butt was... mmm, nice. That swishing tail... even nicer.

Stop it, Min.

She'd been very attracted to a young griffin once who'd come to the shop looking for books on stone carvings. He'd had amazing wings and the same kind of pert butt/tail thing happening. He'd asked her out on the third visit, but she was so flustered, she'd refused. He'd never come back after that. Other than that, and of course the occasional buffed minotaur who walked past (they never entered the shop—minotaurs were not into reading), she had only ever daydreamed over illustrations.

She was so busy daydreaming now, in fact, that she nearly barreled into Ethan as he stopped abruptly and opened a door. He stood aside to let her enter and two species she'd never come face to face with before stood to greet her.

One was a raven, the other a frill-necked lizard.

And clearly neither of them were shifters. Or at least, they weren't inclined to shift in her presence, which some species did when they were presented with a human. Well, good on them. Staying in their original form was a sign of their comfort around their identity.

Unless, of course, like Ethan, they *couldn't* shift.

That, Min reminded herself, was just as commonplace as shifters. Monsters being purely *monsters*.

As Ethan introduced her, the raven stood and extended her wing, softly brushing it against the back of Min's hand in greeting. When she sat, she used the same wing to deftly bring out a laptop and her claws, tipped with red shellac, started to tap on the keyboard.

The frill-necked lizard, Troy, shook her hand with a cold claw and took out a thick file of notes.

"Let's begin, shall we?"

Troy handed them each a page full of events. "Ebony, will you go through the itinerary for the month?" he asked.

"Sure." Ebony ruffled her feathers. "So, the first thing on the agenda tomorrow morning is a press conference about your 'whirlwind romance.'"

Min pushed her glasses nervously up her nose. "Will I be told what to say? I'd hate to get the story wrong."

"Of course." Troy passed over another, thicker document, giving Ethan a copy, too. "You'll both need to learn your lines before tomorrow morning."

Min cast a look at Ethan and he waggled his brow bones at her comically. "Piece of cake. I played Lucifer in a school production once."

"That's a worry!" Min laughed. She liked his knack of being playful to loosen the tension. He'd done the same that first day at Adina's office; that had been one of the things that had sold her on the whole idea of dating him.

Fake dating, remember, Min.

"Straight after that, at 11 am, Ethan, you have a meeting with the Council of Towns, to inform them you are dating Minerva." Ebony passed Ethan another sheet. "They will probably be suspicious of the timing, so you need to stick to the brief and keep your cool. No smoke displays, right?"

Ethan nodded.

"Should I be there, too?" Min asked, not relishing the prospect of being grilled by a panel of Tween officials.

"Not this time," Ebony said. "You will probably be required to sign some documents, and they may seek further proof later. After the press conference, Min, you'll be free to relax and make yourself at home here."

Min nodded.

"After that, the next big thing is the intimate candlelit dinner in the gardens. We've scheduled that for the next Friday, and if Min agrees," the raven paused, "we'll need you to, er, passionately kiss on camera."

Next to Min, Ethan moved sharply in his seat, and she sensed him side-eying her. Min's pulse sped up. She'd expected there would have to be public shows of affection, but…

"As in… really kiss?" She pursed her lips and touched them, then realized she must look ridiculous.

"Yes. A full clincher, I'm afraid. We need to show that the passion between you is absolutely genuine. Fake genuine, I mean." Ebony smirked.

"So… the idea is we're photographed kissing in the gardens of the house?" Min gulped.

"Exactly. There will be a photographer hiding in the shrubbery to take some photos. And then those photos will get leaked."

Min rubbed at her forehead, sensing Ethan watching her. "By whom?"

"By us," Ebony said, "though no one will know that, of course. It makes it more credible if it looks like the paparazzi have invaded your personal space and taken shots when you thought you had total privacy."

There was a moment's awkward silence before Ethan said, "Min, if you're uncomfortable with that idea we can scrap it."

Truth be told, Min was already imagining the kiss in glorious technicolor.

"Min?" Ebony raised a feathered eyebrow in her direction. "You up for a dragon snog?"

"No problem," she squeaked, trying to dampen the vivid images her mind conjured of being bent over in Ethan's arms, tango style, as he kissed her, long and deep and very thoroughly.

"Sorry to subject you to that." The raven smirked. "Though I hear on the grapevine he's a very good kisser."

Ethan glared at his publicist. "Where the heck did you get that from?"

"Does the word *bas-il-isk* ring any bells?" Ebony popped her eyes back at him, then leaned in conspiratorially to Min. "One of my girlfriends from college dated him for a while. I'll probably get sacked for bringing that up." She cast a wicked wink at Ethan, who was now tugging at his collar.

"This is what happens when you employ old college friends," he muttered. "They know too much about your misspent youth."

Min smiled brightly and silenced a little stab of envy. What did it matter who Ethan had dated in the past, for heaven's sake?

Troy cleared his throat and said, "I think we should stick to business, not salacious gossip."

Ebony shrugged, clearly unfazed. "Any other questions, Min, before we move on?"

"Yes, actually, I do have one. How do we explain the sudden nature of our relationship?" Min asked. "Especially in light of the policy change on land buyouts. Won't it look rather suspicious?"

"It's in the script. You've been dating for seven months in secret."

"Why did we keep it secret?" Min asked with a little frown.

"Humans dating monsters is still... not exactly frowned on, but... not encouraged, I guess," Ebony explained. "It's realistic that you might have kept it under wraps until you were certain of your deep feelings for one another. Especially with your surname being Westwind. It's still unusual for a high-breed human to shack up with a monster."

At that, Minerva felt bound to speak up. "I'd like to just be clear that I have no issue with... with... I mean, I wouldn't be at all ashamed to be dating you, Ethan, if it were real, even though it's not. I am not humancentric, or monster phobic in my dating preferences. I have actually considered it before... I got very close to dating a griffin once, so... er..." She pushed her glasses up her nose in dismay at the total knots she was tying herself in.

Three sets of slightly bemused eyes zoomed in on her.

"I don't think I made myself very clear," she mumbled, cheeks burning.

When she glanced up, it was to see Ethan looking... almost touched.

"I got the gist of what you were saying, Min. And I appreciate it."

"Thank you," she mouthed, trying to gather herself back into sensible Minerva again.

But the truth of the matter was, since this big green, gorgeous dragon had walked into Adina's office that day, it felt like sensible Minerva had flown out the window.

And it didn't look like *that* Minerva would be back any time soon.

CHAPTER 9

"I hope you're comfortable with everything we discussed," Ethan said as they stood outside Min's bedroom door later than evening. "Ebony is a great publicist, but she can be a little... enthusiastic with her ideas at times."

He wished he could see her eyes better. Damn, if he could only take those thick frames off, he'd know what she really felt.

Still, she smiled, and it seemed genuine. "Everything was totally fine with me. I would have said so if it wasn't. I knew that this would involve us touching, obviously—if we were in love we'd..." She took a breath, her smile a little too bright. "And now I guess we both have to learn our lines before tomorrow morning. Wouldn't want a slip-up on our first public engagement." She glanced down at the papers in her hand, and he watched with pleasure as with her free hand she twisted a curl of her bronze hair and tucked it behind her ear. He was getting to enjoy her little idiosyncrasies.

"We could have a practice run in the morning together, over breakfast, if that suits you?" he suggested.

"Just a cup of tea for me."

His lips quirked. "Ah yes, tea. I must not forget your

morning routine." He nearly made a comment about her unicorn pajamas, but stopped himself. "There's one other thing I wanted to check with you. If I were to loop my tail around you in the interview tomorrow, are you okay with that? It's not a human gesture of affection, but dragons do show affection with their tails in committed relationships."

A long moment of silence ensued, in which he hoped he hadn't gone too far.

"Perhaps you should just, um, show me what you mean." She wasn't looking at him, and two little swirls of color rode across her cheeks.

"What, now?" Surprise mingled with a frisson of excitement.

"It's as good a time as any, I guess."

Ethan suddenly felt like a gauche teenager.

She smiled at him encouragingly.

Stroking a horn, he took a step closer. Tentatively, he let his tail reach out and curl around her waist. He made sure he gripped her gently, sensing the soft indent of her waist, the feel of her ribs rising with her breath.

"How's that?" he asked. "Not too tight?"

She made a little hum. "That seems quite loose. How close would you hold me if—if I was really your mate?"

Ethan's scale tips tingled. "Do I have permission to show you?"

"Yes, absolutely."

Now she was holding her breath, he could tell. But he couldn't smell fear, just the warm, sweet scent of her body, and her floral perfume, heady and delightful.

He let his tail tighten around her waist and pulled her gently into his flank.

She let out a small squeak and he quickly loosened his grip. "No, no, sorry that was fine, I guess I just wasn't expecting your tail to feel so... so powerful."

He laughed. "We use them when we fly, for stability.

They're pure muscle." *And for other things, best not to mention.*

"I can imagine you'd have to. Okay, can you do it again, because I really don't think I should suddenly squeak out loud in public. I'll aim to be very relaxed, like it's the most natural thing in the world."

"Tell me when you're ready."

She brushed her hair behind her ears, smoothed her hands down her skirt. "Ready."

This time he curled his tail tighter, trying to ignore the way the tip itched to explore up her body.

He sensed her tense up again and was about to let her go when she suddenly relaxed against him, almost leaning her head into his torso. His tail tingled. Then, to his utter surprise, her hand lifted and touched it.

"It's warm," she said.

"Dragons can regulate their blood from cold to warm. It's a—leftover—from our ability to shift." Ethan barely dared breathe as he spoke. He didn't tell her that warmth was associated with affection. Desire.

If she'd looked down, the swell in his pants would have been unmistakable. Her body felt pliant against him, and his tail itched to flick higher, up to the swell of her breast.

To his utter surprise she started to stroke his tail with her fingertips, as if the damn thing fascinated her.

Shit!

He uncoiled her so fast she nearly went spinning across the corridor.

"Oh." She looked shocked. "I wasn't quite expecting that."

"Just—um—don't touch my tail. Not in public."

She looked chastened. "I didn't even think… I'm so sorry if it was unpleasant."

"No," he gritted out. "Quite the opposite."

She was silent for a moment, then she said stiffly, "I beg your pardon."

Ethan hauled in a breath. "It can be an erogenous part of a dragon, particularly when stroked."

"Oh gosh." She stood chewing on her lip, then smiled up at him. "Like earlobes on humans. At least, so I've heard."

He grinned, relaxing a little. "I did notice you have nice earlobes."

"You did?"

"Yes. When you tuck your hair behind your ear, they're visible." Before he realized what he was doing, he reached out a hand and gently traced around her ear.

She blinked at him from behind her lenses, and he saw the sharp rise and fall of her breasts under her dress. Small, high breasts. He took in the hollow of her neck, the way her chin tilted and almost stepped closer. Then he came to his senses.

"Sorry," he muttered. "I forgot to ask if I could touch you then."

"Well, I guess we're quits now, then," her lips quirked almost mischievously, "on touching erogenous body parts."

"I guess we are. Good night, Min."

He sighed as the door closed softly behind her and turned to enter his own room, right next door. Just a thin wall between him and her. That was it.

He really needed to keep himself in check.

It was only day one, and he was already enchanted by her.

If he went on like this, fake dating Min wouldn't feel fake at all.

It would feel like the real deal.

Min woke with a start to a loud crash, followed by a tinkling sound, like glass breaking. And some very loud cussing.

She sat bolt upright in bed, struggling for a moment to work out where she was.

Then she remembered. She wasn't in her bed above the bookshop.

She was in a dragon's home.

More loud cussing, but not in a language she understood. Then a plume of light backlit the curtains. Something was going on outside.

Flames.

Goddess on high. Was that Ethan fire-breathing?

An answering plume of fear skittered down her spine. She'd really thought Ethan was trustworthy. Her whole being had felt safe with him. But what if in the middle of the night he turned into a monster—of the unpleasant kind?

Yanking back the covers, Min ran to the window and flung it open. There, lying sprawled on the manicured lawn below, was a dragon.

But it wasn't Ethan.

This dragon was smaller than Ethan. It was writhing and kicking its leather-clad legs around, flapping its wings, and yes, shooting great arcing flames from its nostrils.

"What the fuck, Beau?" The shout came from the balcony next to her. Turning her head, she saw a very irate-looking Ethan, all the scales on his head and back standing up. She also noticed—gulp—that he was naked from the waist up. And his chest muscles were ripped and powerful and golden and glimmering.

Not the moment to notice that, Min.

"Who closed my fucking bedroom window?" Beau screamed from below.

Min noticed now that there were shards of glass scattered around the dragon, who'd propped himself up on his elbows and was glowering up at them—well, at Ethan, to be precise. Min stepped back into the shadows. The smaller dragon's eyes were bright yellow and pissed to the max, and he seemed to be able to throw flames a loooong way.

Already a bush was alight in the garden.

"I closed your window!" Ethan shouted back.

"What the fuck for?"

"To teach you that it's not okay to party mid-semester."

"Fuck you!"

"No, fuck you."

The language then descended into something she guessed was dragonish, and equally insulting, judging by its tone.

Finally, a winged figure swathed in a billowing satin dressing gown flew out from a window on the other side of the house, wailing and puffing little bursts of flame and smoke as she descended. "Oh my baby boy, are you hurt?"

"No, I'm fine. Get off me, Mom." Beau sat up, pushing her away. A staff member ran past with a fire hydrant and began to put out the fires that had sprouted in the shrubbery.

"I think I've broken my wing," Beau whined, standing up and flexing his shoulder blades.

"No, you haven't."

"And I've got a blood nose."

"Bring out the smallest violin in the world," Ethan sneered.

"Ethan. Don't be so cruel to your brother," Cressida sobbed. "Can't you see he's hurting?"

Min didn't know why, but she suddenly found herself leaning over the balcony. "Could you please stop fighting?" she said in a loud, firm voice. "It's not at all pleasant to listen to, and you're both upsetting your mom."

There was silence except for the crackle of the burning bushes.

Min stared down at the dragon, who was actually quite cute now that he wasn't throwing flames. He was a lot younger than Ethan, probably still in his teens. She could feel

Ethan's eyes boring into her from the balcony next door, and see Cressida gaping up at her, open-mouthed.

"Who are you?" Beau said finally, squinting up at her.

"I'm... Minerva."

"Yeah? What are you doing in Ethan's apartment?"

"I'm... I'm..." Min firmed her voice again. "I'm Ethan's girlfriend."

Beau burst out laughing. "You're a human."

"So?"

"Humans don't date dragons."

"I do." Min crossed her arms. "I understand you've been out late to a concert, and I'm sure you had a great time, but you've woken everyone up, Beau. Now, since you are standing up and your wings look fine to me, and you've been breathing fire beautifully from both nostrils, blood nose or not, I think maybe we should all get some sleep," she finished firmly.

Beau stared up at her, his mouth gaping. "Wh—"

"Do as my girlfriend says," Ethan growled.

"Not if you say so, butthead," Beau gritted back.

"Please don't start up again," Min said, firm and clear. Where on earth was this coming from? Never in all her life had she felt so in command of a situation. "We all need to get some sleep. And I'm sure you need yours too, Beau."

Beau huffed, but it sounded good-natured. "A human dating my scaly brother." He chuckled and, helping his mom up, he put an arm around her shoulders. "Is it true, Mom?"

"Oh yes dear, and she's an angel," Cressida said.

"Well, she sure speaks her mind." Beau chuckled again, his arm still around his mom, and they ambled toward the house. "Night, Minerva. Night, butthead," he threw over his shoulder.

Min watched them disappear inside, her lips forming a smile; she already sensed she was going to like Beau. But the fact he'd responded so well to her firm words was quite a surprise. As were the words themselves. She'd never addressed anyone in her life like that before.

Taking a breath, she turned to the eyes that she knew were trained on her.

"Good goddess," breathed Ethan. "Exactly how did you do that?"

"I don't know." She shrugged. "It just came over me." She felt her lips quirking again. "You were both being pig-headed."

Ethan shook his head and walked over to where their balconies joined. "Thank you. I'm sorry about that. Beau and I are like oil and water. We don't mix. And Mom just gets hysterical. If you hadn't been so calm and firm, that would probably have ended in the whole lawn being set alight. Yet again."

"Oh dear," Min said, trying to not be affected by the soft smile edging his mouth, the warmth in his gaze. Or his rather glorious chest, green and gold and iridescent in the light from their rooms.

She saw him haul in a breath before he said, his voice husky, "Thank you again. Good night, Min."

She watched him go, hugging herself, imagining it was his tail wrapped around her, not her own arms.

"Good night, Ethan," she murmured to the sound of his French doors closing.

CHAPTER 10

Ethan lay in bed nursing a double-trouble boner from hell.

He'd slept fitfully, tossing and turning, thinking about Min, replaying her surprising interaction with Beau; the way she hadn't been at all fazed by his brother's behavior, and the two male dragons screaming abuse at each other in dragon tongue.

And a fair bit of human tongue.

He winced now as he remembered the expletives he'd hurled at his little brother.

What must Min think of him?

But then he smirked as he remembered how Beau had meekly, good humoredly even, taken himself off to bed like a docile lamb rather than an angry dragon. As if just the sound of Min's voice, calm, yet commanding, had been enough. And how Mom had simply floated back to the house with a bemused little smile on her face.

No hysterics at all.

Then as he lay there staring at the ceiling, realizing she was in the room adjoining his, he'd begun to think about other things... the curl of her copper hair around her elegant neck, her slender fingers, the little indent at the base of her throat, the swell of her breasts in her... gods, frankly ugly, baggy unicorn pajamas. And that's when his imagination started to undress her, piece by piece.

Which had turned his cocks rock hard. Both of them. Like his wings, his tail, his dragonish features, his two cocks were an anomaly in his partially human form. And right now, their behavior was confusing him. Because usually his smaller second cock, known as a dragon's groc, did not get aroused until the actual act of sex. The fact that it was tingling and weeping, primed and ready to give his female pleasure when she was nowhere in sight was... highly unusual.

His groc had never been this responsive to a female before. That kind of sensitivity was only supposed to happen when a dragon met his mate.

His life's mate.

But... a human?

That had never been on the cards before. And this was exactly the wrong human for this to be happening with.

With a muffled curse, Ethan threw off the covers and strode into the bathroom, turning on the shower full blast. Before he stepped in, he glanced ruefully down his ripped abs. Both his cocks obligingly jerked. His groc, a thick nub of golden flesh nestled on the inner side of his main cock, was positioned just right to stimulate the clit of many different species (as he'd found out in his late teens—it had made him a very popular date). When stimulated, it gave him a rippling pleasure that would not culminate in an orgasm but would certainly intensify his final release.

And then there was his second cock, the monstrous thing between his thighs that was swollen and winking at him right now.

His primary cock was huge, ribbed, with flesh almost like soft scales down the shaft. Some women he'd slept with, mostly larger species, had waxed lyrical about the size, shape, and feel of it inside them, the intensity of the orgasms they had riding it.

But heck, it would be a lot for a human to take. If she even wanted to. Which, of course, she wouldn't. He resisted the urge to touch it because it was just not acceptable to bring himself off to thoughts of the woman he was fake dating. It would be too embarrassing to face her afterwards.

Ethan scrubbed at his body under the jets until his scales stung. He'd calm down if he went and played the piano, but there wasn't time. He had to meet Min for breakfast.

His only hope was to think of work. Spreadsheets were dull enough, surely.

But in the breakfast room shortly after, he found himself trying to picture spreadsheets all over again as he watched Min sashay toward him.

She looked—amazing.

Up until now, he'd reacted more to her energy and the small, tantalizing glimpses that delighted him and set off his imagination, but now her body was being showcased in the most incredible figure-hugging dress.

She had tits. Not large ones, but perfectly rounded. And hips, wide enough to shout her womanhood. The neckline was scooped and draped but otherwise it was a simple dress, but made of a shimmering material, shot silk, he guessed, which reflected the sunlight from the window. It was like... like dragon skin almost. Her hair fell in thick waves around her shoulders and somehow her glasses added a certain something—the studious look they gave her face, the frames dark against her pale creamy skin, that mouth that just begged to be kissed.

She looked like the most hellish sexy librarian. Or bookshop owner.

Fuck. He should have jerked off when he had the chance.

"Wow!" he growled, much more deeply than he meant to. "That is—I mean. You look great."

She smiled sweetly as he jumped up and pulled the chair out for her. She slid in, and again tucked a thick wave of copper hair behind her ear.

When he'd sat down opposite her, she glanced at him over the top of her glasses, and he felt like he was drowning in the dark velvet of her eyes.

"It took me ages to decide which dress to wear."

"You made the right choice."

"They are all lovely outfits. Ebony has great taste. I'm just not used to looking this posh, I guess."

She opened her purse and brought out her rolled-up script. "I've been learning my lines."

Ethan grimaced. He'd barely looked at his, too worried that the words would spark more inappropriate fantasies. He had to face it; at heart he was a total romantic. He had his mom's nature in that respect. She'd adored his father. And like her, Ethan believed in one love for life. Oh sure, he'd dated, frequently. He'd had plenty of sex—unsurprisingly, there was no shortage of species queuing up to ride dragon cock—and he prided himself on knowing how to satisfy a woman.

He was a fucking good lover. He knew that.

But love… that was a different game altogether. One that had eluded him.

Until now.

Stop these romantic notions, Blade.

His palms were sweating as he picked up his coffee cup and took a sip. He could barely look at her for fear his eyes would give him away. Brusquely, he waved to his staff member to take her order. "Tea, for you Min?"

"Yes please, a pot of English breakfast would be lovely."

While they waited, Ethan picked up his script and glanced at his lines, then it down and promptly forgot what he'd just read. "So, um, remind me where we met?"

"When you came in the Westerly looking for a book, one

your brother couldn't get for the course he was starting at Motham College."

"Gods above, why did Ebony put Beau in the mix?" he grumbled. "Surely he'd go get his own bloody books."

"Maybe she wanted you to look like a caring brother."

He huffed. "After last's night performance? Yeah, sure."

"Will he show his face today, do you think?"

"He has classes, I'm crossing my fingers that he gets to them."

"I hope I'll meet him in more pleasant circumstances soon."

"When he's not torching the garden at two in the morning? Good luck with that."

She eyed him solemnly. "There does appear to be a bit of tension between you two."

"A bit. Understatement." He sighed. "Things have been bad between us for a few years now. Beau was fourteen when Dad died—a really bad age to lose your father. Well, no age is good, I guess. Mom was in deep grief, and you know, I wasn't the best, trying to get my head around the company and how to run it. I had little time for him, I'll admit. That's when things really went off the rails…"

He paused as the waiter delivered warm croissants, a pot of tea and refilled his coffee cup. "He got involved with a gang of damaged twilight dragons. He had a major chip regarding our shifting, or lack of it, and I guess he thought if you can't beat 'em, join 'em."

"Are those the dragons out in the Wasteland?"

"Yeah. Real trouble, that species. It took a lot to get him out of that. We sent him away to school over the mountains for a while, but he's been back now for a year at college. So far, thankfully he's stayed away from the gangs, but he hangs out with a lot of rich young college kids from Motham Hill who have more money than sense."

"It sounds like he's still not happy."

"He's restless, and I don't know why. Honestly, I don't know how to help him." Ethan sighed heavily. "I've thrown money at the problem, given him the best education, but it's never enough. Managed to get him into the top aviation course at Motham College, even though his grades were terrible, but he'd rather just party"

"Maybe aviation isn't the right subject for him."

"Aviation is what Blades do. End of story."

"But what if that's not Beau's story?"

She was challenging him, but strangely he didn't feel defensive. Ethan looked out the window at the lawn, where a couple of minotaurs were re-laying the burnt parts, planting new shrubs. So many times his brother had torched the garden, so many times he'd had the gardeners patch it all up —and threatened to deduct the money from Beau's allowance. Which he'd never done. But maybe he should have, to teach him a lesson. Oh gods, trying to do the right thing as a father substitute was exhausting.

"He refuses to have a civil conversation with me, so I wouldn't have a clue what his story is," he muttered.

"Maybe you could start that conversation, being the oldest?"

"And say what?"

"Talk to him about his interests, ask him what his goals are, what he wants to be doing five years from now."

"What Beau wants is irrelevant. This is what Dad would have wanted him to do."

He sensed her serious gaze on him, sensed she didn't find his answer at all adequate, and shifted awkwardly in his seat. "Besides, you saw how he was with me last night. He'd tell me to get lost."

"You might be surprised if you went in with an open attitude."

"Well, maybe you could coach me" He managed a

crooked smile. "After all, you gave him a good dressing down last night and he went to bed meek as an angel."

"That was pure shock value." Min laughed. "A strange human woman in your apartment telling him to calm down and go to bed? That strategy would never work again, I'm certain."

He chuckled. "You could be right. But I'm still astounded. What is it about you and dragons?"

"How do you mean?"

"You just seem to have a knack. I guess. Of making us feel… comfortable with you." Before she could reply, the clock on Motham Tower struck eight. In another hour the journalist pack would be downstairs, demanding to know his and Min's love story.

"I think we just went right off script," he said with a rueful smirk, picking up his papers, "and we probably need to get back on it."

CHAPTER 11

"Tell us how you first met?" the wolf journalist asked, pen poised.

"I was looking for a book—to help my brother in his studies at Motham College. I walked into the Westerly Bookshop and this... angel," Ethan squeezed Min's hand gently, and she squeezed back, "was standing behind the counter smiling at me. Alas, I did not find the book, but we had a long conversation about dragonology, and she gave me her card."

"Purely for business reasons," Min interjected with what she hoped was a coy smile.

"Ah, but was it love at first sight, Min? Is that the real reason you gave him your card?" another reporter, a lynx, asked with a cheeky grin. Min glanced at Ethan. They'd only just rehearsed the "we're in love" line, and it felt kind of awkward saying it in front of this crowd of reporters. "Yes, yes it was. For me at least." Her hand fluttered in his and she wondered if he would read anything into it.

"And for you, Ethan? Was it love at first sight?"

"Sure was. I called her up the very next day with some lame excuse about another book I wanted her to find for me." She felt his eyes gazing down at her and his wing wrapped gently around her shoulders. "We never did find the book, did we? But we found each other."

Goddess, if she didn't know this was just an act...

"What attracted you to each other?"

"Min? What attracted you to my scaly frame?"

She hesitated, recalling the script. "Oh, you know, I think it was your eyes." Heck, this was true, his eyes *had* held her attention. "They're very intelligent, you know—and his smile, obviously."

"Not his money?" a sharp-faced fox person called out from the back of the group.

Min felt herself blushing. That was also the truth, wasn't it?

"No, not his money," she said firmly, then to her surprise she went completely off script. "It was his kindness, and... um, consideration. His integrity. Ethan is a true gentleman, which is quite rare these days." Well, *that* was true, wasn't it? She did sense these qualities about him.

The journalists were writing fast, then one piped up, "We can sure sense the chemistry between you. The room's sizzling with it." She felt Ethan's hand jerk in hers, and his wing tightened.

"Sooo," grinned foxy, "when can we expect the wedding announcement? Patter of tiny feet?"

Min felt another jerk of his wing around her shoulders. Out the corner of her eye, she saw his tail twitch. After last night's embarrassment with his tail, they'd agreed to go slow with that.

"Ah, well, you wouldn't want us to tell you all our secrets, would you?" Ethan said. "Oh wait, yeah, you would—you're the press." He rubbed a hand up his jaw in good-natured mockery, and everyone laughed.

"Right now, we're taking it slow," Min said coyly.

"Well, you sure haven't taken it slowly so far. One minute

Ethan Blade is the most eligible bachelor in town and the next, here you are, all loved up and committed," the lynx said.

"Yeah, I won't deny that. When you find the one… it kind of hits you right between the eyes," Ethan said. "Though we have actually been dating secretly for the past seven months."

Min stayed very still. It sounded so… genuine. He said it with so much emotion, his blue eyes gazing down at her intensely. So real, in fact, that she could hear some sighs among the assembled paparazzi as they closed their notebooks and brought out cameras with huge lenses.

Afterwards, they smiled and posed, his wing around her, his tail hovering as if he was dying to wrap it around her.

"Lovely, that's right, heads together. Maybe a bit closer. Kiss for me," said a fae photographer.

Ethan drew back, hesitating, his look questioning. She gave him the tiniest nod, hoping the pack of journalists hadn't witnessed their wordless exchange.

She let her eyelids flutter shut and parted her lips slightly as the sweet, warm scent of him drew close.

And then, just like last night, his mouth found hers, gentle and oh so soft, and as she pursed her lips, she sensed him draw in a breath and found herself pressing her lips to his, seeking more. The pressure of his mouth intensified; she put a hand up to his cheek and felt the softness, the slight sharp scrape of his scales. His lips firmed against hers and her mouth opened wider. For a moment they stayed like that, and Min felt like a bee caught in a honey pot as silky warmth swirled between her legs. The big hand that had been lightly cupping her waist tightened, as if wanting to draw her closer, and heavens, she wanted that, wanted to lose herself in his kiss, feel his tongue sweep into her mouth.

Suddenly Min was aware of the busy click of cameras.

This was not real.

They were just acting.

Min drew away, still tasting his warm sweetness, her body still betraying her arousal.

She didn't dare look at him.

The photographers started to put away their cameras, and a few journalists applauded.

Oh gosh. How embarrassing, the way she'd responded so ardently. She wanted to cross her legs to stop her body's reaction.

Neatly, she tugged her skirt over her knees instead.

Ethan had dropped his hand from her waist, unfurled his wing from her shoulder. He stood abruptly, and she couldn't help noticing the sharp twitch of his tail.

An erogenous zone for dragons.

Was he affected by their kiss too?

"I have a meeting to get to, so if you will excuse us..." He held out his hand and Min dutifully slid hers into it. His grip was firm, intimate and a little possessive, and oh goddess, she *loved* it.

The journalists thanked them and started to leave.

As Ethan swept along the corridor, Min had to hurry to keep up.

But as soon as they were out of sight, he dropped her hand. Min swallowed back her disappointment.

But when he glanced down at her, his eyes were twinkling. "I thought we made a great team."

"Yes, I think we pulled it off. And, um, you touching me was perfectly okay."

"Hmmm, that's not the greatest compliment I've ever had."

She was silent, her heart pounding. If she went on instinct, she'd respond by reaching up and pulling him down into another kiss. Longer this time.

"It was... very pleasant, thank you."

He laughed, harder this time. She liked his laugh, it was rich and deep and mellow. "I'm not sure if that was much better than your previous statement. Not that there is any expectation you should enjoy it. Anyhow, you have some alone time now. I have to go to the office for my meeting with the Council of Towns. I'll be back sometime this evening. Enjoy yourself, feel free to explore—the gardens are particularly lovely. At least, the parts my brother hasn't burnt. And I daresay my mom will want to see you again, if you can cope with that."

"I will cope just fine with your mom, Ethan."

"Be warned. She'll drag you into her cave room. She has so much jewelry it's obscene. And she'll be bound to want to give you some pieces. Stay firm. Otherwise, you'll be covered in bling from head to toe."

She laughed. "I'll survive."

"Yeah," he grinned, "I think you will. And for the record, I don't think you need extra bling. You look lovely just as you are."

She nodded, feeling her cheeks heating. "Thank you."

"I'll be off then. We'll meet for dinner, yes?"

"Yes." Still, he didn't move, staring at her out of those magnificent eyes. His tail flicked, as if it was tempted to stretch toward her, maybe even pull her close. Then it snapped back and he curled it close to his upper thighs, tightening his wings into his shoulders.

Then he turned on his heel and strode away.

After Ethan left, Min felt a little deflated. It had been a whirlwind morning of excitement and now she was all alone in his apartment. It was tempting to look around, try to find out more about the guy she was fake dating, but that would be prying, and she had her standards. So she resisted the urge to go into his music room. Didn't *dream* of walking into his bedroom.

Needing something to ground herself, she called Bonnie at the Westerly. All was going well, Bonnie told her. Quiet, just a few customers so far. Gingerbread was refusing to eat anything except lightly sautéed chicken livers. Min sighed. That cat alone would be the reason she needed extra money.

After she'd rung off, she went onto her balcony and gazed out into the garden. The sun was shining, and it looked beautiful. Nature always calmed her, made her feel happy. Why not go and spend some time down there? she thought. Maybe she could get some ideas from the beautiful, manicured beds for her own garden when she returned home.

After all, she'd have enough money to buy heaps more plants after this.

With that in mind, she took the elevator down to the ground floor and immediately became overwhelmed by the passages leading this way and that from the main hallway. Luckily, a small lizard girl came out of a room carrying a vacuum cleaner that was almost the same size as her.

"Do you know how to access the gardens at the back of the house?" Min asked.

"Oh yes, follow me. There's several ways—through the grand ballroom, or down past Mrs Blade's apartment. As staff, we go through the kitchens."

"Through the kitchens is fine." She wasn't sure she was ready to face Cressida quite yet, after Ethan's comments about being decked out in bling.

She got chatting to the lizard, who said her name was Sadie, and that she'd worked here for two years. "Good employer is Mr Blade, very generous with our pay and rates," she explained.

In the kitchens, a group of staff in uniforms and white hats were preparing food. It all looked very busy. After Sadie had introduced her and explained why Min was here, Min asked the chef, a cheery-faced goanna, "Are you preparing for a dinner party?"

"No ma'am, just the usual. Mrs Blade likes a lot of choice."

"Please, there's no need to address me as ma'am."

"But... you're Mr Blade's partner, it's only proper."

"I'm Minerva, most people just call me Min."

"You run the Westerly Bookshop, don't you?" a rosy-faced goblin woman kneading pastry piped up. "My daughter has been there to get 'er books on reading and writing and math. She's just started at Motham College," she said proudly.

Min beamed. "I'm so pleased. That was my father's intention—to get books to monsters again after they'd been banned by humans for so long. Anyway, the garden beckons, so I'd better go."

"I'm so pleased for you and Mr Blade," the goblin woman said. "And I've never seen his mom happier either."

Before Min had to think of a reply, in dashed a slightly harassed looking gazelle. "Mrs Blade requires breakfast—fruit and yogurt and croissants today, and her favorite cherry jam."

The goblin started to bustle off to the pantry. "Better get to it, she doesn't like being kept waiting. Mrs B is prone to getting hangry, and I tell you what, you don't want a dragon hangry anywhere near upholstery."

"Oh, ah, yes." Min couldn't help a grin at that. "This way to the garden," said Sadie, opening a door. Min thanked her and slipped out into the sunny garden, where she was greeted by rows of herbs and vegetables in low walled beds. Nearby, a number of small green species with pointy ears carrying trowels and buckets were being ordered around by a bearded troll with an even larger spade.

Min's nose twitched at the smell of the herbs. She smiled and waved, and the workers stopped and pulled at their caps.

Min kept moving swiftly until she came to the more formal garden area around to the left. Lawns and sweeping beds of brightly colored flowers and topiary bushes in all kinds of animal shapes drew her attention. As she walked along winding gravel paths, she stopped to examine the plants, and even took her cell out of her pocket to take some photos. Some of these would look lovely in the bookshop garden.

Next, there were fountains and a formal area of box cut shrubs that looked like a small maze, and beyond that, an orchard full of orange trees covered in blossom, the sweet scent pervading the air. She kept walking, amazed at how large this patch of land was, and soon found herself climbing up a small hill. At the top, amid some trees, was a marble building with a domed roof supported by pillars. It looked like a folly. She walked round the side and let out a surprised sound.

Because there, on a stone bench, sat a dragon. With a sketchbook, drawing.

She recognized him immediately. It was Beau.

She was about to back away when he looked up.

They stared at each other. His eyelids blinked rapidly across striking golden eyes, before he grinned cheekily, showing a row of sharp white fangs.

"Well, if it isn't Ethan's girlfriend."

"Hi Beau." Min hid her surprise behind a smile. "How did you pull up this morning?"

"After you hauled me over the coals?"

Min's lips twitched higher. "I did not."

"Yeah, you did. It was like a voice from the heavens commanding me to go to bed."

"I'm sorry for being bossy. It just didn't seem like you and Ethan were achieving much by arguing."

He shrugged. "Yeah, well, that's pretty much how it goes. He treats me like a fucking kid most of the time. And not surprisingly, I get mega pissed off."

Remembering her conversation earlier with Ethan, Min

said, "He's probably just worried, and wanting what's best for you."

His golden eyes glimmered. "What's he told you?"

Now she was a bit stuck. If she said Ethan hadn't told her anything, that would definitely make it look like they weren't an item. But if she said he'd told her a lot, she might not gain Beau's trust.

Why does it matter if he trusts you?

She had no answer to that.

The fact that she cared about this dragon family enough to want them to be happy was kind of strange, considering she barely knew them.

"Oh, you know." She shrugged. "Just that you've started at Motham College."

"And…?"

"—and that you had a bit of a rough patch after your dad died."

Beau stared at the sketchbook on his lap. "Did he tell you I got involved with feral dragons?"

"Mmm, maybe."

"Well, FYI, I've cleaned up my act and you know what? He's still not happy. Always on my back. And I'm sick of it."

Seeing a puff of smoke curl out of one nostril and the scales on the top of his head flutter, Min knew not to pursue it.

Instead, she took a tentative step forward. "What are you drawing?"

"Nothing." He pulled the pad up against his chest, eyeing her warily.

"I'd love to see, if you'd care to show me?"

For a moment more, he hesitated, then he smirked, as if unable to stop himself. "Okay."

He shifted sideways on the bench to accommodate her.

"Sit down, I won't throw out any flames, promise. I only do that when I'm wasted."

Min sat next to him on the marble bench, and he flicked the pad open.

The page was filled with sketches of dragons with beautiful swirling wings and tails, and goblins and orcs and beautiful elves and swords and amulets. The pencil images were drawn with expert precision.

Min gasped. "These are amazing, Beau. Are they prep for a painting?"

"Nah, it's for a game me and some mates are designing. I'm creating the characters and all the graphics. My friend Tom is a programmer. We reckon it'll be a hit."

"What's it about?"

"Basically, the humans and the dragons fight, usually to the death. But there's ways to tame a dragon, see, and the humans have to go through a number of tests to earn the dragon's trust. And there are other monsters who will get in the way, to thwart both humans and dragons. We're aiming to sell it on the human market; we reckon the time is right now that we're trading with humans more. Besides, humans have money to spend on gaming, a lot more than monsters do, that's for sure."

"I love the concept. Where did you get the idea?"

He shrugged. "Dunno. Just came to us." She sensed him side-eyeing her. "Do you know the rumors about dragons and humans—"

"I've read a little about it. There's not much information around. Your brother said..." she hesitated, and Beau took up where she'd left off.

"That dragons burnt all their books so humans couldn't steal their magic." He shrugged. "We're all told that as dragonlings. Apparently, humans are responsible for us getting stuck like this." He moved his legs restlessly in his leather pants. "Twilight dragons. That's what they call us around Motham. We're a complete fucking mess, if you want the truth. That's why I like drawing the dragons of old—real dragons, you know, who could conquer the world and inspire fear, not fuckin' ridicule. This," he swept a hand over a spectacular drawing of a fire-breathing dragon, "is what I really want to do, not study aviation."

"Why don't you tell Ethan that?"

"You've got to be kidding. He'd torch all my drawings. Erase all the files I've been working on off my computer."

"Maybe I could talk to him sometime."

Beau gave her the side-eye again. "Why would you do that?"

"I guess I know a little of what it's like for someone to have a passion others don't support." She hesitated, and sensed Beau was listening intently. "My dad, when he was young—his family tried to force him to go into the military, because that's what Westwinds had always done, but he was quiet and shy and loved books, and he was fascinated by humans' interactions with monsters." She smiled softly, sadly. "He wouldn't have survived five minutes in the military. For a start, he was completely myopic. I take after him, I guess, neither of us can see an inch in front of our noses without glasses."

"Was?" Beau said. "Is he dead like our dad?"

"Yes, he was killed in a car accident last year."

"That sucks."

"Yeah, it does."

"Sorry, I won't talk about it if you don't want to."

"It's okay, it's just, it was only me and him. My mom died when I was a baby, and I have no siblings so..." She pulled herself together. "Anyway, what I was trying to say was, Dad hated the idea of going into the military. So he ran away, over the mountains, and studied monster history at university. For a while his family disowned him, but then eventually, when my grandmother got sick, they made peace to some extent. Enough for him to have contact with his parents before they died. He was their only child. And while they never approved of Dad's choices, in the end they accepted it was the right path for him."

Beau looked at her properly now, his golden eyes studying her thoughtfully. "Your dad must have passed on his love of monsters to you."

"Yes, he did."

"Which is why you're dating a dragon, I guess. And my bro is clearly mad about you."

Min's heart beat a little faster. "What makes you say that?"

"He's asked you to move in, hasn't he? He's never got close to doing that with any other girlfriend."

Min fidgeted. Was it having to live a lie, or the mention of Ethan's previous girlfriends that made her uncomfortable?

Who he's dated is none of your business, remember.

Beau was chewing his lip now, frowning. "It's funny though—he hasn't said a word about you, and now suddenly you're living here."

"We kept it secret for some time." Min schooled herself to stay on script, repeating the lines they'd practiced this morning.

"Why?"

"Just because, humans and monsters openly dating is… er, a newish thing, I guess."

"How'd it happen?"

"He came into the bookshop. And it was… love at first sight, really. We kept it hush hush for a while, but we soon knew… that we wanted to be together, so we… Yeah, so I'm here for a little while."

"What do you mean, a little while?"

Oops.

"I said I wanted to get to know his family, and he wanted me to, and then…" She realized she didn't know what happened next.

"Then…" he prompted, his golden eyes perusing her steadily now.

"I… guess… er…"

"Are you going to marry my grumpy brother? Please fucking do, Min, it'll get him off my back."

"It's still a bit early to think about that, but yes, it's on the cards." Min cringed inwardly as she dug herself deeper into a hole. But she'd promised to make this look as real as possible, and that meant lying to everyone, his family included.

"Flaming dragon's balls, Mom will drive you mad going on about babies. She'll think you're the answer to all her grandkid prayers."

Min's chest constricted. She hated knowing she was going to disappoint this whole family.

"That is the plan, isn't it? Marriage, then babies…" Beau mused. "Must say I'd find it cool to be an uncle."

She laughed. "Oh, Beau, you're rushing ahead. At present we're just loving having this time together, and I'm really looking forward to getting to know you all."

"Yeah, well, maybe don't tell him about this yet." He turned over his pad, and she got the feeling a dark mood was descending over him. "Just forget I showed you, okay?"

Goddess, dragons' moods shifted like the weather.

"I don't think I could just forget. Those images are so powerful. You've really got talent, Beau. I'd love it if you'd show me more of your work sometime."

He looked at her, chewing on his lip, his eyes unblinking, as if taking her measure. Min made sure she met his gaze squarely.

"Okay, maybe I will. I like you—dunno why, but I do. For once in his life my dumb-assed bro has done something I approve of."

Min grinned. "It's been lovely to meet you properly, Beau. And I promise not to boss you around in future."

He glanced up and grunted a farewell, but she could see a little smile playing at the corner of his lips.

As Min walked back toward the house, she realized she was smiling too.

There was something about interacting with dragons, even sulky adolescent ones, that made her feel good.

CHAPTER 12

When Ethan arrived at his office, the Council of Towns officials were already waiting in the reception area. Damn them for always being so fucking prompt. He strode over and greeted the three men, then with a word to Sonia about refreshments, led them into his office.

"Sorry, an important press engagement ran over time," he said, motioning for them to sit. There were the usual two, the accountant, Levitt, and the legal rep, Isaac, but the third guy was new to him. A gaunt, rather ferrety looking young guy, with thin sandy hair.

When they were all seated, Ethan asked, "Where's Simon?"

Ferret-face said with a sniff, "I'm Simon's brother, Quentin Jordak. I am currently acting on his behalf while he sees to more important matters within the Council."

Was this little squirt implying this deal wasn't important? When the airport went ahead, the Council would get an injection of cash they'd not seen in years. So, this was Simon Jordak's brother, eh? Simon was a pious prick, one of the descendants of the first mayor of Tween, but Ethan's gut told him his brother was worse. There was something about him that felt untrustworthy, and he smelled slightly acidic, like his clothes were damp.

While Sonia laid out the refreshments, Ethan purposely slouched in his leather executive chair, his wings flung over the back to show he was not the least bit intimidated by humans.

When they'd all stopped rustling papers and opening laptops, he sat up straight, cleared his throat and announced, "Gentlemen, the reason I have brought you here today is to inform you of a change in my circumstances."

They stared at him cautiously. "I am officially in a committed relationship with a human. We will be getting engaged shortly. I thought it best to tell you in person, as the news will be in the press shortly. I understand that this changes my legal right to retain the bid on the lands north of Motham."

"How convenient." Quentin's thin eyebrows rose almost to meet his receding hairline. "That you should find yourself in a relationship with a human at this time."

Ethan raised his own eyebrows in answer. Only his were far more imposing. "I'm not sure I grasp what you're saying, Quentin."

"In light of our recent policy change."

Ethan smirked. "Oh yeah, that. We've been dating for some months out of the public eye, but once this policy was announced, my partner insisted it was time to go public with our relationship."

Levitt said, "I hope you are aware your partner will be expected to sign official documents that will perjure them if they lie. You will suffer heavy fines and will lose the deal, and they could be fined also. Do you understand?"

Ethan inclined his head. "Of course."

Quentin cut in harshly. "To be eligible, you must have been in a relationship for a minimum of six months before we will consider moving to the next step. How long have you been dating?"

"Seven months."

"You have proof?"

"Of course. Min will testify to that."

Quentin nearly shot out of his seat. "Who?"

Ethan frowned. The skinny little guy's face had gone beet red. Weird.

"Min. She would be known to the Council of Towns as Minerva Westwind." Ethan maintained eye contact. "I believe the family name is very well respected in Tween."

Quentin was sitting bolt upright now, almost quivering with what appeared to be incandescent rage. Either that or he was about to have a heart attack. "No way are you dating Minerva Westwind."

Ethan felt the scales all the way up his spine bristle, no doubt making ridges in his fine linen jacket. What the fuck was up with this little creep? What did he have to do with Min? Trying to keep his thoughts from spiraling, Ethan composed his features. "I can assure you, I am."

"That's impossible. I saw her less than two weeks ago, she didn't mention a thing about dating… a dragon." Quentin spat the final word like it was poison.

Why the hell had Quentin seen Min so recently? That was just before… just before their arrangement started. Under the desk, Ethan felt his claws flex. He curled his fists together to stop himself from tapping on his leg, and his chest heated ominously. He really wanted to torch this little runt into oblivion.

The other two humans cast a concerned look at Quentin. Ethan guessed that the more mature men had the good sense to know the Council actually needed his money. Not this little jerk, though, who was muttering "impossible" under his breath.

It took all Ethan's self-control to keep cool and not smoke

out the room. "I can assure you, Min is very happy to be dating a dragon. At least, she was this morning when I left her in our bed."

The scowl deepened on Quentin's thin face. "You're saying she—she's—"

"Sleeping in my bed? Yes. And living in my home."

"Minerva would never leave the Westerly. It's her life."

"Well, clearly you don't know Minerva the way I do." How the fuck *did* he know Min? "Someone is managing her shop for her, and feeding…" Ethan cast his mind back, "Gingerbread, her cat."

"She should have told me," muttered Quentin.

What an arrogant little shit. "Clearly, you're not important enough in the scheme of things for Min to think it worth mentioning to you," Ethan bluffed, though really, he had no clue if that was true. Had Min ever dated this creep? She'd told him she'd never dated, and he had believed her, but… why then was Quentin Jordak's reaction off the scale? His last comment clearly hit the mark because Quentin's face was now a shade of blotchy purple. One of the men touched him on the arm, whispered something in his ear. At last, he seemed to pull himself into line.

"How long did you say you have you been dating?" he asked stiffly.

"Seven months."

"How did you meet?"

Ethan had practiced this enough now with Min, he could almost see the day in his mind's eye. "I walked into the shop looking for a book for my brother's studies. I have it here on my computer diary." He turned the screen around for them to see. Ebony had very cleverly marked a heart emoji on his diary entry seven months ago, and the word "Min" against it. "I guess you'd say it was love at first sight—on both our parts."

A muscle ticked madly in Quentin's jaw, his mouth a thin, tight line.

Ethan continued with his scripted lines. "Min is a private person. My life is, as you know, led very much in the public eye here in Motham, and it's a big step, going public, with our relationship. But with the policy changes, Min insisted. She wants to support everything I do, and she knows the new airport means a lot to me."

Quentin made a choking sound as he tapped something viciously into his laptop.

Levitt took over. "Proof of legitimacy and long-term commitment is essential. Firstly, we will require Minerva's signature on a monster/human de facto statement, acknowledging that she is, of her own free will, cohabitating with you. We also will seek proof that you are living together *as a couple*, if you understand my gist."

Ethan inclined his head.

"You are aware that the Council of Towns reserves the right to do an inspection to prove the legitimacy of your relationship."

"I understand."

Quentin butted in aggressively, "You will be given no notice. Our officials will turn up whenever they choose. And they can and will investigate your most intimate living arrangements. There will be no chance to cover your tracks."

Ethan stared him down. "I expect the courtesy of an appointment being made in advance."

A little sneer shaped Quentin's top lip. "If you want the privilege of buying our lands, we reserve the right to walk into your home and prove you are not just another…"

"Another what?" Ethan said, cold as steel.

"I think we'll leave it there, Quentin," Levitt muttered.

Quentin looked like he was attempting to swallow a knife. Finally, he gritted out, "Anyone can sign a piece of paper. We will go to whatever lengths we need to prove you are not bluffing. Interviewing family members, turning up at any time of day—or night—inspecting your shared quarters. Every little detail will be examined. Humans don't need a permit to enter monster homes." His supercilious smile spread. "We are not going to be duped, Mr Blade. Do you understand?"

Ethan gave a casual shrug. "Buy yourself a copy of the *Motham Times* tomorrow. I think our interview will give you plenty of proof of our legitimacy."

Quentin Jordak looked like he might just vault over the desk and clout him.

If he did... well, bring it on. Ethan would be very happy to singe the thin hair off his feeble human skull.

"Someone from the Council will visit Minerva tomorrow for her signature," Levitt said, then he stood and snapped his briefcase shut.

Ethan rose. He knew better than to hold out his hand. Humans never shook hands with monsters. Except Min. Min hadn't hesitated. "I trust representatives from the Council will be attending the Blade gala ball this year," he said.

Levitt nodded tersely.

Ethan swallowed a cynical sneer. Yeah, you bet they'd be there. The humans wouldn't be able to resist: the food, the entertainment, the glitz and glamor. They'd never have hosted anything like that in their conservative little municipal buildings.

"Goodbye, gentlemen. Sonia will see you out," he said to their departing figures.

Quentin didn't say a word as he stalked out.

Rude little shit.

After they'd left, Ethan threw himself down in his chair, grabbed a pen and started madly flicking the top. The frown deepened on his browbone as he tried to untangle the meeting he'd just had.

He didn't like this squirming feeling in his gut, the tightness in his temples when he thought of Quentin's reaction when he'd mentioned Min.

She's mine.

Not yours, squib face.

When he got home, he'd raise it with her, if only because it had ramifications for their professional arrangement.

Who are you trying to kid? You're fucking jealous.

He tried to scrub that thought away, but as he did, another one surfaced. They were at real risk of a surprise visit from the Council officials to check on their relationship's validity.

Quentin Jordak's words echoed through his head. Truth was, they could turn up at whatever hour they chose, inspect his and Min's quarters. Every little detail would be examined.

It would be bad news if they were found in separate rooms.

Shooting forward, Ethan grabbed his internal handset and called Ebony.

"Come up to my office now. We have a problem," he demanded curtly.

When she arrived, he was pacing the room, still flicking the pen in tense fingers. After he'd explained the situation, Ebony said, "Well, there's no other option. You'll have to share a room."

"I can't ask Min to do that."

"You can't be in separate rooms, Ethan, not now they've threatened to visit. They can descend at any time to search for evidence, *intimate* evidence. There was a case recently where the human was living over the mountains, and they were photoshopping pics of them together in bed and got caught. End of deal. So obviously they're clamping down big time now."

Ethan swore under his breath.

"There's something else that's weird. Something about this guy and Min. He went nuts when I mentioned her name."

"Well, she is a Westwind. That would put their high-breed noses out of joint."

Ethan grunted. He knew there was more to it than that.

"I've got a solution to the bedroom thing. You can sleep in your dressing room and let Min have the bed," Ebony chirped brightly. "We'll put a sofa bed in the closet. That way you can close it up and hop into bed together quick smart if they turn up." Ebony chuckled. "Poor Min, you'll have to pay her a bonus for this."

"It's not fucking funny," he growled as she sashayed to the door, still chirping to herself.

After she'd left, Ethan threw the pen across the room, then called his chauffeur.

It was time to go home and have an awkward conversation with Min.

CHAPTER 13

Min was just about to take the stairs to her room when a squeal of delight pierced her ears.

She turned to see a billow of rainbow silk and sequins descending on her. And then she was engulfed in a dragon hug that smelled of exotic spices.

Cressida, of course.

When Cressida released her, she had tears in her eyes. "Oh, my dear girl, I was coming to thank you for your intervention last night. So bold. So confident. So *daring*. And yet, it worked. I have never, ever seen Beau calm down so quickly. How did you do it?"

"Honestly, Cressida, I don't know. I just felt... knowing Ethan and how upset he gets about Beau, and seeing them arcing up, that I needed to intervene."

"Have you been around many dragons before, Min?" Cressida had already linked arms with her, and seemed intent on accompanying her to the elevator.

"A few, in the bookshop." Very rarely did dragons appear in the bookshop, to be honest. Hardly surprising if all their books had been burnt.

"Generally, dragons are somewhat distrustful of humans.

Sad really, since we used to have such a great relationship with your kind. Many moons ago."

"Do you know much about that, Cressida?"

"Only hearsay, my dear, passed through the Delawares and Blades verbally from one generation to the next. And obviously we have these human aspects to our form." She held out a chubby arm, then stuck out her foot in a little scrappy sandal, with its bright red shellacked claw tips. "So, we all know there are links... You know, mating bonds that must have happened way back. It would be good to know, but I guess we may never find out. But then there's you. The bright light in our lives. Arriving like magic. A human mate for my Ethan!"

Cressida stopped at the doors of the elevator and gathered Min's hands in hers. "Look at your lovely long white fingers. I bleached mine once to try and make them less green, but it didn't work."

"Bleached? Oh, Cressida, why would you bleach your skin? It's so... beautiful."

"You think so?"

"Really yes. And so soft."

"We dragons probably have a bit of a chip... you know, about..." Her voice trailed off. Then she brightened. "You need to come and view my cave room. I have some wonderful pieces of jewelry that would suit you. And we *must* go shopping. I'll help you choose a gown for the gala ball. It's a very special time for me. I took over giving away the prizes after Clifton died. The yearly wheel-out-the-widow thing. Let the old girl make a speech and give out a trophy to a few up-and-coming monster businesses." She tinkled a laugh. "I absolutely insist you let me help you choose a dress for the occasion."

"Oh, yes, that would be lovely." Min decided it would at least be different from her usual taste.

"I will have so much fun matching colors to your skin tone, rather than my awful sallow skin."

Min wished Cressida would stop putting herself down.

"So, when?" Cressida blinked at her.

"When what?"

"When will we go shopping?"

Min opened her mouth to answer when suddenly Ethan appeared beside them. "Are you purloining my girl, mother?"

"She's going to have lunch with me and then we're going shopping together." Cressida was still holding and squeezing Min's hands, pumping them up and down in her excitement.

"Mother, please don't monopolize Min. We need time together. Just the two of us."

Cressida pouted. "But I need time with her too!"

"Yes, Mom, and you will have it. Minerva is here... for a while."

Cressida looked alarmed. "A while? I thought she was here for good."

Min felt Ethan stiffen. "We're trialing living together, Mother."

Cressida's face drooped. "Dragons don't do trials. They know at once when they've met the one. It... it vibrates through them, an energy. You must have felt it Ethan, it's like nothing else. I daresay humans feel it too, yes?" She raised an eyebrow at Min, her golden eyes alight.

Min made enthusiastic noises and cast a look at Ethan, trying to ensure he didn't upset his mom any further.

He returned the look with an eyebrow waggle that was both endearing and slightly... panicked.

"Mom, I have something rather urgent to discuss with Minerva. Alone."

"Oh, poo." His mother pouted. "Well, I will arrange for you to have tea and scones with me in my apartment later then. How does three o'clock sound?"

Min looked at Ethan for guidance. He inclined his head. "If Min wishes."

"Of course," Min said warmly. "I would love that, Cressida."

With that, Cressida gave her a smacking kiss on each cheek and let her go, sashaying down the corridor in a blur of bright color.

Ethan huffed a sigh. "Sorry about my mom—yet again."

"Stop apologising. She's lovely. Why are you home? I thought you weren't back until this evening."

"I wasn't planning to be, but something has come up, in relation to... us, and I need to talk it through with you."

"Okay," said Min. What on earth was going on? Ethan was more antsy than she'd ever seen him.

When they reached his apartment, Ethan strode into the open-plan living area and motioned to one of the large leather sofas. "Sit down, Min," he said. "Something has come up that we need to discuss urgently."

"Is everything okay?" Min asked, her gaze following his tense body as he paced up and down the room, noting the twitch of his tail tip.

He turned and his eyes sparked. "Does the name Quentin Jordak ring any bells to you?"

Min's scalp tightened. "Yes. He's handled my rental agreement for the bookshop for years. He's the one who told me the property was going on the market."

Ethan stared hard at her, as if trying to read the truth of her words, then pivoted and continued pacing. Now his tail was swishing sharply from side to side. Was he angry? And if so, why? Suddenly he stopped and burst out, "Is there... is there anything going on between you two?"

"No, of course not," Min said indignantly.

He pinched the long bridge of his nose. "Because obviously if there was, this could seriously disrupt our... arrangement."

"Do you really think I'd agree to fake date you if there was?"

"No. Or at least, I hoped not. But does he know anything about—us?"

"No! Absolutely not. I'd never tell that man anything about my life."

She thought his shoulders relaxed a little at that. Min sighed. "If I'm honest, I find him... kind of creepy."

"Yeah, well, I can understand why." Ethan gave a distinct shudder. "Officious, nasty little dude, was my conclusion."

Min couldn't help a smirk. "I'd say that's a fairly accurate description of Quentin. But why are you asking me about him now?"

"He's currently heading up land sales for the Council. His brother Simon has moved into some other role, apparently. I had a meeting with him and other officials this morning."

"Oh, that's a step up for him, he was just in charge of rentals before."

"Yeah, well, he's in charge of the whole shebang at present, and when I announced our relationship, he made it patently clear he doesn't believe we are... together. Said you didn't mention dating me when he met you last."

Min bristled. "Because who I'm dating is none of his business."

"He seemed really put out. That's why I'm asking. I guess I wondered..."

Min hesitated. Why not tell Ethan her misgivings? "This is going to sound like I'm up myself, but he... he does give off a vibe when he's with me."

Ethan stopped pacing. "What kind of vibe?" The look in his blue eyes was almost possessive. And she liked it, Min realized, with a frisson of excitement.

"Just a... He looks at me like... Sometimes I catch him looking at my..." She gulped and waved a hand over her chest.

Ethan's eyes darted to her breasts and then rapidly away. He cleared his throat. "Yes, well…that would make sense of why he seemed…"

"Seemed what?"

"Enraged, I guess, as well as disbelieving." His blue eyes held hers intensely.

Min straightened her spine. "Well, we'll just have to prove him wrong, won't we?" Her heart skipped a beat as she said it.

Ethan abruptly broke eye contact. "Ah yes, well, speaking of that, there's something I need to run past you, Min. He also said that the Council will be doing a home inspection. To check that we are bona fide. They could come at any time, day or night, without warning."

Min frowned. "Can they just invade people's privacy like that?"

"They can do whatever they want." He shrugged, his eyes suddenly pensive. "I may be wealthy Min, but I'm still *just* a dragon. Humans have lorded over us monsters for centuries; they still hold a lot of power."

Min sat clasping her hands, her breathing fast and shallow.

"I'm sorry if this is upsetting. I've discussed it with Ebony, and we think we've worked out a solution. But you need to be totally comfortable with it." He stopped pacing and huffed a sigh.

"Go on, Ethan."

"We will need to look like we're sharing the same room. In reality, I'll sleep on a pull-out bed in my dressing room, one that can easily be folded up if the authorities arrive." He cleared his throat. "You will need to leave your belongings in the bathroom, your toiletries and such, and put your clothes in the closet."

"I see."

"I'm really sorry, Min." He was looking so apologetic now, she couldn't bear it.

"Really, Ethan, It's fine."

More than fine, truth be told. Her whole body was fizzing and popping at the thought of being in such close proximity.

"Of course, I'll pay you more for having to do this," he muttered.

"You will do no such thing." She went over and stood right in front of him, flicking her hair almost angrily. Yes, she actually felt angry with him. She didn't know why exactly, but it felt like he was insulting her, treating her like she was just a service, when...

When what Min, exactly?

His mouth twisted. "Min, I need to at least compensate you for..."

"It's not all about money, Ethan. I like you and your family; I feel an affinity with you. Maybe because we're both trying to fulfil our fathers' dreams... I don't know, but I just do. And I totally agree with the principle that monsters should be allowed to buy human-owned land without all these stupid shenanigans. I just feel bad for being part of this human shitshow. I even feel bad for my heritage—"

"How do you mean?"

"Oh, you know." Now it was Min's turn to pace, and his to watch her intently. "The Westwind name and the suffering Colonel Westwind perpetrated on monsters."

He shook his head. "That's ridiculous."

"It's not. I feel ashamed every time I have to say or write my name around monster kind."

"Min, for the gods' sake, my ancestors probably killed a fair few humans in their time. You can't feel guilty for what Colonel Westwind did two hundred years ago. I mean, look what your father achieved, what you're doing now..."

"It's not enough. We humans did something to stop dragons from shifting."

"There's no proof of that, Min."

"That's because you had to burn all your books." She slumped on the bed, feeling utterly wretched.

"Min, why are we arguing?" His voice cut through her angst, and she looked up at him in surprise.

"Are we?"

He laughed at that, ruffling a hand over the scales on his head. "I don't know. Feels a bit like we are."

"Oh."

"We're almost behaving like…" He stopped abruptly.

Min cocked her head, her eyes questioning him. "Like…"

"A married couple." He grinned sheepishly and she found a smile shaping her own mouth.

"Ethan, I guess I just went off on a tangent, but what I really meant to say is I'm fine with sharing a room with you. Honestly, you've been an absolute gentleman and I know we can work this out. Also, I own very modest nightwear."

His smile widened. "Oh yeah, the unicorn pajamas."

Now they were both grinning, rather stupidly. "I'll just pretend you're Gingerbread," Min said.

Ethan's eyebrows shot up. "Your cat? Now I think I might be insulted."

She decided not to tell him that Gingerbread slept curled up on the bed next to her most nights. Instead, she said, "And I'm sure the bathroom door has a lock on it, doesn't it?"

"No. But I'll get one fitted."

"No, don't worry, we'll just use a sign. Or I can call, 'human in unicorn PJs desperate for a pee.'" Min dimpled, and their eyes met and danced. And then suddenly they were both outright laughing.

"Ethan, really, it'll work out. I'm already feeling at home here. I um, saw Beau again this morning, by the way. We had a very pleasant chat."

Ethan raised an eyebrow. "What about?" His blue eyes were curious.

"Oh, you know, his studies." That was kind of true.

"I bet he told you that he doesn't like his course. And that it's all my fault."

"Yeah, well, he did say it wasn't really his thing."

"Did he mention his gaming obsession?"

"Oh, er, not really," Min said quickly. "He's a nice kid, you know, Ethan. Under his bravado."

"Yeah, well, I wish he'd show *me* his nice side." His face tightened. Time to change the subject, Min decided.

"So us rooming together, that's settled then?" she said brightly.

"Yes. Seems so." He looked relieved. "Thank you, Min, I really appreciate your understanding about this." He made a move toward the door.

For some reason she really wanted to keep him here, chatting. "When is our next formal engagement?"

His face tightened again. "Next Friday. The intimate dinner à deux. In the garden."

"And being photographed kissing in the bushes." She giggled nervously.

"Yes, we've employed a photographer who's known for his celebrity shots." He ruffled his head scales. "I'm asking a lot of you Min, more than you signed up for."

"Don't forget you're helping me too. We're both doing this to fulfil our parents' dreams," she said gently.

His lips twisted ruefully. "Glad you see it that way. Well then, I guess I'll go back to work. And Min—"

"Yes?" She stood up from the bed, hopeful, though for what, she didn't really know.

"Thank you for being so accommodating." He strode to the door, then turned to face her. "And—for…"

She cocked her head and held her breath, waiting.

"Just being… you." And then, before she could reply, he was gone.

CHAPTER 14

"Why are you still at work? Don't you have *the* romantic dinner with Min tonight?"

Ebony poked her beak around the door of his office, her head cocked and her eyes bright and beady.

"I'm giving her space to get ready."

Ebony strolled into the office. "How's rooming together going?"

"We're making it work," Ethan said stiffly, avoiding her curious gaze.

Truth was, it was awkward, but with his dressing room being almost as big as a bedroom, he could at least go in and close the door. Knowing she was so close had kept him these past few nights, nursing not one but two eager cocks, and as for navigating the bathroom… well, so far, they'd only *nearly* bumped into each other once.

If he was honest, he was so damn nervous about tonight that sitting here looking at the latest plans for the airport was the only thing calming him down. That was why he was doing all this, he reminded himself. It had nothing to do with Min's full, soft mouth and her big dark eyes behind those glasses.

Meanwhile, Ebony showed no signs of leaving. She pulled up a chair by his desk and sat down.

"Hmm, so is the pull-out comfy?"

"Lumpy as shit."

"But at least if the authorities raid in the middle of the night, you can turn it back into a sofa and just hop into bed together and cuddle up. That's so adorable." Ebony was smirking; he knew she was enjoying this. At his expense. Could she tell his feelings for Min were heading off the professional cliff so fast he was at risk of falling flat on his scaly face?

He merely grunted and turned back to his computer screen.

Ebony picked up his glass dragon egg paperweight and started playing with it.

"Isn't Pete expecting you home?" he grumbled finally, envious suddenly of her real loved-up relationship.

"He's cooking tonight, so I don't have to rush. We take it in turns. Guess we'll just snuggle up on the sofa and watch a movie after. We're so dull and domesticated these days."

The thought of doing that with Min floated into his head, and he felt even more envious. He imagined them cuddling up in his big movie room together. Sharing a huge bowl of popcorn maybe, or take-away noodles.

Ebony leaned forward, her chin on her wings. "So, Mr Dragon, are you quite sure this whole fake dating thing is fake?"

His head jerked up. "Of course it is."

Ebony shrugged. "Just, you know, there's a vibe between you two. A bit of smoldering chemistry. I've seen the way you look at her. Caught her looking at you that way too."

"Really?" A warmth crept up his neck.

"Yep. I think she may have a bit of a crush. And you sure as hell do."

"Keep your bird brain in check, will you?"

But still the damn raven pushed. "She's cute, right, in a kind of serious way, don't you reckon?"

"Mmmm, maybe." The plans danced in front of Ethan's eyes as an image of kissing Min came into his head.

His stomach churned.

Tonight. After their candle-lit dinner for two in the orange grove, they had to simulate a serious make-out session that a minotaur from the purple lantern district would be proud of. Already he had trouble containing his imagination—and his cocks. Because this couldn't be just a peck on the lips, it had to be a passionate kiss—one that would leave no doubt in anyone's mind they were mad about each other.

Hell's goblins.

He'd definitely embarrass himself with a hard-on. His cocks had been giving him merry hell. And he couldn't even jerk off in the bathroom beforehand in case Min walked in.

Ebony got up and strolled over to the doorway, where she stood smirking at him.

"Just go home," he muttered.

Enjoy '*The Kiss*,'" she said, making air quotes around the words, then finally left him in peace.

Huffing a sigh, Ethan powered down his computer and flicked a look at his watch.

Time to head home.

And yet... his nerves were shredded, and he really needed to cool down before he saw Min. He got up and strode over to the window. He couldn't go home feeling agitated like this. His chest was tight and hot and full of flames. He'd probably singe the limo.

Any other time, he would go to the gym in the basement of his offices and do a vigorous workout, using the flying machine to exercise his wings. But there wasn't time for that tonight, and he needed to let off steam. A *lot* of steam.

Damn it, yes, by gods, he would fly home. Ignore the rules for once.

He called his chauffeur and told him not to wait, then stripped off his shirt and jacket and strode over to the windows of his office. Sliding open a panel of the floor to ceiling glass windows, he stepped onto the narrow ledge.

He was twenty five floors up, and the feeling was exhilarating.

Ethan took a deep breath and, for the first time in ages, spread his wings and took off. And soared over the Motham rush hour traffic toward home.

Toward Min.

~

Min had not had the best few days.

After the honeymoon period in the grand Blade mansion, having fully explored the gardens, frankly, she was bored. With Ethan at work for hours, she felt lonely and out of place in all this grandeur.

The fact that she barely had to think of something she wanted before a servant was at her side, ready to take her request, was a novelty that soon wore off.

She nearly snapped at one poor snake girl that she could get her own damn glass of water, thank you very much.

She missed her simple life, her little shop, her garden, Gingerbread curled up asleep by her side. And worse, she felt like she was moping around waiting for Ethan to light up her day. It only made it worse, knowing he was sleeping in the dressing room, while she was alone in his big bed.

Even so, there were things to keep her busy.

The highlight had been Cressida showing her round her cave room, which was actually a whole interconnected system of rooms, with domed ceilings decorated to look like there were stalactites everywhere. Though it wasn't exactly to Min's taste, she found it fascinating. And Cressida's jewelry stash was, by any standards, completely staggering.

The lowlight had been the arrival of a rather officious woman from the Council of Towns firing nasty personal questions at her. Luckily, she and Ethan had gone over their stories several times, so she was pretty sure she'd got the details right. The woman's mouth had puckered as she told Min to sign on the dotted line, and then she'd left in a hurry, as though being in a dragon mansion was akin to spending time in a sewer.

Such a snob.

That evening over dinner, Ethan had commiserated with her over the document signing, then politely excused himself, citing work commitments. As usual since they'd been sharing a room, he was impeccably polite and distant.

Except Min didn't want *this* dragon. She wanted the dragon she'd seen glimpses of, the little jokes and quirky comments he made, the twinkle in his bright blue eyes when he looked at her, his deep resonant laugh and the way it made his throat bob.

She wanted—oh goddess above—to catch him naked in the shower.

Minerva Westwind. Really!

Not that she'd tried to, of course.

She'd kept to the rule of checking before she entered. Not that it was ever a problem. He was never in there. He'd come to bed really late, tiptoeing through the bedroom so as not to wake her. (She was of course, wide awake.) She'd hear the soft pad of his feet in his dressing room, and in the morning he would creep out of the room before she was awake. What woke her were the sweet strains of his piano floating down the corridor.

And each morning she'd get out of bed, open the bedroom door a crack and listen, enthralled.

He'd lied to her. He wasn't an amateur.

This guy could play piano like a pro.

She'd stood transfixed, almost wanting to weep from the

melodies, longing to tiptoe along the corridor to his music room, but not daring. And when she heard him stop playing, she'd run back to bed and listen to his footsteps, hearing him pause briefly at the bedroom door before striding off down the corridor.

It was a really strange existence, but she kept reminding herself that at the end of all this, she would be able to buy her bookshop freehold. That it was worth it, even if her heart was filled with a longing she couldn't quite put words to.

But right now, as she decided she'd wear the beautiful silver dress hanging in her wardrobe, she was filled with excitement.

Because today they were going to kiss. Really kiss. No more tantalizing grazing of lips. No more pecks on the cheek for the camera.

Would he use his tongue? She'd seen the forked tip from time to time, when he was concentrating, and she wondered what it would feel like tangling with hers.

Wriggling into the dress, she was just about to add some jewelry Cressida had insisted on loaning her when a shadow passed by the window. She ran to the balcony to see a winged silhouette against the sunset.

Beau? Headed out for a night on the town, maybe.

She hoped he wouldn't arrive home like he had the other night. She hadn't seen him since their interlude in the garden, so hopefully that meant he was going to college as well as doing his drawings.

But no, *this* dragon was heading toward the house, and he was bigger and more buffed than Beau.

It was Ethan, she realized, her breath hitching. Bare-chested, his wings beating in slow, powerful strokes, his face intent and focused on his goal, which was clearly the middle of the lawn.

Min watched him come in to land, totally mesmerized.

His chest, so buffed and human, his pecs and six pack

accentuated by his green and golden shimmering skin. His human arms moved gracefully in sync with his wings, like he was swimming, not flying, and his tail moved to the same rhythmic beat. He was the picture of beauty and harmony as he soared and circled.

Peering over the veranda, she watched him glide elegantly onto the lawn, knees bent, his feet taking one, two, three long strides before furling up his wings and brushing them down casually. Already a uniformed lizard was running toward him with a bathrobe. Ethan shrugged it over his shoulders, his wings poking through the slits in the back of the gown as he strolled nonchalantly toward the house.

Min stood completely still, her heart beating hard in her chest. Watching him fly had completely taken her breath away.

She was just about to take out a diamond on a white gold chain and pair it with the diamond droplets that hung from her ears when there was a soft knock at the door.

She flicked her hair over her shoulders, clasped her hands in front of her and then called out primly, "Come in."

Ethan's head poked round the door. "Hi—all fine to enter?" Then he saw her, and she noticed the scales around his horns stand to attention, then flatten. Something hot and sexy flared in his eyes.

"Wow! You look incredible."

"Thank you," she said, color chasing across her cheeks.

He entered the room in his robe.

"Nice work outfit," she quipped, eager to take the limelight off herself.

"I flew home. This is what the staff gave me so I wouldn't be bare-chested."

"I know. I watched you land."

"Oh." He grimaced. "It was a bit clumsy, I got caught in a wind gust."

"No, on the contrary, you were very elegant."

He gave a self-deprecating laugh and strolled across the room, little glimpses of his chest shimmering from the gap in his robe. Min gulped hard.

"Well, thank you, but you're being kind. I'm pretty rusty. Not like Beau, who flies all the time despite knowing he shouldn't."

"Is there a law against it?"

"Not exactly, but there are regulations we've agreed to with the gargoyles from Tower Security. Besides, it's not a great look if the family who own all the aircraft in Motham City fly everywhere on their own wings. Doesn't exactly inspire confidence." He sighed. "But, heck, I sure miss flying."

"But if Beau does... surely you can?"

"Beau does *not* represent this family," he said, almost fiercely. "I'm constantly being made aware of how I need to compensate for his rash behavior."

Min pinned her lips. Now was clearly not the time to go into bat for his little brother. What right had she to interfere anyway? She was, after all, nothing to this family. And at the end of this arrangement they'd all forget about her. Ethan would find a suitable monster partner, probably a dragon, and... and... why did that thought make her feel so sad suddenly?

Min blinked away the moisture in her eyes. Her usually steady emotions were all over the place. Was it because she had no family of her own? Or perhaps it was the idea of kissing Ethan when really it was all a sham, however much she'd like to pretend otherwise.

"I've finished in the bathroom if you need to get ready," she said stiffly, and turned toward the window. Suddenly she felt less like a princess in her finery, and more like a kid playing dress-ups.

She heard him mutter something and disappear into the bathroom.

Who was she kidding? She wasn't a princess with her prince. This wasn't a fairy tale with a happy ever after. She was a human woman down on her luck, fake dating a dragon for economic gain.

She looked down at the beautiful necklace Cressida had lent her, and shut the box with a snap.

CHAPTER 15

"Will that be all, sir?" The skink waiter removed the dessert plates with a little bow. "Can I bring you coffee, tea, chocolates?"

"Min?" Ethan raised his eyebrows at her across the candle-lit table, and she smiled and shook her head.

After their awkward conversation when he got home, which Ethan put down to nerves on both their parts, it seemed a few glasses of fine Avella Hills champagne and a delicious meal, the smell of orange blossom all around, and a soft, nearly full moon hanging in the sky had put them both in the right headspace.

Which was a fucking good thing, since very soon they'd get the cue that there was a photographer poised and ready.

"Maybe just another half glass of bubbles, please." Min smiled, a little boss-eyed, at the waiter, who poured it and then left.

"Are you sure that's a good idea? You don't usually drink much."

"Not champagne, I agree. My drink of choice is rum."

"Rum!"

She shrugged, twirling the glass between her fingertips. "I

keep a bottle under the counter, so I can take a swig between customers."

"Min!"

She giggled again. "Westwind humor, just ignore me."

Ethan's lips quirked. "I should know by now."

"Comes out when I least expect it, so I don't even know myself. Dad was prone to making very inappropriate jokes about high-society humans—usually when they were within earshot."

"That would have made him popular. My experience with high breeds is they're generally a humorless bunch. Present company excepted, of course."

"Very glad you added that addendum. I would hate to be associated with high breeds. Dad loved stirring the pot, poking fun at their conventions. We rarely got invited to Tween events. Not, may I add, that we were worried by that."

"I guess opening a bookshop dedicated to monster books would have been enough to ensure that."

"Most definitely. They loved our name… just not us."

He watched her put the glass to her lips and slug back two big mouthfuls. She smiled hazily at him across the rim.

"Delicious." She sighed. "I feel like I'm really living it up."

"Min, maybe slow it down a bit, or I'll be carrying you back…"

"Mmm, we could just fly up to the balcony."

Fly with her. To their room. Ye gods. A sudden fantasy overtook him of gliding with her in his arms, landing on the bed, nuzzling into her neck. Feeling his cocks nudging into the soft, dark heat of her pussy. His secondary cock would tease between her folds until she cried out her readiness to take all of him.

Back up the truck, Blade.

But how could he when she was looking at him like that,

twirling a little copper lock of hair around her finger, those two little dimples playing close to her lush lips.

"Shouldn't we be flirting wildly? To get in the mood..." She drained her glass and blinked at him, her eyebrows bouncing comically.

Ah, *this* Min, when she loosened up, how he loved being around her. And hey, why not? Flirting would definitely loosen them both up, make their kiss look like the real thing.

He poured himself half a glass more of bubbles. "Okay, you start."

"Oh no, no. You're the experienced dater."

"Not of late." He grimaced.

"What? No gorgeous ladies lined up?"

I only want you. He gulped down the champagne to stop himself from saying the words out loud. "Nope, not right now. I mean—present company excepted."

"You are saying that a lot this evening. I will *accept* being *excepted*, thank you."

He threw back his head and laughed.

"What?" Another innocent blink.

"Westwind humor and dragon humor do seem to fit well."

She reached over and touched his hand with her pinkie. He startled.

She bit her lip. "How about Westwind flirting and dragon flirting. How do they fit?"

He opened his mouth, trying to think of something witty to say, but the soft stroke of her pinkie grazing the side of his hand was doing disturbing things to his cocks.

"So, tell me, how should I flirt with you?" she asked.

"I—I think," *gulp,* "you're doing just fine."

She cocked her head. "So how would you flirt with me? Just say you met me in a bar, what would you do, what would you say?"

"Er," he stuttered, all his scales fluttering.

Min giggled. "Don't tell me the handsome dragon is lost for words."

"Handsome — I'll take that."

"So you like compliments?"

"Yeah, dragons like compliments the way we like bling."

"Except you don't like bling."

"Compliments are verbal bling. I'll accept them."

"What have your other girlfriends complimented you on?"

"Oh, I don't know, my smile, I guess. "

"Yes, I can agree with that," she murmured, and he glowed. "How about your kissing prowess?"

He chuckled. "Maybe. You'll have to give me your opinion on that a little later."

"So, what else have your previous dates said about you?" She was leaning her pretty chin on her hands now, elbows on the table, batting her eyelashes behind her frames, and there was no denying it, it was a turn-on.

"Oh, this and that. You know…"

"No, I don't know, that's why I'm asking."

"They often quite liked the things I did with my tail, I guess."

"Oh." Her chin retracted, her lashes sweeping her cheeks. Oh gods, he'd gone too far.

But then, flicking her hair off her shoulders, she leaned closer. His eyes panned to her breasts, pressed together, milky white flesh glittering under the fairy lights. Ethan gritted his fangs, remembering what she'd said about Quentin. He would never want her to put him in the same box as that creep. But then she whispered, "So, Mr Blade, what *can* you do with that tail?"

For a second, he just stared at her.

Oh, to hell with it, he was enjoying himself too much. Ethan leaned forward in his chair until their foreheads were almost touching.

His tail twitched and he felt it moving toward her chair

under the table. "Apparently I play a mean game of tailsy," he husked.

"Tailsy!" Her eyes popped, her cheeks pinking as she put down her glass. And then she moved her leg under the table and her foot engaged with his tail.

Gently, very tentatively, he let it curl around her ankle.

He held his breath. Didn't move his tail. Not even a twitch.

But she didn't take her foot away. Instead, she inched it closer.

And then she breathed out, "How would it go from here?" Her lips were parted, glistening, ripe, her eyes an invitation.

He hesitated, then edged his tail up her calf. "Okay so far?" he asked gruffly.

In answer, she reached across the table and traced over his lips with a fingertip.

His body jerked at the frisson of lust that went from his lips to his tail, and his cocks jumped from fluffed to fully alert.

Oh gods, that was it. He was going to show her some real tail play. Right here. Right now.

His tail curled up around her calf, the tip exploring, quivering, stroking up over her knee, onto her inner thigh, and she... she opened, sank back in her chair, panting little breaths that made her breasts rise and fall sharply.

"Min?"

"Mmmm..."

"Want me to stop?"

"No," she hummed. "It's nice."

Now his tail flicked higher up her inner thigh, marveling at the softness of her skin. His cocks were hard against his fly, painfully so, his groc leaking copiously. Thank the gods above they were seated, because there'd be a mighty big stain on his pants at this rate.

Tentatively, he let his tail tip probe higher, flicking at the lace edge of her panties, watching her face as her head arched back, exposing her long white neck, her teeth biting at her lower lip.

She was—gods! Min was hot for this. He could smell her arousal wafting across the table from him, sweet and intoxicating, and he wanted nothing more than to thrust his tail up into the apex of her thighs, peel aside the little scrap of material and stroke the tip along her hot, wet cleft.

He held himself back, his body taut, tail quivering with the effort to restrain himself.

And then, fucking hell, her little hand curled around the end of his tail, stroked the tip and moved it under her panty line. Ethan let out a muffled curse as delicious wet heat registered. Oh yeah, his groc was going crazy now—he could feel the fluid seeping into his pants.

And... gods, she wasn't stopping.

She moaned softly as she gently tugged his tail along her seam. Heck, she was drenched. The musky aroma mingled with the heady scent of orange blossom, making it all the more tempting—so fucking tempting. Unable to stop himself, he moved his tail tip faster between her slick folds and then, finding the swollen bud of her clit, he let it curl around it, quiver. Inside his pants his groc started to vibrate, and his primary cock nearly burst through his zipper.

Hell, if this continued, he'd be creaming himself spectacularly.

And seeing her, slumped lower in her chair, eyelids fluttering, her lips swollen on her little gasps, it seemed Min wasn't far off coming spectacularly too.

Her thighs spread wider under the table, her fingers gripping his tail. Her hips snapped and jerked, and... and... out the corner of his eye, Ethan caught the flash of a camera.

Shit!

He had to be the responsible one here. She was a virgin.

And somewhere in the bushes, that photographer was capturing her teetering on the edge of release.

He leaned forward and stroked her cheek. "Min. There's a guy with a camera nearby."

She opened her eyes, blinked dazedly at him from behind her glasses. Even through the lenses, he could see how desire had darkened her gaze. How her whole body was almost tipping over the edge. So beautiful, so vulnerable. It made him want to protect her more than anything.

He started to reel his tail in.

"Oh, I—" Her fingers loosened their grip, and, trying not to weep from frustration, he scrolled it back close to his butt.

She gasped, staring at him out of desperate, hungry eyes. Her glasses had gone wonky on her nose, and her cheeks were flushed bright and rosy.

And Ethan's hard-ons were about to cripple him.

CHAPTER 16

As Min came down from the peak of pleasure she'd been climbing, two things struck her.

Firstly, she had drunk way too much champagne, and secondly, she'd almost ridden a dragon's tail to orgasm. Except she hadn't. Because there was someone in the bushes with a camera, and Ethan had been gentleman enough to stop.

But would she have? If he hadn't pulled back? Her pussy was clenching with longing, and the dampness around her thighs was enough evidence that she would have gone the whole way.

She managed to straighten in her chair and brushed the hair back from her hot cheeks with shaky hands.

"I think that prepared me for the, um… the second act," she tried to joke, at the same time squeezing her thighs together to ameliorate the throbbing desperation in her pussy.

Ethan just stared at her, his eyes in the moonlight full of raw emotion, a muscle in his jaw working.

He didn't seem to appreciate the joke.

She took a sip of water. She probably needed to throw the whole glass over herself just to cool down. Goddess, she'd take so much more than a kiss right now. He could bend her over the tabletop, do wicked things to every part of her body...

Another camera flash.

"That's our cue." Ethan got up and held out his hand to her. And as she stood on jelly legs, his arm came around her, his wing gently folding her into his chest.

"So, um, now what?" She gazed longingly up at his mouth, the musky sweet smell of him doing nothing to dampen her cravings.

"We play to the camera."

"I thought we just did," she said on an almost hysterical laugh.

"They will *not* be using those pictures," he gritted out, and you had to love the growly protective way he said it.

"But maybe I should, ah, start by, er, nuzzling into your neck?" he suggested.

"After what you were doing with your tail, I hardly feel you need to ask." She giggled.

"I'll have to lift you up."

"More than happy for you to—oh, nice." She gasped as two strong arms suddenly swung her up and her breasts were crushed against his powerful chest. She registered his hands—or was it his wings—pinning her thighs around his flanks, and when his hot mouth touched her neck, Min keened with delight and stretched her neck into his caresses.

Vaguely she was aware of another flash coming from the direction of the shrubbery.

Whether it was the champagne or her body's cravings, she couldn't care less right now. Being cradled in a dragon's embrace was like floating in heaven. She felt his tail now, looping around her thighs, one hand splayed against the back of her head.

"May I kiss you now?" he asked, his eyes glittering and so deliciously non-human. Min nodded, her lips parting, ripe and oh so ready...

At first his lips barely grazed hers, his forked tongue tip softly circling her lips. Min trembled and opened wider, begging on little wheezy breaths, and as if that broke the dam of Ethan's self-control, suddenly the kiss was taking no prisoners. With a groan deep in his chest, his tongue plunged into her mouth, demanding, thrusting, almost indecently mimicking a far more intimate act.

Min clung on for the ride, kissing him back with all her might, grinding her wet seam against the long hard ridge in his pants.

There was no mistaking it. Their kiss was turning Ethan on just as much as it was her. And dragon dick was huge.

Another flash, and with a growled expletive Ethan lifted his head. His wing loosened and then his tail was gone. Gently he put her down on her feet. "I think that will be adequate footage," he said stiffly.

Min stood unsteadily, her pussy greedily spasming on thin air, empty, needy, wanting so much more of him. His eyelids blinked one, twice, then two tendrils of smoke curled from his nostrils. "Sorry. The smoking thing tends to happen when I get... aroused," he muttered.

Some little demon made her say, "You mean you're not faking it?" It was daring, but it didn't feel like they were play-acting anymore.

And to hell with the cameras.

His face contorted. "Oh Min, can't you tell?" It was guttural, harsh, the need in his voice unequivocal, and she dared take a step forward, put her hands around the back of his neck and whisper in his ear, "Take me somewhere private."

As she heard his sharp inhalation, she wondered where the old Min had gone. The Min who quietly ran a bookshop, tending her garden as if waiting for that special someone to come so she herself could blossom like one of her plants.

"Gods, Min." He buried his head in her neck. "Don't tempt me."

She pressed her body against him and almost gurgled with delight at the feel of his desire, still rock hard against her. "Please be tempted," she begged softly.

He cradled her now in his arms, still kissing her as they strode out of the orange grove.

Inside the elevator, he continued kissing her, her spine pressed against the cool mirror and his tongue wreaking havoc with her hormones. His tail slid around the inside of her thigh and flicked the little nub of her clit, nudging her right to the edge.

Somehow, they made it to his room, still kissing and caressing.

But just inside the bedroom, he stopped abruptly.

"This is madness, Min."

It was like he'd thrown a bucket of icy cold water over her.

"H-how—what do you mean?"

"We're... this isn't real. We mustn't. Gods, this could get complicated." His grip loosened, he took her arms from around her neck and slid her down his body.

She stumbled back, blinking. "W-what?"

"Min, I'm *paying* you. It's an imbalance of power. I'm... I shouldn't have flirted with you or forced my tail on you. Or kept kissing you like this once our agreed time was over."

Hands on her hips now, she glared at him. "You did not force your tail on me," she said, righting her glasses on her nose indignantly. "I invited you to play tailsy with me, if I remember rightly."

The fizz of the champagne was wearing off now, and she felt suddenly drab and dull, as if the magic spell that had bound them had suddenly lifted. Her pussy ached miserably and her whole body felt empty. And he was so tantalizingly close, yet so far away.

She shook her head, pushing her hair violently behind both ears. "Oh, now I feel totally cheap."

"NO, Min, gods no. I loved it... It's just... This could get very tangled if we allow ourselves to become... intimate. And you are..."

"I am what?"

"Sexually inexperienced."

"How do you know?"

He looked suddenly bewildered. "You implied you were a virgin."

"Yes. But I have a vivid imagination... and hands... and maybe even... *toys* that you know nothing about," she huffed out. "Just because I haven't had *physical* sex doesn't make me a non-sexual being."

He raked a hand over his horns. "I didn't mean that."

"Just because I held out and never went for a human. Because I have my standards. Maybe—well, maybe my tastes are different..."

"What?"

She dropped her gaze. "All my fantasies are about non-humans."

He said nothing, just stared at her, unblinking.

"I guess now you know. So there's nothing to stop us, is there?"

His eyes flared. "Gods, Min, it's not that simple. I just—what if you get emmeshed with me and then you or I realize it's a mistake? Then what? At least if it's a clean business arrangement, I can keep my head clear. I have to keep my head clear or I—"

A lick of flame escaped his nostrils.

"See what I mean? Min, this is what happens when I'm aroused. I throw flames. Dragons are beasts. We have beastly instincts and beastly anatomy. A sexual liaison with a dragon, it's not something many humans would be prepared to enter into."

"I've enjoyed it so far," she mumbled, giving him a little glance from under her lashes.

He smirked at that, even as he shrugged helplessly.

"Min, I am going to bed, you are going to bed. Separately."

"Is that what you really want?"

"No, actually, it's not what I want. Look what you do to me." He stood wide, magnificent in his pants and swept a hand down past his crotch, which was bulging so much the zipper stood out proud.

"I'm fucking suffering here, Min."

"Then... please, Ethan."

"You don't want to see what's inside my pants."

She raised her head and her eyes sparked. "Yes, actually, I do."

He cursed softly under his breath. "No!" He covered his crotch firmly with big green fists. "Min, have you even seen a human penis?"

"No. I mean, yes—in an anatomy book." She didn't add that they'd always looked woefully inadequate, comical even.

"Well, I am telling you, if you haven't seen human dick, dragon dick is not where you want to start, sweetheart."

Wild-eyed, he grabbed her neatly folded PJs from the coverlet.

"Min, please. Go to bed. Dream of unicorns. They're safer than dragons."

And with that, he stomped into the dressing room and slammed the door behind him, leaving Min clutching her PJs and trying to swallow the lump of shame and disappointment in her throat.

CHAPTER 17

"Not this one," Ethan growled, tossing aside the picture of Min, head flung back, eyes closed, her mouth forming a perfect, ecstatic circle. He knew exactly when that photo was taken—right as she almost came around his tail. "No way are we using this one."

The ferret photographer gave him a sly look. "Makes it look genuine though, eh?"

Ethan tore the photo into shreds.

The ferret looked surprised, then smug. "I've got the originals."

Ethan was out of his chair and around his desk faster than wildfire, grabbing the ferret by his grubby collar.

"You work for me. You are paid by me. And I will choose the photos. This was not a peep show, and you do not get to lasciviously decide what you will and won't show. Understood?"

"Okay, hold your scales together. Got it, loud and clear," the ferret placated.

Ethan gave him a little shake for good measure before dropping the pesky creature and returning to his seat.

He tried to stay calm as he flicked through the shots again.

Goddess in heaven, they sure had gone for it. Apart from the ones of he and Min tail-playing at the table, there were a dozen of them kissing, her slender thighs clasped around his strong ones, her dress falling away from her legs and his finger digging into her butt. Heck, he wanted to preserve Min's dignity. These were going to be splashed across the press, and suddenly it *really* mattered that she wasn't humiliated.

He was involved, whether he liked it or not. Admit it, that very first day when their eyes locked, he'd felt a stirring that went way deeper than his cocks. It went to his soul.

Something about him and this human went beyond logic.

Fuck Adina. She was supposed to have arranged a business agreement, not a fucking love match.

Love.

He shook himself, turned his attention back to the photos, trying to view them as anything other than the most erotic things he'd ever set eyes on.

"These," he said. "Only these three. No others." He chose the ones that preserved a skerrick of Min's modesty, just his hand on her butt, before her dress had rumpled in his fist, showing her beautiful skin in the moonlight. "Now go hand over all the negatives to Ebony. If any other picture ever shows itself, we will come after you so hard you'll wish I'd set a pack of hounds on you instead."

"Right-o, boss." The ferret moved carefully toward the door, one wary eye on him.

"Yeah, take that, you little vermin," Ethan muttered as the door closed behind him, feeling somewhat ashamed of his outburst.

It was just that he was so freakin' wired after last night.

He'd sneaked out this morning before Min woke.

Her shape in the bed as he tiptoed past, the tumble of her gorgeous hair on the pillow, had made him want to dive onto the bed and gather her into him, sniff her hair, the scent of her arousal still embedded in his brain, the feel of her human, pliant body.

He'd stood in the guest bathroom staring helplessly at his bursting cocks.

It was the smaller one, the way it pulsed and oozed pre-cum that had him really worried.

Sure, his main cock was hard as a rod too, the ripples and veins standing proud, but it was the fact that his groc wanted to pleasure Min, give her orgasm after orgasm before his own release, that was what worried him.

If his big rod was willing to wait, then that could only mean one thing.

It was commitment shit with a capital C.

He'd never had it this bad, not even close.

Never felt this way toward any other creature.

With an exasperated growl now, he picked up the internal phone and called Ebony.

When she arrived in his office, he motioned for her to sit.

"Has that ferret left the premises? Because if he hasn't, I will torch his mangy ass until he's racing around in search of a water hydrant."

"Yes, he's gone. And I have disposed of the negatives."

She came over and looked at the pictures on his desk. "Which ones should I put out there?"

He practically flung the three photos at her. She frowned. "What's bitten you?" She glanced at the pictures and her beak clacked in surprise, her bright eyes wide. "Oh, um, that kiss is quite... saucy."

"These are the least saucy."

She blinked across at him, smirking. "So I was right about the chemistry, then."

Ethan pushed back his chair, got up and stomped around his office, ruffling the scales on the back of his neck. "It's... got awkward. Not in a bad way — well, probably not in a good way either, but er, yeah, seems we do have a bit of a mutual "thing" for each other."

Ebony let out a musical chuckle, her wing fluttering to her mouth. "Ooh, I love it when I'm right."

Ethan rolled his eyes. "Well, hooley dooley, why don't you quit working for me and start up a matchmaking service then?"

"I just might." She plumped up her feathers, her eyes dancing.

"Get out of here," he grumbled, swallowing his own smile, "before you burst into fucking song."

"Love is good… Love is great," Ebony chirped as she sashayed to the door. "And these pics are going to get so many hits on social media."

Ethan threw himself down at his desk and buried his head in his hands.

∽

"Hello Min, how is everything going?" Adina Thrimble's voice trilled down the phone.

Min huffed a sigh. How on earth could she tell Adina that her business arrangement had turned into one hot mess?

That she nearly rode a dragon's tail to orgasm last night, pleaded with him to take her virginity, and that ever since, she'd been a whimpering mess of need and sexual frustration.

"Great," she lied through gritted teeth. Glancing in the mirror on the dresser, she decided she looked like a crazed ventriloquist's doll with that fake smile plastered on her mouth.

Fake smiles for a fake date.

No, not fake—not for her at least.

Adina's melodic voice brought her back. "I've been following you both in the media, out and about together. I have to say you make it look very real. I must commend you on your acting prowess."

Min groaned inwardly. "Yes, we've... worked hard on it."

A little more working on it would be welcome.

"Well, my dear, you are doing admirably, and after the gala ball you will be free." Min's heart dropped like a stone. That was only three weeks away. So little time left with Ethan. "Hopefully there won't be a visit from the Council of Towns before then, but they do like to spring them on people, so be prepared. Their visits can be challenging."

"In what way?"

"Oh, they'll check on *everything*. Go through your private belongings, usually in the middle of the night."

"I see." Min gripped the phone tightly.

"Don't worry, given how much you've been in the limelight, they may take that as proof enough."

"Hopefully." Min winced. The next set of photos would more than put them in the limelight. The spotlight more like.

"Don't hesitate to call my office if you have any questions or concerns."

"No, none, it's all going fantastically."

"Good, good. Must dash, I have another call coming in. Goodbye, my dear."

"Goodbye, Adina."

Min sighed as she put the phone down. Sadly, there was nothing remotely fantastic happening between her and Ethan.

She'd woken this morning to find a note from him on the dresser, saying he thought they should put a little distance between them. That it would allow them to get back into their professional roles.

Well, *oof.*

What a slap in the face.

And now the day stretched empty in front of her, her head ached from the champagne she'd drunk, and her pussy ached from frustration.

Suddenly she knew where she needed to be. She needed to be at the Westerly, to ground herself among familiar things, the shelves of musty old books, her garden, with the birds singing in the trees and the spring flowers in bloom, and Gingerbread asleep in the snug, with a beam of sunshine on his back.

That would bring some sanity back to her brain. And body.

Min pulled her shoulders back and exited the room.

As she made her way toward the helipad, where there always seemed to be a limo ready and waiting to take off, Beau appeared from a room off the main hallway with an excited grin on his handsome young face.

"Hey Min!"

"Oh Beau, hi." She smiled at the eager look on his face.

"Have you got a moment?" he asked. He looked a lot less grungy today. He was bright-eyed and excited, and he was wearing jeans and a white tee instead of his usual black leather.

"Sure." She guessed she had all day, in fact.

"C'min here. I want to show you the program prototype." When they entered, Min was presented with a row of screens. Beau sat down in front of one and started tapping at the keyboard. "I've just got it back from Tom who's putting it all together. And I've gotta show someone or I'll self-combust. I'm so fucking excited. Here. Sit down."

He pulled up a webpage. A huge, fire-breathing, red-eyed ancient dragon coiled across the screen, with the title emblazoned across it:

Dragon's Lair.

Enter if you dare.

"Just let me take you through the intro." A screenful of characters came up on the screen.

"Oh Beau, these are incredible, I recognize them from your sketchbook, but they're more detailed now."

"I know, I've been working like fucking crazy to get them finished."

"Dare I ask if you've been to college this week?"

"Nope. But don't tell Ethan, he'll go apeshit at me."

She didn't even know if she was talking to Ethan after last night, so there was no risk that she'd tell him anything.

"Once the game is live, I'll tell him, I just need to prove this is going to work first. When he sees I can make a success of what I love, what I'm good at, then—yeah, I'm hoping he'll get off my back."

"When does it go live?"

"In two weeks. Fuck, Min!" His eyes goggled at her. "It's freakin' scary that this is actually happening. Can you at least keep Ethan busy? If he gets suspicious now it could hold up our plans."

"Okay—I… I'll try."

"You're amazing." He gave her a big hug. "It's so good having you here Min. I finally feel like there's someone in this house who's got my back."

"Your mom always has."

Beau guffawed. "Mom just spoils me rotten. Buys me tasteless gear to wear, tacky sneakers with bling all over them. I'm still a dragonling in her eyes. I think she thinks I hatched out of the fucking egg yesterday."

"Oh Beau." Min smothered a smile; that had kind of been her observation too.

"You've barely been living here and it's like you just get us, you know? Mom loves you, Ethan loves you…" He smirked. "And I don't think you're so bad either."

"Stop flattering me." Min turned to leave.

"It's true, you should be an honorary dragon, Min." He looked at her out of suddenly worried wide eyes as she stood in the doorway. "Just don't split with my brother, will you? Don't leave us. We need you, Min, you make everything better."

She froze with her hand on the doorknob, squeezed it until her knuckles hurt.

"I won't leave, Beau."

How on earth was she going to keep that promise?

～

She'd just got to the helipad when she heard a familiar voice calling out behind her.

"Min, Min. Where are you off to, darling?"

Turning, Min saw Cressida dressed in a jaunty little jacket and hat, a big glitzy purse in her hand, which she was waving wildly to catch her attention. "Where are you going, darling?"

"Back to the Westerly, just to check everything's going okay."

"Oh, but darling, I had plans to take you shopping today." Cressida stood pouting and puffing on the gravel driveway.

"Well, I won't be there long." Cressida looked so crestfallen that she added, "Maybe we could meet somewhere… afterwards."

"Oh yes, let's be girls who do lunch. Won't that be jolly? Meet me at The Right Bite at 1 pm, and after lunch we can go look at some dress shops in The Hole In The Wall." Cressida was all smiles now as she waved her off.

Min quickly got into the hover cab before there were any more interruptions.

"Where to, ma'am?" Vincent threw over his shoulder, putting the limo into a sharp upward thrust.

"The Westerly Bookshop please, Vincent. And it's Min, remember."

"Yes, ma'am."

CHAPTER 18

Min sighed with relief as the limo hovered over the bookshop and then landed on the perimeter road.

As she walked up the path, the smell of spring flowers and cherry blossom met her nostrils.

It was a beautiful warm day and there were bees everywhere in the garden, and small birds drinking from the bird bath.

She wanted to walk into the shop and stay there, get busy behind her desk pricing books and chatting to customers.

What had she been thinking, getting involved in this crazy scheme?

Face it, she was so out of her depth she was at risk of drowning.

It didn't help that when she walked inside, Bonnie looked at her a little strangely.

"Hi Min. I, er… wasn't sure whether to contact you or not."

"Is everything okay?" Min asked. A sudden horrible thought hit her. "Is Gingerbread okay?" Her heart stuttered. She always worried that one day he'd streak across the perimeter road and get hit by a car.

"Oh, Gingerbread's fine. The shop's fine."

"Busy?"

Bonnie seemed to hesitate. "It *has* been busy. Not with sales, though." From the way Bonnie's snakes were squirming, she was clearly embarrassed.

Min took off her jacket and moved behind the desk. "Well, I guess more customers is good, though it's a shame they weren't buying."

Bonnie hesitated. "The subject of conversation hasn't been about books really. Folks have been asking about you and… er… this Ethan Blade guy." Bonnie's eyebrows waggled. "Either this was a very whirlwind affair, or Minerva Westwind, you've told me some whopping great porky pies about this internship."

Min huffed a sigh. She'd been naïve to think that just because Bonnie didn't like social media, the news wouldn't reach her somehow. Of course, customers talked. "Do you want to put the kettle on, and we'll sit down and have a chat?" Min said.

Bonnie nodded and trotted into the little back office.

Min felt strangely displaced, like she'd been away forever.

And while the shop looked much the same, she was irrevocably different.

But as she glanced around, she couldn't help feeling comforted when she spotted Gingerbread, curled up on the lumpy old easy chair in the snug. She went over and stroked his ears, and he stretched and opened one eye, then closed it.

"Lovely to see you too, Ginge." Min smirked.

Bonnie soon returned and handed Min a steaming mug.

"Okay, so what's this all about?"

Min hesitated, then sank down into a chair. Bonnie sat opposite, cupping her mug in her hands.

"I—um—the day I started my internship, we… I met… that is…" Min ground to a halt, biting her lip. This was stupid, she couldn't lie to Bonnie. They'd been friends for too long. She trusted her to keep a secret.

She stared at her fingers, wrapped around her favorite mug, the one that read "Monster Boyfriends are better." She wished it was true.

"I'm fake dating Ethan Blade," she blurted.

"*Fake* dating?"

"Yep."

"My oh my! But... but those photos of you together... and that article. It looks so... real. You mean it's all a lie? You're play-acting?"

Min nodded miserably.

"Why?"

"Because I'm trying to save the Westerly."

Bonnie's eyes looked like they were about to bounce right out of her head.

In a halting voice, Min explained about Quentin's visit, and the rental agreement terminating, about Adina and the peacock coat, and Midas Touch Partnerships, about meeting Ethan and their fake-dating arrangement.

When she was finished, Bonnie looked genuinely sad. "Oh, if only I was rich, then you wouldn't have to pretend to be in love with a dragon."

"Honestly, it's not so bad." Min thrust a lock of hair behind her ear as a memory of Ethan's tail between her legs made her pussy clench. "I mean, he's a real gentleman and... His family, his mom and his brother, I kind of... I don't know, I just seem to get on with them really well."

Bonnie laughed. "You have always had an affinity with us monster kind, like your dad I guess."

"I'm sorry I didn't tell you, Bonnie. I hate lying, especially to you, but since you don't go on social media, I thought you wouldn't find out, at least not until it was all over."

"I probably wouldn't have if it wasn't for the customers.

They started coming into the shop and showing me their news feeds. One of them brought in an article from *The Motham Times*. You both looked genuinely in love. The way he was gazing at you... and you him."

"He's a good actor," Min said, gulping down a mouthful of hot tea.

"Yeah, you must be too." Bonnie looked pensive. "And then another guy who knows you came into the shop yesterday. Right peeved, he was."

Min frowned. "Monster or human?"

"Human. Said he works for the Council of Towns. Quentin somebody or other."

Min sat bolt upright. "What did he want?"

"He more or less demanded to know where you were. I think he said, where *the hell* were you. He was rude, I didn't like his vibe."

"What did you tell him?"

"That you'd had to go away for a month, and I didn't know where. I'm sure he didn't believe me, because he kept ranting and raving about you playing games. I'd seen the pics by then, but I kept quiet. He just went on and on about you selling out on the Westwind name."

Min's forehead tightened. "Then what?"

"He stormed out, saying he was going to get to the bottom of this, and that if you thought dating a dragon was going to help your cause you had another think coming. I didn't know what he was on about, but now I realize he must have been talking about the bookshop."

Min shrugged helplessly. "Well, there's no other way I could afford to buy it, Bonnie."

"We could start a petition," Bonnie said brightly, "call it 'Save the Westerly.'"

"Yeah, and the folks who would sign it would have *so* much influence. Not." Min couldn't help the sarcastic note in her voice. "It would be monsters who are trying to get themselves an education, and maybe a few sympathetic humans. None of them come from Tween. And that's what matters in the end." She huffed a sigh. "Humans who live in Twill and Be-Tween don't count. It would have to be high breeds, and they'd never give us their signatures."

Min tried not to let the sense of panic take over. Clearly, she'd blown it. She'd fallen for her fake date.

And now Quentin Jordak was angry, and on the warpath, too.

It had all turned into a horrible mess.

Her eyes blurred suddenly. She'd always been so level-headed, always kept her fantasies and dreams tightly bound and wrapped. But now she was unraveling like a ball of string. Or worse, like the snakes on Bonnie's head.

Her lip wobbled and she let out a little hiccupping sob. "Oh Bonnie, I think I've messed everything up." Min put down her tea and covered her face with her hands.

Bonnie came and put her arms around her. The worst of it was that when she got emotional, so did her snakes. Min smiled, even through her tears, as several of them got entangled in her hair.

"Sorry," Bonnie said. "They're just worried for you."

"Sure, I get that."

As Min pulled away, something landed with a plonk on her lap. Gingerbread. He stared up at her, kneading his paws on her legs, and meowed. Min couldn't help a laugh, wiping her eyes with the back of her hand. "Have you come to tell me to pull myself together, Ginge? I know, I know, I'm behaving like a pathetic weak human."

The cat meowed again, then plopped off her lap onto the floor and padded toward the back of the shop. Curious, Min followed him. He stopped outside her father's study and turned to look at her again. Min had kept the study locked since her dad died. It was full of unsorted books and mostly unpaid bills that she still couldn't bring herself to do anything about.

And she certainly didn't feel strong enough to unlock that door today.

Gingerbread meowed again.

"Maybe he's telling you that your dad would understand," Bonnie said, at her side.

"I'd love to believe that." Min looked at her searchingly. "Do *you* understand, Bonnie?"

"Of course I do. This shop is everything to you," Bonnie said fiercely. "And it's a shining beam of hope to monsters who've never had a chance to read a book before. Monsters are going to college because of this shop. They're getting an education and finding out about their heritage. It took your dad years to build this up. Do what you've got to do to keep it running. If that means pretending you're in love with a dragon, who cares? There are worse ways to earn money."

Min had to giggle at that. "Yeah, well, I don't think I'd be a good fit for the Purple Lantern District somehow." And then she thought about her make-out session with Ethan in the orange grove and bit her lip, blushing. She would have done a succubus proud.

"I have a friend who works as a pole dancer." Bonnie grinned. "Guess she could get you a job if you need one."

As they giggled together at the thought of Min pole dancing, Min started to feel a little stronger. As she wandered back to the snug she took in the shelves crammed with books, the slightly musty smell of old paper, the strange little lamp her dad had found in an antique shop, with clawed feet and a faux fur covered shade. The medieval map of the world, showing the volcano site where monsters were said to have burst out of the earth's crust many centuries ago.

It was as if the shop lived and breathed, and still had so much to achieve. She would not, could not let it be knocked to the ground.

Firming her lips, Min finished the dregs of her tea, then looked at her watch.

It was nearly lunch time.

"Oh, goddess above!" She looked around for her purse. "I'm meant to be meeting Ethan's mom for lunch. I better go."

Bonnie gathered up the cups. "I'm so glad you came by, and I absolutely promise I won't let on that you're fake dating Ethan Blade, not to anyone."

"Thank you, Bonnie."

"You're doing a great job. I really believed you two were in love."

Min forced a bright smile. "Well, I guess acting is another career I could pursue if..."

"Shhh, don't say it. It will be okay. You'll keep the shop," Bonnie said firmly.

Before Min left, she went to find Gingerbread. Not that he was any good at farewells, but it made her feel better. He was still sitting outside her father's study, slowly and meticulously cleaning his whiskers.

"Goodbye, Gingerbread," she called out.

Gingerbread looked up from his task and stared at her, as if she'd mortally offended him.

Cats, Min decided as she left, were unfathomable creatures.

CHAPTER 19

Ethan needed a coffee, a strong double espresso, and he needed to get some fresh air to clear his head.

He took the elevator to the ground floor, crossed the polished marble foyer of the Blade Wing Air building and strode into the sunny Hole In The Wall District. Everywhere was buzzing with shoppers. There were spring sales on in the shops, mannequins wearing pretty dresses in the windows. He paused, gazing at one that would look perfect on Min.

Min. There he went again, unable to get her out of his freakin' head for two minutes.

Really, he needed to be focusing on the final plans for the airport, which were sitting on his computer, waiting for his sign-off so they could be submitted to the Council of Towns. Their meeting was in a fortnight, and everything had to be finalized by then.

And after that…

When the papers were signed…

Deal done, and this fake-dating fiasco would be over.

Min would return to the Westerly, and he would… he would…

A black hole gaped inside him at the thought that she would no longer be in his life.

He ignored it, focusing instead on the aroma of coffee wafting through the open door of The Right Bite.

The cafe was crowded. Ethan always enjoyed the buzz of different species. Two humans gossiped loudly, high and fast spoken, but not as high-voiced as a fae couple nearby. There were the rich, gravelly voices of minotaurs, orcs, and griffins at another table, and the braying laugh of a centaur somewhere nearby. A table of husky gelfin girls chatted raucously, probably grabbing a bite to eat before working their beat.

And then... the booming laugh of a female dragon.

Mom?

Followed by a soft, gentle human laugh that made his claws curl in his designer shoes.

Min?

As he stood in the coffee queue, his eyes scanned the tables.

"Hi, Ethan. Your usual?"

"Yeah, thanks," he said absently to Bianca, the pretty elf serving him. She'd made eyes at him sometimes, and before Min he'd had the occasional thought of maybe a brief fling, but... nope.

He only had eyes for one woman now. And he was certain she was in here somewhere.

His gaze panned more sharply around the room. His mom's laugh came again—she was clearly enjoying herself.

And then, just as he grabbed his coffee, he saw them, tucked into a corner booth.

Eating, drinking, laughing like they'd known each other forever.

His heart lurched hard in his chest.

He hadn't seen Mom looking this relaxed in... since... before Dad died.

He forced himself to stroll over nonchalantly, while his

claws gripped his coffee hard enough to make holes in the cardboard cup.

"Oh Ethan!" Cressida reached out a hand covered in rings. "Min and I are having a mom/daughter-in-law lunch."

He wanted to shout, *you're not her mom-in-law, nor will you ever be*. But that just intensified the gaping hole inside him.

Min looked up at him and her face suddenly pinched into a frown. He needed to rectify this, or his mom might think they weren't getting on.

He swooped in and kissed Min fair and square on the mouth.

He felt her little indrawn breath. Damn it, he should have asked permission, but desperate measures were required to make sure everything looked normal between them, whatever normal even was at this point.

As he drew away, the sweetness of her breath and the softness of her surprised mouth lingered on his lips.

He wanted to do it again. Real bad.

"Hi babe," he said casually.

She gathered herself, the panic in her eyes softening. "Hi—gorgeous."

Gods, if only she could keep saying that, in that little breathy voice, until the end of time.

"Oh, look at you two." Cressida clasped her hands in glee. "Just so in love."

"Yes Mom, okay, we got that."

"Sit, sit down." His mom waved a hand at the seat next to Min. "Drink your coffee with us."

"I can't really, I've got so much to do."

"Oh, you can. Don't be such a workaholic. You are getting like your father." Cressida's face momentarily crumpled. Min reached out and touched her arm, and to Ethan's relief, his mom's face immediately brightened. "Silly me, let's not go there. Seeing you so in love just reminds me, but

I'm so, so happy that you are. Look at you, just perfect together."

Min cast him a glance, the smallest twitch of a smile on her face, and he smiled back.

It suddenly felt... okay between them again. The tight band around his chest loosened, and he let his wings relax down on his shoulder blades.

"I'm taking Min to get a dress for the gala dinner after this," Cressida continued, stuffing her face with pasta carbonara.

"What, already?"

"Ethan, it's barely three weeks away. Have you been hiding under a rock?"

On a whim, he said, "Min has been distracting me." He saw her startle slightly as he said it.

"Aw, that's so adorable. But darling, the gala dinner has always been the year's highlight. How could you forget, even for this gorgeous being?"

"I know, Mom, I know. It's the event of the year." Ethan managed not to roll his eyes. His mother lauded it up at the Blade gala dinner, giving out the awards to small businesses on the up and up. It was her night really, not his. But he went along with it, and this year with humans from the Council of Towns attending for the first time ever, he did need to take it seriously.

He and Min had to look absolutely rock solid.

"Tell him, Min, that he has to come shopping with us. Ethan has such great taste in dresses. Whenever I... Well, let's say, the few times I've got a bit overwrought and set light to my entire wardrobe, he's always helped me buy new outfits."

"Sounds like that's happened a few times," Min said with a gentle smile.

Cressida smiled sadly. "Oh dear, yes, quite often after Clifton died. Less so of late. Don't you think I'm improving, Ethan?"

Ethan gave a tight smile. "Yes, Mom, you are getting better on that front."

"Thank you, my darling boy. Now let's go." Cressida went and paid the bill, then bowled out of the cafe like a ship in full sail, clearly expecting them to follow, all her silk billowing behind her.

Out in the street, Ethan glanced at Min.

She smiled up at him, her lips a little tremulous, her eyes questioning.

Gods, how he wanted to touch her, put his tail round her, claim her.

Mine.

But then, they *were* in public, and he guessed it was appropriate to touch her. They needed to be seen together as a couple. He glanced down at her hands, neatly clasping her purse in front of her. Tail might be too much though, bearing in mind their wicked game of tailsy the other night.

"May I hold your hand?" he asked, feeling ridiculously shy suddenly.

She nodded and reached one small slender hand toward him.

Ethan enveloped it in his and couldn't help the smile that panned his features as they walked along the busy street hand in hand, just like *real* lovers.

When Min disappeared into the change rooms buried under a pile of dresses, Ethan was still smiling, just as he had been all the way down the street as he walked along swinging hands with his human.

He was used to this clothes shopping gig with his mom, he'd always accompanied her, even as a little kid; helping to tone down her tastes a little, steering her away from the most over-the-top bling.

He'd always had a good eye for what suited a woman.

Glancing at his mom now and the dresses she was feverishly piling over her arm, he really had to step in.

"No Mom, that will *not* suit Min. Too many frills."

Cressida pouted. "But it's a *Kominsky*," she said in an awed voice.

"Mom, Min turning up at the gala dinner in a gown made by a disgraced vampire family is not going to be a good look."

"If anything, their brand has got even more popular since the scandal."

"Yeah, well—not on my girlfriend," he huffed. The fucking Kominsky family were the reason buying human land had become so difficult, after one of them had abused their land rights with shady vampiric practices.

"Please?" His mom batted her eyelashes at him, and he guessed he should let Min decide.

Luckily, the next dress his mom presented was simpler, in a beautiful rich red silk that would complement rather than clash with Min's deep copper hair.

"I'll pass these through to her," he said, placing the red one strategically on top.

He went over to the curtain and hiss-whispered, "Min."

"Yes?" She poked her face out between the two curtains, like a little squirrel. Her hair was a mess, no doubt from pulling the dresses over her head, and her glasses sat at an angle on her nose. She was too adorably cute.

"Any you like so far?"

"No, all way too fussy." She grimaced. "They make me feel like a wedding cake. Can you tell your mom thanks but, um…"

"Here." He held up the simple red dress.

Her eyes widened. "Oh, that *is* nice."

One slender arm came out, and as she grabbed it, he couldn't help but catch a glimpse of her simple cotton bra with the pale sphere of her breasts above it. So modest, which somehow made it even more of a turn-on.

Ethan quickly turned away and stood with his back to the cubicle, waiting. Then he heard her say "Ethan" in a small plaintive voice from behind the curtain.

"Yes?"

"I, um, think the zipper might be stuck. Could you..."

He looked helplessly around for Cressida, but she'd flitted off to another part of the shop, out of earshot.

Nothing for it. He moved the curtain aside.

Min was standing in front of the mirror, the dress on, but the zipper only half done up, exposing the curve of her spine, the little knobs of her vertebrae, the smooth, milky white of her skin.

His mouth suddenly dry, Ethan stepped forward and gave the zip a tug. It didn't budge.

"Maybe if you pulled the sides of the dress closer," she suggested huskily. He did, and that meant his fingers grazing her skin.

He tugged again and the zipper moved up a fraction, then stuck again.

She moved her hair aside, giving him a full view of the long line of her milky white neck.

Instinctively, he stepped closer.

And then he swore, yes, swore, that she arched her back enough for her butt cheeks to graze his crotch.

Arousal surged through him, almost making him dizzy.

The warmth of her body, the sweet scent of her, the glow of her skin, he wanted to place his lips on the nape of her neck and nibble at it with his fangs. Suck her soft skin, give her a hicky to claim her as his.

She let out a little sigh.

Slowly, he did the zipper up to its full length. She turned, and her eyes raised to meet his.

"Min," he said huskily, shakily. "Min." He was going to

fess up, wasn't he? He was going to let everything spill out, right here in this little cubicle. Tell her to tear up the stupid note he'd left about wanting to put distance between them. That it was the biggest lie. Because in reality, he couldn't stop thinking about her, wanting to be the one to pleasure her—the only one, for eternity—and he'd do it better than her own hand, making herself come to monster fantasies. He wanted to tell her that hell, he was *jealous* of her fantasies, and so fucking jealous of that little hand that pleasured her while she dreamed of beasts.

Because *he* wanted to be the beast in her bed.

Every single fucking night.

They stared at each other. Ethan's mouth opened, but no words came out.

"Yes, Ethan?" she breathed softly.

"I just wanted to say..." the words stuck in his parched throat.

She stared up at him, her eyes huge behind her glasses.

"That this dress—it's definitely the one."

CHAPTER 20

For what felt like the hundredth time since it had appeared in the paper three days ago, Min flicked through the pages of the *Motham Times* until she reached the photos of her and Ethan in the orange grove. Tingling all over, she stared at the images of them passionately kissing. Truth was, when she looked at these, she could *almost* imagine they were in love. The way they laughed up into each other's eyes, his big green hand splayed intimately on the swell of backside, the other tangling in her hair, angling her face to his.

The kiss, so deep, so intimate. There was even a glimpse of his long tongue visible in one photo. Her gaze kept catching on the way his fingers indented her thigh over the material of her dress. How her body was pressed against him, reliving every nuance of the feel of him against her yielding flesh.

Min squeezed her thighs together with a little moan to try and ease the throb in her pussy. Placing the magazine down, she went over to the window and gazed out at the darkening sky.

She'd eaten with Cressida and Beau tonight.

They weren't so very different from a human family

really, with their own foibles and idiosyncrasies. Except for the fine silverware and the bejeweled cutlery and the seemingly endless array of dishes and serving staff.

And the fact that her *supposed* lover, Ethan, didn't join them.

It had been nearly a week since the kiss, and truth was, he was keeping her at wingspan length. They'd been to an art gallery launch and the official opening of some new hover cab station way over in the east quarter of Motham, but as soon as they got back to the Blade mansion he would disappear, either to his office or his music room.

Late into the night, he would play the piano. And she would lie in bed, her body ripe with longing, until finally the beautiful melodies would chase away desire and let her slumber.

But not tonight. The music room door was firmly shut, the piano silent.

She sighed, went and cleaned her teeth, and put on her PJs.

She'd just hopped into bed with a book, a historical novel about orc kind set in the era of Atholrose Motham, when Ethan burst through the door, a look of sheer panic on his features.

She got such a surprise that she dropped the book and sat bolt upright with a squeak.

"Min, I'm sorry, but we've just had word the officials will be here in twenty minutes."

"What officials?" Totally discombobulated by him striding around the room in a panic, she pulled the sheet up to her chin.

"The visit from the Council of Towns officials... to check whether we're..."

"Oh, shit!" Min's hand went to her mouth. "What do we do now?"

"We... um... we need... to be found in the same bed."

Min gulped. "Right. Well, you better get in then."

"Yep. I'll go undress." He raked a hand over his head, his eyes wild. "I'll put my PJ bottoms on, leave off my top, as if…"

Min rolled the cover down and cast a glance at her modest nightwear. "Should I… keep these on?"

He grimaced at her baggy faded unicorn PJs. "Not quite the right look for a loved-up couple. Here." He grabbed a negligée from one of the dresser drawers and tossed it to her.

"This would look more… authentic."

'Right-o." Min swallowed hard.

As he disappeared into the dressing room, Min tugged off her PJs and slipped the silk negligée over her head. Ebony had provided it for her to wear in the event of a raid like this, but it was the tiniest scrap of silk, barely covering her tush. And there were no panties with it. It literally skimmed the top of her thighs, almost exposing the soft v of hair around her cleft.

Totally indecent. Oh well, she'd be in bed. They'd only see her top half, and then Ethan would go back to the dressing room as soon as they left. Sadly.

She flicked her hair around her shoulders and hopped back into bed just as Ethan bounded out of the bathroom in a pair of loose pajama pants, his torso gloriously naked and glistening. His wings furled closed to his shoulders, which were muscular and buffed. Min couldn't help staring at his body as he climbed gingerly into the bed next to her.

Her breath hitched as she felt the mattress indent, the warmth of him already seeping into her. Dragons definitely did not run cold. Not this one at least.

"Maybe put your arm around me," she ventured. As she spoke, they heard footsteps outside, then there was a sharp rap on the door.

"Come in," Ethan called out.

Snibs, Ethan's valet, put his head around the door. "Ethan, sir. The authorities are here. Are you okay if I let them in?"

"Sure, er, just give us a moment." Ethan's arms came round her, and he tugged her against his flank.

Min gave herself permission to *really* nestle in and put her hand on his chest. She could feel his heart beating fast under her palm.

He glanced down at her. "Ready for this?"

"Ready as I'll ever be," she said, trying not to smirk too broadly. There was definitely an upside to this visit.

"Okay," Ethan called out. "Tell them they can enter."

They flounced in, a woman and a small, bearded man. They were both wearing white coats, like doctors. Oh gods, they weren't planning on a physical examination, surely? Taking semen samples off the sheets?

It was a shame they wouldn't find any, Ethan thought ruefully.

The woman advanced, her spine stiff and her mouth turned down. "We have ID." They pointed to the identity badges on the lapels of their coats. "MHRM," Ethan read.

"What's that stand for?"

"Monster Human Relationship Management."

"Make this quick," Ethan growled. "My girlfriend wants to go to sleep."

The woman and her companion prowled around the room. They checked the dressing table, looked underneath it, opened all the dresser drawers. The man went into the bathroom. Ethan heard him calling out in a flat, nasally voice, "Toiletries in evidence. Both sexes.

"Two toothbrushes. His and hers.

"Her dressing gown is on the door hook next to his."

The woman checked them off on her paperwork. "Any evidence of sanitary wear?" she called out.

"Yes."

"Contraception?"

"No contraception is in evidence."

"We're not using any," Min piped up. "Leaving it to fate."

Ethan eyeballed her. Her face was deadpan, but he saw the hint of a dimple in her cheek. Westwind humor at its best.

Now they went into the dressing room.

"What is this?" the woman said.

"Looks like a couch," her companion replied. "Yeah, seems to be a sofa bed. Made up."

Ethan looked at Min and winced. "I forgot to fold it up."

The woman said, "Hmmm. Very suspicious."

"Sometimes he snores," Min called out. Ethan gave her an outraged look and was rewarded with two dimples this time. "I make him go and sleep in there sometimes. I guess when we're married, I'll boot him out more often." She giggled as the woman stalked back into the bedroom. She didn't raise a smile as she stood by the side of the bed and gestured impatiently.

"Pull back the bedclothes."

"What?" Ethan spluttered.

"Get out of bed, both of you."

"What the fuck for?" Ethan growled.

"Mind your language," the woman snapped. "We need to check that you're dressed appropriately for an intimate relationship."

"We could be naked," Ethan said.

"Exactly the point," snapped the woman.

Min flung back the covers. Ethan glanced at her and almost salivated. That negligée was something else. Even so, he was still outraged on Min's behalf.

"This is really fucking not okay, you hear me?"

"It's fine, Ethan," Min said calmly and stood up. He tried not to ogle her gorgeous body. She had fantastic legs, slender yet muscular, and her tits bobbed, almost falling out of the lacy garment. His cocks obligingly thickened. Well, he guessed if these officious little shits copped an eyeful of what was tenting his PJs there'd be no room for doubt.

Min held her hands out to the sides and her beautiful breasts lifted, giving him a tantalizing glimpse of her nipples. "You think I'd be wearing this with a guy who's not my partner?"

The woman sniffed and wrote something down.

"While you're at it," Min said sweetly, "would you like to see our drawer of sex toys, or maybe I could show you our sex dungeon downstairs? We've got whips, chains, butt plugs —you could put that in your little book too."

Whips, chains, butt plugs? What. The. Heck.

Ethan tried to catch her eye. If this woman called Min's bluff they'd be done for. Though the idea of setting up a sex dungeon with Min did hold a certain appeal.

The woman didn't look up from her paperwork. "We don't need every detail."

"Could have fooled us," Ethan grumbled.

"I'm just doing my job."

"Surely you could find a better one," Min said. "One that doesn't humiliate monsters." The woman thinned her lips and kept ticking boxes. "You're not from Tween, either of you, are you?"

Ethan glanced at Min's face. Where was she going with this?

"Nah, Twill," the woman said.

"What have they promised you? A nice new condo in Tween? Folks will always know you're from Twill by your accent, you'll never be fully accepted."

The woman scowled at Min, who was now standing with her hands on her hips, staring the woman down.

What had got into her? Was it the little silk negligée that was breaking down her inhibitions? Did she turn feisty from lack of sleep? With her copper hair blazing around her shoulders as she glared over the top of her glasses, she looked like every boy's schoolteacher fantasy. But hot and adorable as she was, it was time to shut her up. The last thing they needed was a bad report from this pucker-mouthed human who'd probably never had a skerrick of sex in her life.

Ethan flung back the covers and strode over, not caring about his fluffed-up dicks. He bent Min over his arm and kissed her full on the lips.

For a moment she was rigid with surprise, but as his tongue tangled and coaxed hers, she went limp against him with a tiny moan.

With difficulty, he pulled away, keeping his arm around her. She looked up at him, her eyes full of awe, and then gently pulled his head down and kissed his scales, just below his left horn. The gesture was so sweet and loving, his big dragon body almost melted into a puddle of goo.

He snaked his tail around her, and she leaned into him.

The two officials had the grace to look away. "Hmm, well, it all seems to meet the criteria for intimacy."

"Really, are you sure?" Min said archly. Ethan gave her a little slap on the butt with the end of his tail. This farce did *not* need to be prolonged.

The bearded man said, "The Council of Towns have to protect humans from shonky land deals, they make no apology about that."

The woman added, "Despite your back-chatting, you're in luck—I'll be reporting that this all looks genuine. We do expect, however, that an engagement will be announced within the next few weeks."

"Right, of course," Ethan said, his tail tightening around Min.

Of course.

CHAPTER 21

After they'd left, Min guessed she should disentangle herself from Ethan's embrace.

Trouble was, she had no desire to do so.

And it seemed like he had no inclination to move away from her either.

She loved the feel of that strong tail looped around her hipbone, the wing that was still draped around her shoulders, and her body hummed with adrenalin from the last few minutes. She'd never stood up to another human before, let alone while dressed in a tiny scrap of silk. Plus, she'd felt Ethan staring at her, and had been sure her nipples had hardened beneath his gaze.

Gosh, it should have been a humiliation, but instead it had empowered her. And it made Min realize she was prepared to take this further between them, whatever the consequences. She was going to make a move.

For a moment they both stood staring at the door.

"Well, I think we convinced them," Ethan said, removing his wing from her shoulder.

"Yes, I think so." When she felt his tail loosening, she

curled her hand around it, and with feather light fingers stroked up and down its length.

Ethan let out a low groan.

"Min... I told you..." His voice was deep, husky, his whole body coiled tight.

"Told me what?" She glanced up at him, blinking innocently.

"Don't stroke my tail unless you want..."

"Want what?"

"Stop being obtuse." A muscle in his jaw ticked.

"Unless I want trouble? Like the other night, in the orange grove?" she asked softly, and turned into him, lifting his tail and curling it around her. "I like that kind of trouble."

He groaned.

"Ethan." She buried her head in the velvet softness of his chest. Sniffed the musky sweet scent of him, felt his tail flick over her butt cheeks, the tip tweaking at the crack between them. Oh, that was interesting.

And even more enticing, standing pressed into him like this, she felt the hard ridges of his cock, getting harder by the moment.

Oh, how she wanted to free it.

See it.

Touch it.

He let out a guttural groan. "Fuck, Minerva, you're messing with my head. I—I don't know what... if we... if we... take this further, I—"

"I'm actually planning to mess with something else right now." She giggled, her hand panning lower. "Ethan, if we made love, surely it would be easier to pretend our relationship isn't fake."

He barked a laugh. "That's an oxymoron. Pretending something isn't fake."

"No, it's totally logical." She nuzzled her nose deeper in between his pecs, then glanced up at his long jaw, smiling cheekily as her hand crept still lower. He turned his head and one bright ice blue eye gazed at her, humor and wonder reflecting back at her in equal measure.

His big hand came over hers and stilled its path. "Min, you know I want you. Badly. But... this could get complicated." He gathered her exploring hand in his and held it firmly, his eyes suddenly cloudy with concern. "You're a virgin. I can't take advantage of that."

"What if it's not taking advantage, Ethan? What if it's what I want? What if I want to lose my virginity to a dragon?"

"You don't know what you're asking, sweetheart."

"Yes. I do." And with that, she wiggled her hand out of his grasp and moved it between them until she'd cupped his huge swollen girth.

He groaned and threw back his head, and courage surged through her. "Can we both stop fighting this?" she husked, her hand moving up his length, marveling at the feel of him, the ripples and ridges of a cock that felt so alien, yet so right.

"Let's lie on the bed, get our breath for a moment." He gasped. She nodded, and with his wings around her, they lay down. With shaking hands, he removed her glasses, put them on the bedside table and then stared at her, stroking her cheek. "Your eyes are so beautiful without the frames."

"I can see you better up close without them." She traced her fingers over his lean nose, the little scales that flattened as she touched them. Over his horns.

"Do you like what you see?" he asked softly.

"So very much." She sighed. "But I want to see all of you. Just tonight, let's... let's not think of the consequences, let's just..." She was in freefall, but she was sure of one thing: she knew that this dragon would catch her. "Let's make love," she finished, burying her face in his chest.

Another deep groan, and then he gently cupped her chin and kissed her long and deep, his tongue thrusting into her mouth, exploring every nook and cranny. Oh, how she'd missed his kiss since that night in the orange grove. It had only been a few days, but it felt like a lifetime ago. Immediately she could feel her response, the wetness of her arousal flowing liberally between her legs. Her nipples were as hard as two little pebbles, her breasts swollen and yearning for him to touch them. She thrust her breast out to meet his mouth as he moved down her neck with little kisses, but he paused and lifted his head. "Min, one more thing—"

Min huffed a sigh. Couldn't he tell how desperately she needed relief here?

"I need you to know that dragons have no sexually transmitted diseases. It's one of the few good things that came out of losing our shifting powers, we didn't inherit human diseases. And you don't need to worry about pregnancy... males are fertile only on quarterly cycles. I am not in one, and I don't know if I even could... with a human..."

Min felt a little pang of disappointment. Could she birth Ethan's dragonlings? How would that even work? But now was not the time to think of that. She touched his cheek. "Thank you for reassuring me."

Ethan sighed, and then finally his mouth went to her breast. He nipped and grazed her nipples with his fangs, working her there. As he did, his tail curled tight around her, bringing her hips up to him as he knelt above her and she squirmed beneath him.

Min keened and writhed. Oh yes, he was prepping her, well and good. But it wasn't enough, she needed to hold his cock.

Her hand went to the band of his pjs, slid below.

"You're really sure?" he asked her.

"There's nothing I want more, Ethan. Please," she heard herself whine. "Let me see you."

"Oh fuck, Min." He stood up, the material tenting at his groin.

Min gulped.

He slowly shucked his pants, and she gasped as his cock sprang free.

There was no denying it was massive, but it was also ribbed and rippled, the skin pulled tight over glowing hues of gold and green, the head protruding, glistening bright green from his foreskin, and just nestled in front, a smaller, bulbous head leaked iridescent silver fluid. As he took his larger cock in his fist, his little finger looped over the smaller head, stroking it, and more fluid fountained out, lubricating the length of both cocks, making them glisten in the light.

Min found herself salivating. "Y—you've got two."

"Kind of." He smiled, shy yet proud.

Min stared. His anatomy looked so natural, so right to her, his double-headed arousal standing magnificent above his big dark green ball sack, between those powerful muscled thighs. That strangely delicious ribbed and rippled appendage with his smaller cock in front, was so much more magnificent than any human penis could ever be.

He gazed at her out of vivid blue eyes. "Min, is this okay? You're not shocked by my cocks?"

Shaking her head, with a little sob of pleasure she reached for him. "They're magnificent. *You* are magnificent. Come here, let me touch you."

"What is this?" She let her fingers move around the smaller swollen bulb, her fingers slipping and sliding in the sweet-scented liquid.

"We call it our groc. It's to pleasure our mate, to prepare them for our primary cock."

"I can see that could be useful," she said, awestruck.

"Will you trust me? To pleasure you right?"

She gulped, nodded.

He lay down on his back and lifted her easily onto him, her legs stretched over his powerful thighs.

"I will not go inside you. Not the first time."

"Oh, but I want to," she begged, her fingers joining his as he worked himself, her pussy poised.

With gentle, explorative fingers, he opened her slit and slid his hot rippled cock along her seam so that his groc rested perfectly against her clit, wet and delicious and... good goddess, *vibrating*. She could feel the head of his big cock all the way along her seam, nudging at the sensitive tissue around her entrance. The combination was electrifying.

"Oh goddess—Ethan!" Min's whole body arched above him as his groc massaged her clit better than any vibrator she'd ever owned.

She clung on to his shoulders, biting, stroking, clawing as the pleasure coiled inside her with each nudge of his cock against her entrance, each vibration of his groc. He worked her so expertly, one big green hand manipulating his cocks into just the right spots to intensify her pleasure, all the while watching her response out of vivid blue eyes.

His groc seemed to know what pressure and intensity she needed, as if it could read her body perfectly. Min's pleasure built to a crescendo. She heard herself mewling, panting out his name, as the pleasure rose higher, coiling tight in her pelvis... and then his voice demanded, guttural and harsh, "Come for me, baby," and just like that the pressure burst, her orgasm pitching her into the heavens. She clung on, imagining herself riding her dragon toward the stars as she peaked and tumbled, keening his name, her hips snapping and jerking with the intensity of her release.

And he husked out, "Oh yeah, that's it, that's it baby," as he wrung the last atoms of pleasure from her, and she slumped against his chest, sated and spent.

When she was finally able to lift her head and look into his face, his gaze was full of awe, and raw longing. Despite her orgasm, she needed more. "Come inside me," she begged him. "Ethan, please."

"No, sweetheart," he gritted out. She felt him drawing his

primary cock away from her seam, his hot wet groc gone from her clit. "Not this time."

"But you..." As he knelt above her, she gazed at his shaft, glistening with both their juices, dark and swollen with arousal. "It must be painful." Her little hand reached for him, but he pulled back further, covering his cock with one big fist.

"Min, now is not the time. You will need me to pleasure you like this often before you will be primed to take me inside you."

"But I can't leave you like this. Besides, I want... you to fill me..."

"Min, I'm an adult, I can control my own arousal. And my release will be amazing when we do finally..." He bent over her, stroked a claw gently along her cheek. "Sweetheart, you need to sleep."

The he kissed her with slow, exquisite sweetness, holding in his need, putting her first.

"Sleep, sweetheart," he said.

It was true, her limbs were limp from her orgasm, her eyelids unbearably heavy. "Where are you going?" she managed on a yawn, aware that he was gently pulling the sheet over her.

"To play you a lullaby."

∼

Ethan had to smirk.

The pleasure center below his waist was probably going to affect his ability to play for her, if only because his hard-on was so large it was grazing the bottom of the piano keyboard.

But he wanted to play his favorite piece for Min, one he'd written himself.

He'd had dreams long ago, stupid dreams, of being a professional pianist, a musician, writing his own songs, playing to a full auditorium.

As a dragonling, he'd shyly showed his father the scribbled notes of a composition and asked if he wanted to hear it. His father had shaken his head. "Another time, lad, when I'm not so busy," he'd said. Then he'd turned his piercing blue eyes on Ethan and said, almost sternly, "Just remember, son, dragons are rulers of the sky. Leave all that soft stuff to the birds, and the fairies."

His father hadn't meant to be cruel, Ethan was sure of that; he just didn't understand the love he had for music. And so Ethan had stifled his creativity after that. Buried it under an inflexible façade, trying to be the perfect son Dad wanted him to be.

After his father died, he'd finally bought the grand piano, although for months he'd felt guilty whenever he sat down and played.

But eventually, he'd allowed himself the pleasure of his music. And now, he was going to share that pleasure with his beloved.

If only his rock-hard cock would get out the way and let him focus!

He breathed slowly, battling to keep his thoughts from straying to how good it had felt having her little pussy vibrating around his cock head, the pleasure in his groc, a pleasure that rippled up and down his spine like... well, similar to the pleasure music gave him.

Pervading his whole being.

He'd left the bedroom door open. Kissed her eyelids and the tip of her nose, then told her to relax and just let the music waft her into a deep sleep.

Now he focused, placed his hands over the keyboard. They shook slightly as he readied himself.

And then the notes danced in front of his eyes, and his fingers danced over the keys.

Somehow, he knew he was connecting his soul to Min's,

that there was a vibration that passed through his fingers to her ears as she lay in his big bed.

And that, unlike his father, she would love that her dragon was a musician.

He guessed she'd be asleep by now. Just as he was feeling like he'd got some semblance of order back into his body, at least enough that he could sleep, a pair of warm human arms slid around his neck and down his chest, fingers exploring under the lapels of his dressing gown until they found his nipples, and gently tweaked them.

Ethan's cocks obligingly hardened, along with his nipples.

"Min," He growled. "You're supposed to be asleep."

"Your playing is divine, Ethan, but I can't sleep."

He swiveled and picked her up, and in one fell swoop, her butt was cupped between his open legs.

Her sweet little cunt nestled there, nudging his cocks into action.

So much for the music calming his libido down.

She was only wearing a towel, which pooled on the ground as they kissed.

"Min, Min, Min." It was like an incantation, a mantra whispered against her neck.

"I want you. All of you. Please, Ethan," she begged.

"Min, this isn't something we can just do..."

"You've already prepared me with your groc, and I've seen you now, and I'm not scared. I'm in a state of wonderment."

"Wonderment!"

"Yes." She snickered softly into his shoulder. "Your cock is the most magnificent thing I've ever seen. And if it hurts, I don't care. The pleasure will drown out the pain. Feel me, feel how wet I am."

She took his hand, and he ran his fingers through the warm dark wetness of her, strumming the bud of her swollen clit. Min writhed on top of him. "More... please..."

Obligingly, he settled a finger into her entrance, and when she begged, he added another,

stretching that tight little space.

"Does that hurt?"

"No."

She grabbed his face and kissed him, her tongue darting in and out, and following her lead, he pulsed his fingers with the same rhythm, moving them a little deeper inside her as Min moaned out her pleasure and begged him to take her with his cock.

Ethan wondered where the quiet, bookish Minerva had gone. This wild creature ready to ride his cock was a different woman altogether. There were so many different facets of Min, and he loved them all.

He closed his eyes as her hand gripped the base of his cock. She looked down, her tongue rimming her lips as she ran her fingers reverently over the ridges and ripples. He saw the color of his primary cock changing, knew that meant he was primed and ready to penetrate her. Pre-cum pulsated out of his groc. As if she knew exactly what to do, Min smoothed her finger over his groc, spreading the silky fluid around his big cock and her own seam.

And when she told him this was the most beautiful thing she had ever seen, and that she had to have him inside her now... *that*... that unraveled him completely.

With a growl, he flipped her around so that her butt landed on the piano keys, and they both laughed at the wild sound that made.

Her legs spread wide, her pelvis thrusting to meet his cock. Ethan gazed longingly at her glistening cleft, the little juicy bud inviting him, taunting him, begging him to pleasure her some more.

She was perfect. And he couldn't hold back any longer.

He tried one last weak protest about it being too soon, but

already her hand was guiding him closer, her teeth nibbling at her lower lip, her eyes hazy.

He let her hand move up and down his length, her little finger catching on his groc and rubbing over it, sending ripples of delight through every cell in his body.

As he nudged the head of his main cock into her entrance, his groc pulsated rhythmically on her clit and her hips rocked, jangling the piano keys.

And then—oh, gods in heaven—the head of his primary cock slipped inside her, swallowed into the tight warm wet cavern of her cunt.

Tight, but not too tight.

Oh gods, he was dying of pleasure here.

"Ethan!" she gasped, and he held her. Stilled his movements. "Okay?"

"Keep going," she begged.

Another thrust, and she gave a harsh little cry, then a laugh. "Oops! There went my hymen."

Even now, that Westwind humor made him pant out a laugh.

Min was everything.

Quirky, feisty, sweet, sexy as all hell. Everything he'd ever dreamed of.

Gently, he kissed away a little tear from her eye.

"Better now?"

"It only hurt for a moment."

"You want me to keep going?" It would be anguish, but he'd stop in a second if she needed him to.

"Yes, oh yessss…"

Ethan eased deeper inside her. She was so wet from her own lubrication and the stream of liquid from his groc, and now, sweet goddess, he was almost in to the hilt, and she'd accommodated his cock like she was… like she was *made* to take it. He could feel every vibration and ripple of her internal walls as she sucked him into her, her little mewls and sobs of pleasure vibrating against his ear.

Ethan flung back his head and a stream of flame burst from his nostrils. It soon disappeared, and little sparks showered harmlessly back onto them.

"Oh, Ethan that is so beautiful."

"*You* are so beautiful," he countered as she clung on, her legs clamped tight around his hips, her hands curled around the keyboard. He pulled out a little, just enough that they could both watch him moving in and out of her.

And soon that proved overpowering.

"Ethan..." she crooned, "I'm... I'm close..."

"Gods, me too Min."

He buried his head in her neck and thrust deeper, the ecstasy building in him like a storm ready to burst wide open. Would she cope with his dragon orgasm?

It was a fleeting worry; he knew his groc was preparing her, lubricating her like nothing else could. She was taking him fully now, and she clung to him, panting, biting at his neck. As they moved faster, lost in each other's bodies, he was vaguely aware of the piano keys playing out their arousal.

Suddenly he felt her spasming, tightening, her vulva rippling around him, and he held her tight, his wings beating out behind him as the volcano of his orgasm drummed at the base of his balls, demanding release.

With a deep growl, he gripped her thighs and pulled them around him, and all that came to mind was that they were riding, together, locked together, to the peak of completion.

The pants and gasps, the sound of their shared ecstasy, his gasped dragonish words of love, all of it was spiraling them higher.

And when he heard her cry, "Oh gods, Ethan, I'm—you're making me—oh, I'm going to..."

And then her internal walls clamped onto his cock as she came, and he couldn't hold back another second.

"Oh gods, Min." He lifted her clean off the piano, her copper hair falling around them as with one final thrust and a deep bellow, he spilled his hot dragon seed deep within her.

It felt for all the world like they were diving, falling through the skies, then flying up, up into the clouds with their release, until finally, spent, Ethan slumped against her, gasping into her neck.

Nothing and no one had ever blown his horns off his head like that before.

He was reeling, seeing stars — maybe he *was* in heaven. As they came back to earth, gasping and laughing almost in disbelief at the magic of it, Min giggled. "I never thought I'd hear music when I lost my virginity."

Ethan threw back his head and howled with laughter.

CHAPTER 22

The morning light filtering through the curtains woke Min. Or maybe it was the soft little kisses Ethan was raining down the back of her neck.

She shivered with delight, remembering last night. Losing her virginity to a dragon on the keyboard of his grand piano.

Now that was something to tell your grandchildren. Or perhaps not.

She leaned back into his kisses, and his rasping dragon tongue curled lower and around one breast, the fork flicking over her nipple, hardening it. At the same time she felt his strong tail moving lower, curling around her waist, between her legs.

Min hummed with pleasure, her eyelids fluttering.

Oh, holy aunt, this was good. She could just lie back and give in to the pleasure.

But sensible Min needed to have her say. She sat up, hugging his tail to her breasts.

He looked at her, disconcerted. "I'm sorry, don't you like it?"

"Ethan, we need to talk."

He sighed heavily. "I guess."

"Last night. Us. This whole fake relationship thing…"

He was silent for a moment, then, quietly he said, "Guess it's not so fake anymore." He had a smirk on his face that was endearingly boyish. "Not sure that it ever was. For me, at least."

"Oh—I…"

"Min, I've had feelings for you from the moment I set eyes on you in Adina's reception. It was like a lightning bolt hitting my heart. Crazy, I know, but that's the truth."

"I know, it was the same for me. It's so weird, Ethan. From the very beginning—actually, the moment I saw your photo on your profile—I was attracted to you, in a way I can't explain."

"So you think you fell first, huh?" He couldn't help teasing.

"Yes, absolutely I did." She mock pouted.

"Hmmm. That kind of one upmanship will get you… kissed!" With that, he rolled her over and his big dragon frame covered her, his thigh pushing between hers as she arched into him.

They kissed, and she felt his cocks hardening against her leg. Such beautiful things, built for pleasure. How could it be that they fit a human woman's anatomy so perfectly? Or at least, *this* human woman's.

And that in itself was… strange. And wonderful.

He looked at her in awe. "Min, for someone who's never had a lover, you're so responsive… Your body felt like it was meant to take me. It's hard to comprehend."

"You think I'd lie?"

"No, no, the evidence was there." He smirked.

Min's eyes widened. "Oh dear, did we mess up the piano keys?"

"I wasn't looking, to be honest; my mind was elsewhere.

Besides, they needed a bit of lubrication. There was one key that kept sticking…"

"Oh you, idiot!" She smacked her little hand against his chest, then buried her head in his shoulder, giggling. She could happily stay here forever, but he lifted her chin with a claw, his blue eyes suddenly full of gravitas.

"Min, on a serious note, we do need to navigate this differently now that we've acknowledged our feelings for each other are real."

Real. The word thrilled her.

"Well, obviously I won't take any money from you."

"Yes, you will."

"No way, Ethan." She sat up, pushing her hair back from her face and glaring at him. "That would make me feel like… like I'm prostituting myself."

"Then I will gift you the bookshop, when this is all over."

Her heart clenched. "When all this is over between us, you mean?"

He buried his head in her neck, laughing softly. "No, Min. When the deal is finalized. I don't want us to end." At those words, her heart bounced back into its rightful place and she wrapped her legs around him and tugged him into her.

"Erm… okay," Ethan husked out, "suddenly I have more pressing things on my mind. Maybe we can continue this discussion later."

Her hand snuck down between them and massaged his big, ribbed member, then the vibrating groc nestled in front, nudging it with her little finger, feeling it wet and ready to pleasure her again. To prep her for that beautiful, gigantic cock of his.

His tail flicked around her thigh, tugging her against him. "So many parts of you give me pleasure," she sighed, and stroked the tail moving up and down her seam.

"Which part would you like to be pleasured by first, Miss Westwind? My tail, my tongue, or my double-headed cock?"

"I'll take all of them," Min laughed.

∽

Quite some while later, seated at breakfast in their dressing gowns, Min was surprised when Ethan said, "I want to visit the Westerly with you, Min."

Her brows raised. "You mean today?"

He nodded. "I need to see the place that shaped you. You've shared my home, spent time with my family, but I don't have a real sense of your life, of where you grew up." He reached across the table and stroked her hand. "It's just not enough to *pretend* I know about your life any more. I *need* to know about your life, Min. I *want* to know everything about you."

Min was touched, but she couldn't help wondering what he'd make of the shop, of her home. "It's just a musty old bookshop." Why was she trying to put him off, when she'd love him to visit the Westerly more than anything? Was she scared that if Ethan saw how simple her life was, she'd no longer hold the same appeal?

But his next words appeased her worries as he said softly, "But it's *your* musty old bookshop. It's where you grew up, it's what made you who you are." He smiled, and she melted into the blue of his eyes. "I've taken the morning off of work so I can be with you, so why not today?"

"We could go back to bed instead," she said hopefully. Gods, she was insatiable for his touch.

"After we've visited the bookshop," Ethan said with a quirk to his lips but a firmness on his handsome face.

"Very well. To the Westerly we will go," Min said, wondering how Gingerbread would respond to a big green dragon invading his space. And what would Bonnie say when her fake date proved to be anything but?

"I'll just make a call, tell Bonnie to expect us," she said.

When the hover cab touched down an hour later, Bonnie was waiting at the open door, bouncing on her heels with excitement.

"Hi," Ethan said, giving her his best smile.

"Oh hi, let me make you both a cuppa." A cup of tea was Bonnie's answer for everything. She dashed into the office and put the kettle on, her snakes going every which way in her excitement. While Ethan looked around the shop, Min followed Bonnie into the office and told her an abbreviated version of the facts.

Min's eyes rounded. "Oh goodness me, so now you're telling me it is real between you? I can't keep up! I can see why, though, he's even more handsome than in the photos."

Min laughed, blushing. She looked around. "Where's Gingerbread? I didn't see him in the snug."

"No idea—mousing maybe? You go be with Ethan, I'll bring the tea out shortly."

Ethan was already wandering along the bookshelves, casting his eye over the volumes. And there at his feet, doing figure eights around his legs, was Gingerbread.

Min laughed. "Oh, he's found you."

"Yes, so it would seem."

"Are you okay with cats?"

"To be honest, I haven't met many. We never had cats at home; dragons aren't really into domesticated pets." He looked down at Gingerbread and smiled, and the cat looked up at him and let out a plaintive mewl.

"Well, he does seem to like you," Min observed.

Gingerbread ambled over and nudged her leg, almost as an afterthought.

Ethan's gaze returned to the shelves. "What a treasure trove. How long did it take your dad to collect all these books?"

"Years and years. So many of them had been hidden away in attics and basements in Motham."

"I've never seen anything like it."

"The only other collection of books written by monsters for monsters is in the Motham Library, but I believe Dad actually acquired more."

Now Ethan was strolling toward the wooden door at the back of the bookshop. "What's in here?"

"That's Dad's study. I've kept it locked since he died. There are still things in there that I—I haven't had the courage to go through yet. I just keep thinking I'll cry so much I won't be able to get the job done."

"I felt like that when I walked into my father's office after he died. Like I'd never be able to fill his shoes." Ethan put his arms around her waist and his wings around her shoulders and laid a kiss on the top of her head. How could you settle for just arms when you could get a double hug with wings as well, Min wondered.

After a moment, she sighed. "I guess I do need to go in there. There are boxes of books that need sorting still. And there's a box they found in the mangled wreckage of his car." Her lip wobbled, tears filled her eyes. "I think that's what makes it so hard. It would remind me of that day too much."

"If you want to go in, I'll hold your hand."

She stood very still, hesitating. "I—I'm not sure. It doesn't feel quite the right time."

"Then honor that," Ethan said gently. "Maybe you need to be alone when you first go through his stuff."

"I'm not sure if it's that even." She couldn't put a finger on it, she just knew this was not the moment.

As if reading her thoughts, he said, "You'll know when it's right, Min."

She looked up at him, her eyes swimming with tears, so glad that Ethan understood without the need for explanations.

"Thank you," she sighed, and laid her head against his chest.

After all the sadness of losing her father, all the pain and loneliness of this past year, as Ethan's wing bound her close, Min finally felt like she'd found home.

CHAPTER 23

The next couple of weeks were the happiest of Min's life. She'd never dreamt that she would ever find someone so right, so perfect. They seemed able to sense what each other needed, physically and mentally.

She discovered that Ethan loved having his spinal scales massaged gently.

He found her G-spot. And a little spot just behind her ear that turned her on when he kissed it. Every. Single. Time.

They went on a whirlwind of dates, spending every evening out on the town, holding hands, kissing, chatting about all kinds of things. And they laughed—a lot. About the silliest things, really.

Ethan was right—dragon humor and Westwind humor were the perfect match.

Every night was filled with lovemaking, her riding his cock, being pleasured alternately—and sometimes simultaneously—by his tail, his groc, and his cock. He had this amazing way of looping his tail along the crevice between her buttocks and teasing her little hole, as she rode his cock and his groc stimulated her clit. And her orgasms were so intense her rippling inner walls would bring him off at exactly the same moment.

Other times he'd lie her on the bed and lick down her body with that long, forked tongue, taking her nipples in his mouth like ripe cherries, suckling them until she practically came just from that.

Then he'd lick down, across her tummy, down to the soft patch of hair between her thighs, and his big green hands, with just a touch of claw — she'd told him she liked the scratch of them — would part her legs. He'd smile up at her lasciviously, showing her his tongue before placing it between her legs and lapping a path that drove her nearly insane with want.

Rimming her. Teasing her.

Until she was like putty in his hands, and if his cock had been twice, thrice the size, she'd still be wide open enough to take it.

In between these encounters she slept, quite a lot. To get her energy back for the next marathon. And she spent time with his family, too.

She and Cressida would trawl through her cave room, going through her jewelry collection and talking about her past. She'd also met Cressida's friends at coffee mornings, a group of loud, fun-loving monster species who teased Min relentlessly about dragon cock. Min gave up blushing after a while. These older women were worldly wise, knew what they wanted in the bedroom and didn't buy the shy virgin act.

Besides, Min didn't have to play that part. She was well and truly not a virgin anymore.

She also spent time with Beau, learning all about the game he was working on. He clearly loved confiding in her, and often showed her the almost finished graphics for his game.

"What do you think of Schelzan?" he'd say as they sat in the garden. They spent time there most days as summer advanced and the weather was perfect.

"He's great, but maybe extend the fangs and horns a bit," Min mused, head cocked as she examined his work. "From what you told me about Schelzan's character, he's a mean, green fighting machine. He looks a bit too friendly to me."

Beau had squinted at the iPad. "Okay, you may be right. I'll make his horns bigger, give him a more scowly look, more flames. Talking of friendly dragons… Do you think I should tell Ethan about this yet? We're getting on better, and I really want him to know before the gala dinner. I don't want him saying anything in public about me joining the family business and having to bluff my way through it."

Min knew all too well how lies could get you in a pickle.

"I could hint that you have something you want to talk to him about. Maybe prep him a bit."

"Would you?"

"Sure."

"Oh Min, that would be great. Usually when I try to talk to him, I say the wrong thing and we end up fighting, but if you've already kind of briefed him…"

Min wasn't sure how she'd raise it, but she'd find a way. Now the brothers were getting on so much better, she knew she had to. "Leave it with me, Beau."

Beau grinned, and Min felt a warm glow in her chest. It was so nice to see the young dragon genuinely excited and happy. Gone was his sulky look. These days, he'd bounce up to the dinner table each night, and he never came home wasted. The garden was looking lovely, no burned bushes.

She loved what he was doing, and how dedicated he was to it. She wanted to help in any way she could.

If she timed it right, Min was sure she could get Ethan to understand.

"I declare, I've never seen my two boys happier together than they are right now!" Cressida, sitting across the dinner table from them, smiled. Reaching across, she took both her sons' hands.

Beau spluttered something about her being the most embarrassing mom ever, while Ethan gazed at Min, and under the table squeezed her hand with his free one. His tail rested gently against her lower leg, and occasionally he let it flick higher, up to her inner thigh, watching the flush of desire build in her cheeks.

Later he would take her, leisurely, giving her a full body massage with his tail, before his mouth would suckle and tease the tight little bud of her clit and his tongue would work her to a screaming orgasm.

The thought sent pleasure rippling down his spine and he hardened. He forced himself to focus on the conversation.

"Good to see you knuckling down to your studies, Beau," he observed.

A definite look passed between Beau and Min. Ethan's brows furrowed. "Are you two plotting something?" He waggled his browbone at Beau. "If you think you're going to move in on my girl, mate, that is taking brotherly love too far."

Min giggled. "Beau, you're gorgeous, but I'm sorry, I'm already taken."

Beau threw his napkin at her. "Don't worry, I'm not pining. There's a queue of others, let me tell you," he snorted good-naturedly.

"La la la la, too much information!" Cressida put her hands over her ears. "You're still a dragonling to me, Beau."

They all laughed, and warmth filled Ethan's chest. Since Min had been here, Beau really had changed. He seemed to be studying hard in his room most evenings, and there'd been no more incidents in the garden.

He couldn't get over how much he adored this woman,

and the effect her presence had on all their lives. Mom was calmer than he'd seen her in years, and she seemed happier in her own skin.

Earlier that night, as they dressed for dinner, he'd asked Min, "What do you talk to my mom about?"

"Oh, this and that. How much she loved your dad. What you were like as dragonlings. All the attempts she's made to shift over the years."

"Has she told you how much she's spent on therapies?"

"Not in detail, but I got the impression she's tried a lot of different things. It means a lot to her, Ethan."

"Yeah, I know, but she seems to be coming to terms with it a bit better now. And Beau, he's been really knuckling down to his studies."

He'd sensed her hesitate. "I think he wants to talk to you about that. When he does, try and listen properly, Ethan. Give him a chance to explain."

He'd promised her he would, so now, as the dinner plates were removed, when Beau said, "Can I show you something I've been working on?" Ethan said, "Sure, I'd love to take a look."

Beau dashed out of the room and soon came back with his laptop under his wing.

Placing it on the table, he flipped it open. Ethan expected to see an essay Beau wanted him to read over, maybe add a few points to.

But what was on the screen were a whole lot of graphics.

Beautifully drawn images of dragons, intricate in their design, exquisite in their execution.

Ethan stiffened. "What's this got to do with your course?"

"I didn't say it was about my course. It's a game."

"You know I don't approve of you gaming," Ethan growled. "Total waste of time that could be spent productively. Don't tell me when I thought you were studying, you've been gaming."

"Please, just listen Ethan," Min pleaded, her hand on his arm. "Let Beau explain."

Remembering his promise to her earlier, Ethan sat, arms crossed, as Beau flicked through different graphics of beautifully drawn characters.

"What is this all about, Beau?" he finally gritted out, unable to hold in his exasperation any longer. "Where did all these images come from?"

"I drew them."

"What the fuck!" Ethan stared harder at the screen. "But these are... professional."

"Are you implying I can't do something professionally?" Beau huffed.

"No, it's just—when did you learn to draw like this?"

Beau's lip curled. "Years ago. You never took any notice."

"These graphics are yours?"

"Yes, for a game me and my friends have been building," Beau said defensively.

"When?"

Beau's head tilted back, his nostrils flaring as his eyes met his brother's challengingly. "For the last few months."

"When you should have been studying?" Ethan sputtered, flames coursing out of each nostril.

"Yeah, and you know what? I'm proud of that," Beau gritted out.

"Oh, Beau." Their mom, who'd been looking over their shoulders, joined in. "These are amazing drawings."

Ethan was aware of Min, very quiet and still at his side. "Did you know about this?"

She nodded.

"And you think this is okay? Beau spending his time doodling?"

"Doodling!" Beau spluttered.

"I think it's great, if you want my honest answer," Min said.

Ethan raked a claw over his head scales. "I'm paying for his damn education."

"Well," said Min, calmly, "maybe you should stop."

Ethan couldn't believe his ears. Was Min actually supporting Beau with this nonsense?

Beau's mouth went sulky. "If you're worried about the money, I'll put my trust fund money into it."

Ethan shot forward, all his scales arcing up. "No. I forbid it."

"You forbid it?" Beau's lip curled. "What are you, the career police? Well, thanks bro, for your support." He slammed the laptop shut and hightailed for the door.

Ethan's eyes sparked. "Where the fuck are you going now?"

"Well, it's obvious you don't want to see any more, so I won't waste any more fucking time showing it to you," Beau hissed from between his fangs.

"Oh boys, please stop fighting!" Cressida wailed. But Beau had already stormed out, slamming the door behind him. Cressida's face crumpled. "We were having such a lovely evening, and now look what you've done."

His mom's golden eyes swam with tears.

Oh gods, now he'd upset her too.

"You should know better, Ethan." She pushed back her chair and flew out the door after Beau.

Which left only Min.

And she obviously thought he was a complete bastard too.

Ethan got up and paced around the table, feeling Min's gaze trained on him. Every scale on his back sensed her disappointment in him. And that was almost the hardest cut of all.

Finally, he ground to a halt. "Well, what are you thinking?"

Min sighed. "I think Beau a very talented artist, and he has a great concept. I think you should have given him time to explain, not just jumped down his throat."

Ethan growled an expletive in dragonish and did another turn of the table.

"You think I'm too strict with him, don't you?" He pivoted and fixed her with a bright blue stare.

"Yes, Ethan, I do." She came over and gazed up at him solemnly, her hands curling around his upper arms. "And I understand why. You're worried. He went off the rails after your dad died, and you're scared it will happen again. I know you're coming from a place of caring. But... remember what you told me about your piano playing the other day, how your father brushed your talent aside?"

He'd confided this to Min in a moment of vulnerability after they'd made love and now he felt a ridiculous lump in his throat. Fuck. He'd be bawling like a chickling in a moment.

"I put that behind me." He fisted his hands at his sides. "I knuckled down, got on with what really mattered. Running the company."

"If you put it all behind you, why have you bought a grand piano, which you play for a couple of hours every day?"

He gulped hard, his eyes stinging now. "It's a hobby."

"No, Ethan, it's a passion. It makes you feel alive. And maybe this is more than a hobby for Beau. Maybe this is his passion." Ethan couldn't answer, because he knew everything she was saying was true.

"What if you let Beau do what he loves? Stop trying to be the disciplinary big brother. Wouldn't that take a weight off both of you? Wouldn't it be better to get along with each other rather than fight?"

He looked at her, his heart wanting to soften. His approach to date hadn't worked, that was patently obvious. If he continued down this path, he'd burn every bridge he'd built with Beau this past month.

Min stepped closer and continued, stroking his chest with her palms. "I desperately wanted a brother or sister, but with no mom, that wasn't ever going to happen. It's hard for me to see you guys having a family and pulling it apart for no reason."

"There is a reason." He couldn't keep the bitterness out of his voice. "You weren't here when Beau was out every night getting into trouble, driving mom crazy with worry, pulling me out of meetings to go get him from the police station."

"But that's in the past, Ethan. It's not happening now. He's got a great group of supportive friends; his concept for this game and the execution are brilliant. And above all, he's an incredibly talented, dedicated artist. Surely you should be rejoicing in the fact that he's found his direction in life?"

Oh gods, she was right. So right. And suddenly it felt like a rock had been lifted off his shoulders.

"Ah Min." He sighed, pulling her against his chest. She nuzzled into him, and his wings enveloped them both in a cocoon. "How come you're so wise?"

"I'm not." She smiled up at him. "But I do think I know what will work for Beau—and maybe for both of you. And that will make your mom very happy."

She lifted her head and they kissed.

"Guess I'd better go and put out a few fires," he said when he finally released her.

"Not literally, I hope," she laughed.

"You never know with us two. But no, I promise I'll stay calm, get him to sit down with me and show me his work. Would you mind going to Mom and telling her I'm making peace with Beau?"

"Of course," she said softly. "You're a good guy, Ethan Blade."

"Maybe," he sighed, kissing her soft upturned mouth, "but you're making me a better one."

CHAPTER 24

When Ethan approached Beau's door, all was quiet. Unusual. He knocked. There was no music, nothing, just silence, which was more worrying. He knocked again, but there was still no answer, so he turned the handle and walked in. The room was in darkness.

"Beau?"

No answer.

He cleared his throat. "Beau, are you in here?"

A tiny little flame thrown from the bed illuminated Beau, who was curled up on the mattress, his wings huddled around him.

He looked so young, so vulnerable with his arm thrown over his horns and his wings curled around his body. It reminded Ethan of how his little brother had been when he'd first hatched. How much he'd loved him. His heart swelled as the memories of his tiny hatchling brother hit him in the solar plexus.

No one had time for Beau when Dad died. Not Ethan, and not his mom. Ethan had been too wrapped up in his own grief, and coping with his mother's. When Beau had gotten involved with ferals, he'd come down on him like a ton of bricks, sending him to a special school, which he'd absconded from.

The therapy, and the cajoling, and… it just seemed endless at the time. He pinched the bridge of his nose, fighting the flood of memories. It was in the past, just like Min said.

Just sit down and hear Beau's story now.

Let him show you his work.

Listen. Be a big brother who cares, not one who resents the worry he's caused you.

Min was right: he and Beau weren't so different. They were both creative—him with his music, Beau with drawing. Ethan could still feel the sting of rejection, like ice, when he'd showed his dad those few pages of music he'd written, the feeling of deep disappointment, the sense that who he was wasn't going to be enough. Not unless he followed in Dad's footsteps.

And now—shit. He was doing exactly the same thing to his little brother.

No. He couldn't—wouldn't—do that to Beau.

He walked cautiously over to the bed, sat down on the edge. He sensed his brother shifting away. "Mate, I'm sorry. I was too quick to react. I really do want to see what you're working on."

Another puff, but it was only smoke, no flame this time. That was a good sign. Ethan sensed Beau sitting up now, hugging his knees.

"Is this just because Min told you to come and talk to me?" Beau's voice was sulky.

He could lie, but Ethan thought better of it.

Just tell the truth.

"Min did persuade me I was wrong, yes. But… hear me out. I've been blind to what I've been doing to you, Beau. I reacted too strongly, and didn't give you a chance to explain." He huffed a sigh. "I guess you know how much I've worried about you since Dad died, but there's more to it than that.

When I was younger than you, I dreamed of being a musician, writing my own music, maybe being a concert pianist." He laughed. "Crazy, huh?" Beau said, nothing, but Ethan sensed his brother didn't think it was crazy. "One day I showed Dad a piece I'd written. I wanted to play it for him. And he shot me down. Not in a fiery way—to be honest, I'd almost prefer he'd shown more passion. No, he just shrugged it off, said he'd hear it some other time. I remember he told me music was soft stuff, for birds and fae." He laughed bitterly. "I waited for him to ask me to play that piece. And waited. He never asked. So I locked away my dreams and got on with being a dutiful son. And I'm only just realizing I've been expecting you to do the same. And that's not fair. When you tried to show me your art just then, I did to you exactly what Dad did to me. And I'm sorry."

Beau said a gruff, "Thanks." But his voice cracked.

There was silence for a few moments, punctuated by a snuffle or two from Beau. Finally, Ethan asked gently, "Will you show me the game you and your friends have created?"

"You mean, now?"

"Yeah, right now."

"Okay." Beau turned on the bedside light, jumped off the bed, and grabbed his laptop.

Ethan sighed with relief. At least Beau hadn't set light to the thing in a rage, or chucked it out the window.

As he sat and looked through the characters that Beau had created, and his brother's voice turned from cautious to confident and enthusiastic, a warmth filled Ethan's chest. This was so much better than the tightness, the scrunched fist he'd had in his heart, worrying about Beau.

Min was right, it was so much better to approve than disapprove. To find merit rather than fault.

Not just for Beau, but for him too.

Min was dozing off when she felt Ethan gently pull back the covers and climb in beside her.

She moved into his chest, smelled his sweet scent of smoky cedar and spice, so uniquely—dragon.

"Mmm, how did you go?"

"It was great, feels like we've broken through to each other. Thank you for making me go and talk to him. You're right, he's really very talented. I had no idea he was so good at graphic design."

"Amazing what you find out when you take an interest," Min said wickedly. She heard him sigh.

"You're right, I stand corrected. We've lived in our silos, me and Beau, ever since Dad died. And that's sad, because I loved him so much when he was a dragonling. I guess it's time we really got to know each other again."

"You're both creative, with so much vision. And you both want to make your mark in the world, for dragons," Min said softly.

"Just differently, I guess." He nuzzled into her neck, and she melted into his kisses. "How was Mom?"

She snuggled into him, loving how it felt to be a couple, a *real* couple.

"She's good. She spent a lot of time telling me about you and Beau's childhood. How you used to be such a great big brother, always looking out for Beau, and how he hero-worshipped you. And then she fell asleep, so I just left her and tiptoed out."

"Min," he dropped kisses on top of her head, "sometimes it feels like you're the missing part, making us whole again."

She laughed. "I'm not sure about that, but I do think I'm developing a sixth sense of when you're about to breathe fire."

"Or make love to you?"

She giggled, and felt his lips moving down her body, her nipples hardening as his tongue flicked over them. "That too."

"I want to pleasure every little part of you. I want you to lie back and let me give you everything a dragon can give."

As he pushed up her negligée, Min sighed and succumbed to everything *her* dragon could give.

∼

"I don't want you to ever leave," he whispered as they lay sated, several orgasms later.

"I'll have to go back to the shop eventually, Ethan. It's my life. It's what I do."

He stiffened a little. "But you won't live there, above the shop anymore."

"I—I hadn't got quite that far in my thinking."

"If we were married, surely you would live here with me."

He hooked up on his elbow and played with a strand of copper hair that fell over her beautiful breast, the nipple turning tight and rosy even at that soft touch. "What do you say to that, Miss Westwind?"

"Is this a marriage proposal, Ethan?"

"I think it just might be."

"I've known you barely a month. And most of that time we were fake dating."

Ah, sensible Min was back in the driving seat.

"It's been six weeks," he corrected.

"Oh Ethan, that's… no time, really, is it?"

"Does time define what we have Min? You and I had something the moment we first met. And it feels like time has nothing to do with it." He wanted to say it transcends time, but he knew that would sound kind of woo woo. "It felt like we were meant to be together from that first meeting."

"Yes." Her voice was small. "And you know I felt the same. But maybe… maybe we were primed to find each other attractive, because we were fake-dating…"

"You know that's not true."

She let out a whispered sigh of assent.

"You don't want to marry me. Is that what you're saying?"

"No, Ethan, I absolutely do, it's just my cautious nature coming to the fore. Apparently my mom was like that."

"I get that. But Min I'm supposed to announce our engagement at the gala dinner, to ensure the contract is approved."

She nodded "I know."

"And when I do, you need to know it's not one iota fake, that even if this deal fell on its face tomorrow, I would want you by my side, as my mate, forever."

"Oh Ethan." Her voice caught. "I want that too, more than anything in the world."

She reached up and kissed him.

As he kissed her back, his heart sang. Because tomorrow he would tell the world he was with Min, honestly, openly, no more lies.

Just the simple, beautiful truth.

That he loved Minerva Westwind with all his heart.

CHAPTER 25

Tonight was the big night, the annual Blade gala dinner, and as Min got ready, it was hard to believe that her month of fake dating Ethan was almost over.

Except, truthfully, it hadn't been fake for either of them, had it?

After tonight, having wined and dined and entertained 500 monsters and humans and, for the first time ever, representatives from the Council of Towns, the deal would be in the bag.

Ethan's company would own a great swathe of human land north of Motham City, enabling him to fulfil his father's dreams.

And their relationship would be really real.

Min smiled to herself, remembering their arguments over whether she would get paid. Now he was mumbling that he would gift her the Westerly as a wedding present.

A knock on the door cut through her thoughts. It was Ebony.

Min had asked her to come up and give her some last-minute advice on her outfit.

Ebony looked her up and down admiringly. "You look absolutely stunning. But I really think you shouldn't wear glasses tonight. Do you have contacts?" she asked, tapping her beak thoughtfully with one of her shellacked claws.

"I do, but I don't often wear them. I don't like touching my eyeballs." She hated slipping them into her eyes, and even worse, fishing them out, but tonight she wanted to lose her studious look, so she decided to take Ebony's advice.

After she'd blinked them in, she came out of the bathroom, and Ebony said, "Brilliant. And the gown you've picked is amazing. Almost on a par with a Kominsky design — except after what happened last year, you couldn't possibly wear a Kominsky dress. That would be a big black mark against Blade Wing Air, and we can't have anything go against Ethan right now."

"What exactly happened? With the Kominskys?"

"You've not heard?" Ebony looked surprised.

Min shook her head. She'd never followed the news much — at least, not until she was in it constantly.

"I guess it was hushed up, but you know, if you're a gossip like me you find out *everything*. Remind me to tell you the story another time. For now, suffice it to say, the Kominsky family are keeping a *very* low profile. Humans are still buying Kominsky gowns and cutting out the labels, but honestly, it's best not to risk it."

"Absolutely," Min said firmly. "Nothing must go wrong before the contract signing tomorrow." She smoothed her hands down the fitted silk of her dress.

"You look bea-uti-ful," said Ebony. "Time to go slay your dragon, hon." She smirked as she left the room. "See you down there."

After she'd left, Min stood staring at her reflection in the mirror, rearranging the diamond and ruby necklace that Cressida had given her to wear. It was more glitzy than anything she'd owned before, but one of the simplest creations Cressida possessed.

Without the barrier of her glasses, her eyes shone back at

her steadily. A sweeping uplift with eyeliner made them seductive and sophisticated, and her lipstick complemented the deep red of her dress.

Minerva Westwind.

Confident. Beautiful. And ready to stand by her dragon.

To undo all of Colonel Westwind's wrongs.

A moment later there was a knock on the door and there was Ethan.

He looked devastatingly handsome in his tux and dress suit.

The green and gold of his skin stood out against the stark black and white of his outfit.

His eyes skimmed down her body, and the admiration in his piercing blue gaze was unmistakable.

She saw his chest rise on a sharp inhalation. "You're not wearing your glasses."

"Nope. Strict instructions from Ebony."

"You look… amazing," he murmured. "With or without them."

She took a deep breath. "You don't look so bad yourself, if I may say so, Mr Blade."

"You may, Miss Westwind." And still he stared into her eyes.

His eyelids flipped sharply across his eyes, then he held out his arm. "May I accompany you to the grand ballroom, my love?"

"You may."

At the double doors into the ballroom, he bent his head and whispered in her ear, "Ready?"

"I'm ready." She beamed up at him, her heart so full of love it drowned out her nerves.

"Then let's do this thing." The staff threw open the double doors to the Blade grand ballroom and in they walked.

It seemed to Min like a thousand eyes homed in on them. Suddenly, she felt a little dizzy. Without her glasses as a barrier, she felt exposed. As if sensing this, Ethan's tail tightened around her waist, steadying her.

A peal of applause erupted as they entered, and Min realized some folks were standing, smiles beaming at them from every direction.

Ethan led her through the packed tables of monsters and a few humans. As they got closer to the stage, she saw Cressida seated, smiling and wiping away a tear. Beau sat next to her, looking very spruced in his own tux. Grinning, he winked at her, and her heart filled with a rush of love. Yes, she loved this dragon family.

It was *her* family now.

Her anxiety started to ease.

But then she glanced at an adjacent table to see a group who were not applauding, not smiling even. Gray men in gray suits. Human men. One face stood out among them, and her heart jolted.

Oh gods, Quentin Jordak.

And Quentin was positively scowling. Right at her.

Min looked away quickly, an ominous feeling of dread filling her chest. It was supposed to be a good thing that for the first time, humans were attending the gala dinner. But seeing Quentin here didn't feel good. Everything came flooding back to her: the way he'd stare at her body whenever he visited the Westerly, the unpleasant things he'd said to Ethan at his office, the way he'd questioned Bonnie when he'd stopped by the shop.

Would he make trouble tonight?

No, of course he wouldn't. Not here. Besides, he'd never done anything to her that would warrant her feeling this worried.

Ethan stopped at their table and reluctantly, the men stood from their seats.

"May I introduce my partner, Minerva Westwind."

Min could hardly breathe in the tight dress as she felt Quentin's eyes boring into her.

"Hello, Simon. H-hello Quentin," she said, trying to sound confident, but she didn't offer her hand in greeting. If they refused to shake hands with monsters, then she would not shake hands with them. Simon was polite, but Quentin greeted her through tight teeth, and his eyes were slivers of ice.

Min carefully avoided his gaze as Ethan exchanged polite pleasantries with the men, and then he led her to their table. "Sorry to subject you to that," he said. "It's a necessary formality."

"I understand. I know how Tween high society works."

He squeezed her hand. "Soon this will all be over, and it'll just be us."

She squeezed back and tried to loosen the rock of dread that was sitting on her heart.

Somehow as the evening wore on, she managed to relax and enjoy the music and entertainment, and the food, which was delectable. Cressida delivered the business awards admirably, hugging each winner with gusto.

Min kept her eyes carefully averted from the Council of Towns table.

As the time for his speech drew nearer, she could sense Ethan getting fidgety, glancing at the papers he'd brought with him. He'd told her he hated public speaking, so this was a big deal.

"I'm just going to practice my speech quickly," he said, getting up.

She nodded. Soon he'd be up on the stage, and she'd join him for the announcement of their engagement.

"How long have we got? I'm dying for a pee," she asked.

He laughed softly. "You've got at least five minutes. Just don't do a runner, or I'll be standing up there looking like a loser."

"I would never!"

He kissed her lips lingeringly and she whispered good luck, then watched him slip away through the crowds, his knuckles tight around the pages of his speech.

Min hurried out of the ballroom, then down the corridor to the powder room. Having relieved her bladder, she reapplied her lipstick and left.

She'd barely taken a step when a voice hissed close to her ear. "Minerva." Harsh fingers circled her wrist.

She knew that voice.

It was not a dragon voice.

It was human.

A shiver traversed her spine. She tried to pull her wrist away, but Quentin's grip tightened. His acrid breath was hot against her cheek as he marched her along the corridor, away from the ballroom. "Time you and I had a little chat, Minerva," Suddenly he dragged her behind a large potted plant in an alcove. Finding her voice, she demanded, "Let me go!" She tried to tug her arm out of his grip, but he slammed her back against the wall, pegging her there.

"No more of that snotty little princess behavior," he growled, his hands digging into her upper arms.

"Let go of me. I have nothing to say to you."

His grip tightened. "Oh yes you have. You need to tell me what the fuck you are playing at."

"I don't know what you're talking about. Let me go, Quentin, or I'll—"

A hand slammed over her mouth. "You'll what? Scream for that scaly dragon? He's about to give his speech, he won't hear you." She stared horrified into his cruel eyes, trying to work out how to escape, her pulse pounding in her ears. His hand was cold, and clammy against her mouth, his narrow eyes malevolent. "What are you doing, lowering yourself to dragon kind. Sullying your family's name?"

Jerking her head to the side, she freed her mouth, but now he pressed his face closer. "Answer me."

"Quentin, go and sit down and maybe I—I'll pretend this didn't happen." Anything to get his horrible presence away from her.

"Oh yeah, of course you will. You're very good at pretending, aren't you? Just like you're pretending to be in a relationship with a dragon."

"My relationship with Ethan is real," she said hotly. "You saw the report."

"And I don't believe it for a second. This kind of thing happens all the time." He sneered. "Cash-strapped humans selling themselves to rich monsters. But you... Minerva, *Minerva*, I thought you had more class. Is he giving you money to keep that ridiculous little bookshop?"

His eyes stabbed into her, full of venom and yes, she saw it now, jealous rage.

And lust.

She'd not mistaken the way he'd looked at her all those times, his filthy gaze undressing her.

"I'd have helped you out. Anything, Minerva, you could have asked for anything," he whined.

"I'd never take anything from you," she spat back.

"But you'll take it from a dragon, eh?" He stroked her cheek, and she shuddered, repulsed. "You must have guessed I have feelings for you. I'd have asked you out earlier, except it would have been kind of embarrassing, you know... for the Jordaks, given your father's monster-loving ways. But I'm willing to overlook that, if you drop the fucking dragon. We'll put it behind us, move on."

Min jerked her hand out of his grip. "You're deluded. I would never have dated you, even if Ethan and I hadn't fallen in love."

"You are not in love with him."

"I am."

"Lying little bitch!" His grip tightened again, his body slamming against hers. "I should have closed your stupid shop down. But instead, I supported you. I can offer you a good life, Minerva, and yet you want to throw it back in my face. You go down this path and the Westwind name will be soiled forever. You'll never be welcome in Tween society again."

"Good." She managed a harsh laugh. "Why would I want to be associated with a name that drove dragons and other beasts into servitude? Locked them up. Abused them, murdered them." She cast him a withering look. "I'm not proud to be a Westwind. I'm ashamed of what Colonel Westwind did. And the Jordak family is even worse. Never in a million years would I want to be part of it."

She smelled the alcohol on his breath as he sneered. "So that's it. You want to be a dirty little monster fucker, do you? If that's how you want to play it, I guess you won't mind if I take advantage either."

Min struggled and cried out as he continued to pin her against the wall, one hand over her mouth, the other shoving up her dress, pushing between her legs, ripping at the gusset of her panties. His body pressed against her, forcing her back against the wall, the thrust of his arousal repulsive, terrifying.

And then suddenly a flare blinded her. A blast of heat. As Min blinked, she realized the plant that had been obscuring them had burst into flames.

The next moment, Quentin was ripped off her.

She spotted a pair of rage-filled golden eyes. Scales raised in a halo around sharp horns.

With a roar, Beau swung Quentin into the air. "Don't you lay your hands on her, you piece of slimy pallid human flesh."

Quentin fought back, freeing his arm and punching Beau squarely in the jaw.

Beau let out a roar and threw a ball of flame, which made Quentin lose his footing and sprawl on the ground. With a mixture of horror and relief, Min watched as Beau picked him up by the collar and forced a squirming, shouting Quentin Jordak back along the corridor and into the ballroom.

Following dazedly on shaking legs, Min was aware that the applause ground to a halt as the dragon and the human tumbled in front of the podium, throwing punches at each other in full view of everyone. Quentin grabbed Beau by the neck scales and twisted. Beau threw a double flame from his nostrils, setting the front of Quentin's hair alight.

Quentin let out a high-pitched scream, grabbing at his head, and someone came running with a fire extinguisher and doused the flames. His hair now covered in foam from the extinguisher, Quentin ran full tilt at Beau and pitched into him again.

Standing at the edge of the grand ballroom, Min leaned against the wall, too weak and shaky to do anything except watch the drama unfold as Beau and Quentin pummeled each other, in full view of the gala dinner guests.

And worst of all—right in front of Ethan, who stood at the podium, about to deliver his speech.

CHAPTER 26

Ethan stood in front of the crowded room, the lights in his eyes.

Even though he'd done it many times, he still hated speaking in public. His hands were sweaty, but he reminded himself that Min was in the room somewhere, waiting to join him.

He squinted at their table, trying to spot her, but the lights were shining in his eyes.

He cleared his throat and smiled at the assembled crowd.

"Ladies and gentlemen, Council of Towns officials, Mayor of Motham, thank you all for attending the seventh annual Blade gala dinner. Tonight, I have—"

Suddenly the doors at the side of the ballroom burst open. Ethan stopped mid-sentence and stared at the scene unfolding in front of him.

It was Beau… Beau, fighting with someone, they were tangled in his wings, and his fists were flying, so Ethan couldn't see what species.

Un-fucking believable.

Rage flared up Ethan's throat. He couldn't believe that on his night of nights his brother could do this to him…

Beau's wing dropped for a moment, and Ethan caught sight of the other combatant. It wasn't a monster, too small... It was a *human*.

And not just any human...

Fuck! Quentin Jordak was attempting to throw punches at Beau's head, while Beau held onto his shirt and easily dodged his fists.

They tumbled onto the floor in front of the stage. For a moment Quentin managed to free himself, and he hit Beau square in the middle of his snout. His brother let out a string of dragon expletives and threw a flame straight at Quentin's lank hair.

It went up like a stack of dry hay.

A staff member ran forward and doused Quentin in extinguisher fluid.

Enough was enough!

Ethan jumped off the stage, grabbed both guys and separated them.

"What the hell are you both doing?" he growled loudly. The auditorium, he realized, was deathly silent except for the pair's labored breathing.

Beau clambered up now, placing his foot on Quentin, who'd dropped to the floor as he tried to wipe foam from his face.

Beau said, "I found this lowlife with his filthy hands all over Min."

"What?" Ethan's blood ran cold in his veins.

"Yeah, he'd grabbed her outside the bathroom."

"Where's Min? Is she okay?" All his thoughts were for her. His gaze flew around the ballroom, trying to locate her in the sea of faces.

"I'm here, Ethan." The sound of her voice had him heaving a breath of relief. Then he spotted her, pale and disheveled, her dress ripped on one shoulder. "Oh shit, Min darling, are you okay?"

"Yes, I'm fine, it's nothing... I mean, yes, he did grab me, but I... fought him off, and then Beau came and pulled him off me."

Ethan's heart clenched. "This piece of shit dared to touch you?"

She nodded. "It's okay, Ethan, nothing happened. Beau got there before—"

Red-hot rage blurred Ethan's vision. He grabbed Quentin by the scruff of the neck and hauled him up until they were nose to nose.

Quentin squinted as extinguisher fluid dripped from his forehead into his eyes.

Ethan glared at him. "You cowardly lowlife. If my brother hadn't already fire-balled you, there wouldn't be a hair left on your head." Ethan marched him over to the table where the Council of Towns officials were standing, stiff and red faced, and shoved Quentin into the midst of them.

Simon Jordak's thin face was white as he stood rigid, fists at his sides. "Expect an assault charge," he said, handing his brother a handkerchief with a contemptuous look that showed he was more worried about his reputation than his brother.

"Do not threaten me or mine," Ethan said softly. "Who do you think you people are? I invite you into my home, show you my hospitality, and your brother dares to abuse the woman I love in the most cowardly, despicable manner. And you call us monsters?" His lip curled and he pumped two bursts of fire from his nostrils, which narrowly missed their shirt fronts. The men hastily backed away. Ethan stood to his full height and snarled, "You may not have noticed, but the days when monsters bowed to your laws are coming to an end. Now, get out of my home before I have the head of Tower Security throw your sorry asses into the Motham lock-up."

"Here if you need me," shouted Grayson Lightfoot from one of the tables.

"Thanks, mate," Ethan called back.

"You've blown it, I'll see to that. No other monsters will ever get to buy human land, not after this, you hear me!" Quentin burst out in a high-pitched whine.

"Shut up, Quentin," Simon snapped, gathering his jacket off the back of the chair. He scowled at Ethan. "You realize you are this close to losing the deal." Simon pinched his finger and thumb together in a gesture that made Ethan want to laugh.

A low-level hissing and booing started up around the room.

Ethan felt Min's hand slide into his, her body close. He squeezed her hand tight.

"And you'll lose the Westerly Bookshop," Quentin sputtered, stabbing a finger at her.

Min held her head high. "Quentin, I don't want you to ever come near me or my shop ever again."

"It won't be your shop for much longer. The Westwind name won't come back from shaming the Council of Towns."

Min shook her head. "Right now, I'm ashamed to call myself human, let alone a Westwind." She turned to Ethan. "But I'm proud to call myself the partner of this incredible dragon."

Smiling down at her, his heart nearly bursting, Ethan turned to his security staff, who were flexing their scales and baring their fangs. "Please escort these humans to the gate."

The group of buffed alligators and crocodiles, barely able to disguise their grins, hustled the humans out of the ballroom.

And then Ethan turned to Min and held her cheeks between his palms. Gazed deep into her eyes. "I love you, Minerva Westwind."

Suddenly the hissing and booing stopped. There was rapt silence.

He cleared his throat, then spoke again, louder this time.

"I said I love you, Minerva Westwind. From the moment I set eyes on you. I knew it was you."

"I love you too, Ethan, with all my heart and soul."

And now Ethan could detect quiet applause, just one pair of hands, soon joined by another, and then another. The sound grew and grew until suddenly the whole ballroom was bursting with applause.

And there, in the midst of it, Ethan stood gazing at the woman he loved. And then he kissed her, long and deep, and she kissed him right back.

Forget land deals.

Forget progress.

Forget fulfilling the dreams of his father.

What mattered to him more than anything in the world was this beautiful brave human at his side.

He pulled her close, whispered in her ear, "I'm going to make a very important announcement."

"Should I be nervous?" she whispered back. He shook his head, his lips quirking. "Not half as nervous as I am right now."

But as she smiled radiantly up at him, he realized his fear of public speaking had evaporated completely.

Ethan turned to the crowd.

"Ladies and gentlemen, ten minutes ago my intention up on that podium was to announce that I was about to sign a deal with the Tween Council of Towns to build a new airport on human lands north of Motham. It seems, after the colorful performance you just witnessed, that—" He looked over at Beau and winked, and was rewarded with a huge grin in return. "That deal is probably off. And er, I want to thank my brother for that. Because tonight, Beau, you did something that matters far more. You warded off a cowardly attack on this precious woman standing beside me." He paused, hauled in a deep breath. "The woman I am madly in love with. Since you've been in my life, Min, you've brought my family together, gone on shopping trips with my mom—and that takes courage. Sorry, Mom." But Cressida just beamed at him. "And you've helped me repair my relationship with brother. Min, there's just one more thing I need to ask you," he turned to her, "while I have five hundred witnesses present." His heart was pounding and all he could do was drown in her eyes. Eyes that told him she was so happy to hear what he was about to say.

"Will you, Minerva Westwind, do me the honor of becoming my wife?"

CHAPTER 27

O NE WEEK LATER

Min turned the key over and over in her slightly sweaty palm.

She'd been standing here for the last ten minutes, trying to pluck up courage to open her father's study door.

She needed to do this. To go in there, tidy his desk, dust. Put away the books still in boxes. She would sort through her father's things. Get organized. It was time.

But still she hesitated. She looked around, then called in a reedy voice, "Gingerbread, are you there?"

Where was that damn cat when you needed him?

She heard the bell tinkling, signaling that someone had entered the shop, and sighed with relief. A customer—she could put off the decision for a few more minutes.

When she walked to the front of the shop, it was Ethan standing at the counter.

He was much earlier than she'd expected, which was probably not good news. After a week of curt email communication, the Council of Towns and Ethan had finally met today to nut out the situation, having been locked in an icy stalemate since the gala dinner.

Min had told Ethan that she wouldn't press charges against Quentin provided he was never allowed to come near her again. A restraining order had been issued by the Motham authorities, which made her feel safer, though it had probably done nothing to advance the airport deal.

Ethan had told her he wasn't worried about the airport, that all he wanted was her, but she couldn't let him leave it there. "No Ethan," she'd told him firmly, "you need to see this through. It's everything you've worked toward."

But now, she couldn't read his mood at all as he gazed at her, his expression inscrutable.

"Min, can we sit down?" They went into the office, and he sighed heavily as he sat down.

"It's not going through, is it?" she said.

He shook his head, and she reached for him. "Oh, Ethan, I'm so sorry."

"They've offered me some other land, just not where I wanted."

Min's heart sprang with hope. "Well, that's good. Surely you can make that work. Where is it?"

He looked down at his hands. "It's here, Min. It's the Westerly."

Min stopped breathing for a moment. "Right here—this land?"

He nodded. "It's not what I hoped for, but I can make it work. So, I've agreed."

Her eyes flew to his face, confusion and hurt jostling for supremacy.

"Y-you agreed."

He nodded, tight-lipped.

Min gulped back the huge lump in her throat. Of course, she wanted him to fulfil his father's dream... but her shop... *her* father's dream. She looked helplessly toward her dad's study, her enthusiasm for making a fresh start dying in her chest.

"Without... without asking me—or telling me?"

"There was no time. It was sign then and there, or forget it. Besides, I didn't really think it was necessary."

"Not... necessary." She barely got the words out through her parched lips, her world turning over, tumbling into pain. This guy, who only a mere week ago had declared his love for her in front of 500 people, was going to build his airport on her father's beloved bookshop.

She ground her hands tight in her lap, dug her fingernails into her skin to stop the tears from falling.

"Min, look at me." Ethan's words were soft, gentle.

"Please, Min."

She looked at him. His blue eyes were full of love. "It wasn't necessary to tell you because I won't be building an airport."

She shook her head, trying to hold back the blur of tears. "W-what are you saying, Ethan?"

"The Westerly will always remain the Westerly Bookshop. Nothing will change, except maybe..." his mouth twisted into a smile, "the gardens could expand a little. In fact, we could landscape this whole area so the road into Motham is an oasis."

"What? Oh Ethan. You mean that?"

"You think I would put an airport before you? Never ever, Min."

No, of course he wouldn't. She realized how silly she'd been to think that for a single second. Min flung herself into his arms and hugged him tight.

"But the new airport," she finally managed.

"Is on hold," Ethan explained. "But when we build it, it will stay inside the boundaries of Motham City. I've already got ideas. I'm going to talk to the authorities about whether we can start cleaning up the Wasteland. It's a huge task, and one that may take a long while. But in the long run, it's a viable option."

She smiled at him through her tears. How could she have doubted him?

They cuddled for a long time, then Ethan eyed her curiously. "What were you doing when I got here?"

"Standing outside the door of Dad's office, stiff as a twig, trying to make myself open the door and go inside."

"I thought as much when I couldn't see you at the front desk. Maybe it's time. After all, you will be the proprietor for many years to come."

Min smiled at him, a sense of certainty settling over her. "You're right." After all, her father would want her to use his study, not cram herself into the tiny office behind the counter.

"If you're ready?"

"I'm ready." Min took another deep breath and straightened her shoulders, then she walked to the study, turned the key in the lock and stepped inside.

The room smelled musty, but then again, it always did, with all the old books and papers her father had hoarded over the years.

It was just as he'd left it, other than the boxes that had been taken out of the wreckage.

Min walked around the room, gently touching her father's artefacts, remembering his face, the furrow he'd get on his brow when browsing through books, his glasses on the end of his nose. The way he'd smile at her and say, "Guess what I found about merfolk?" Or krakens, or orcs. How he was always searching for more books on dragons.

And all the while, Ethan stood quietly watching her. "How does it feel?"

"Okay. So far." She moved around, touching the spines of books. "Good, actually."

She smiled at Ethan, deeply grateful that he'd put his ambitions on hold for her and this shop.

"What's in those boxes?" he asked.

Min grimaced. "They were in the boot of the car when it crashed. After the police brought back all Dad's belongings, I just hid them in here."

"Maybe it's time to open them, Min," Ethan said gently.

She drew in a big breath. "Yes." Her smile was wobbly, her glasses fogging up with unshed tears as she watched Gingerbread rubbing his chin on the corner of a box. "And I guess if there's anything decent in there, it's best to put it on the shelves for folks to purchase."

Ethan nodded. She got her father's pocket knife and sliced the boxes open. "Move over, Ginge," she said. The cat obligingly went and jumped up on Dad's desk, watching her as she opened the box.

Min knelt on the floorboards, and Ethan came and crouched down next to her.

Out spilled a few volumes of general monster reading. Some kids' picture books of the golden days before The Great War. The usual kind of thing they found when trawling around Motham. But then, at the bottom, Min spied a very old looking book.

She picked it up and blew off the dust. It looked like it had been buried in a pile of rubble, or a cave...

As Min dusted it with her hands, the title sprang out at her.

Verigo te Muto Draconis
by Bartholomew Blade

"The Truth of Dragon Shifting," Ethan whispered. "Ancient dragonian language. Bartholomew Blade was my great, great grandfather."

He was staring at the book, transfixed, his eyes bright blue and unblinking.

Min took it to the desk and gently put it down, then brushed off the dust carefully. The pages were yellowed and aged, but the illustrations of dragons were impeccably hand drawn and colored with gold leaf.

"It's all written in calligraphy," Min observed. One page was in dragonish, the passages translated into English on the other side.

The most powerful dragons to emerge from the volcano of Dolpha, around the year 47,100 were the dragons of the great Saulus clan. Gaining flight after eons confined to the underground labyrinth, the clan took to the highest mountains, living in caves for several hundred years. Eventually, violence from ogres and other dark species threatened to drive their clan back to the darkness of central earth.

Around this time a group of peaceful humans appeared in the mountains from the west, escaping similar unrest. They brought with them transformative magical powers, a green liquid in a golden vial. This magic had been harnessed from the Winds of the West by powerful mages, and carried within it the Alchemy of Shifting.

The humans became known as the people of the Westwinds, and with the dragons of the Saulus clan they set up a symbiotic existence, guarding both human and dragon young from the evil of devious demons and malicious ogres. As unrest grew, with the armies from the north gathering forces, it became imperative that humans and dragons combined their powers to fight this evil.

It is not known exactly how the first shifting dragon happened, but it is believed to have been the result of a dragon and human simultaneously drinking from the magical vial, under the guidance of a powerful mage. Thus, the first mating occurred that allowed dragons to take on human form — to shift.

Certainly, the first recorded citing of shifting hatchlings was in the year 47,750, more than a century after dragons and the people of the Westwinds set up home in the mountains together.

Many matings took place during the next five centuries, and it was, in the main, a time of great love and harmony between dragons and humans.

And yet, alas, just before The Great War was perpetrated upon us, a prestigious member of the Westwind clan was corrupted by humans promising wealth and status. He sold the magic vial of the Westwinds for personal gain. The shifting powers of dragons were weakened by this breaking of trust, and further dark wizardry was used to finally destroy the ability for dragons to shift.

That is the tragedy of the dragons of Motham. Destined to live in a twilight world, caught between human and dragon form. Being neither fully dragon, nor human. Their magical powers curtailed, and many of their treasures stolen.

When evil forces take hold, as they surely do during dark times such as ours, the spell of the Westwinds will lie dormant for many centuries. It is decreed that at some future time, the magic of Saulus and the people of the Westwinds will rise again, and that although it was a Westwind who betrayed dragon kind, it will be a Westwind who will unite us, once again.

Praise be to Saulus and to the magic of the winds from the west that shall finally transport our species back to their rightful status as proud shifter dragons.

Draconi eta surrexi agat.
Dragons Will Rise Again

As Min closed the book, all she could hear was the pounding of her heart against her ribs. Everything she thought she'd known about her past had irrevocably changed, become imbued with a magic that her soul had always sensed but never known for sure. And even more importantly, Ethan was by her side, strong and steady, *her* dragon, his heart beating to the same rhythm as hers.

Finally, he spoke in an awed voice. "Min, *this*—you and me, the sense we had from the beginning that we were mates, it wasn't a coincidence. You are a descendant of the original people of the Westwinds."

She looked up at him, and tears pricked her eyelids.

"The Westwind who betrayed the dragons must have been Colonel Westwind. He killed the magic between humans and dragons, destroyed their ability to shift." She covered her eyes with her hands. "That is so awful."

Gently, Ethan peeled her hands away and held them. "Min, the magic didn't die, it just got buried, like a..." He laughed shakily. "Like a dragon buries its eggs, ready to hatch when the time was right. When I met you."

"When you met me," Min echoed in wonderment.

"We both knew there was a bond that ran deep between us... didn't we?"

"Yes," said Min. And then she frowned. "But there are still things that aren't explained. Like how we came to meet."

"Through Adina."

"Exactly," said Min. "Adina. There's more to Midas Touch Partnerships than meets the eye. I sensed she was—different—the day she came in here. Her coat... and... and Gingerbread behaved very strangely around her."

"In what way?"

"He *loved* her, Ethan. He actually went and sat on her lap. It took him a year to sit on mine after he came to live here, but he hopped onto her lap immediately, and I could barely get him off."

"He liked me too," Ethan protested.

"He rubbed around your ankles. That was nothing compared to how he responded to Adina." Gingerbread was now curled up on her father's chair. "Look at him. He would never have sat in Dad's chair when he was alive." She went over and tickled under his chin. "Gingerbread, what do you know?"

Gingerbread's purr rumbled like a jet engine, but his eyes remained firmly closed.

Min sighed. "I think you are deliberately obfuscating, Ginge."

"He can't talk, Min, he's a domestic cat, not a shifter," Ethan pointed out.

At that, the tip of Gingerbread's tail swished.

Min shook her head, pushed her glasses up her nose. Gingerbread knew exactly what was going on, even if he couldn't—or wouldn't—talk.

Which meant they needed to get the truth from someone who could.

CHAPTER 28

When they walked into Adina's office, Min was flooded with memories of the last time she'd been here, sitting there so nervously, about to meet a dragon.

The dragon who was her fated mate.

That electric pulse that had shot through her when she'd locked eyes with Ethan. She'd known somewhere deep inside that this was who she was destined to be with.

And since reading Bartholomew's book, it all made sense.

Because she was a person of the Westwinds. One of a clan who had harnessed the magical powers that allowed dragons and humans to mate, and dragons to shift.

But she still needed to know why this magic had activated *now*, between her and Ethan, in the Motham City of today, centuries later. And she was sure Adina had played some pivotal role in it all.

So here they sat, holding hands quietly. Tiffany, Adina's receptionist, who today was wearing earrings like tiny fireflies and glitter streaked up her cheeks, told them Adina was expecting them.

Min and Ethan exchanged perplexed glances. They hadn't booked an appointment.

A moment later, the little bird jumped out of the clock on the wall and merrily started chirping the hour. As it finished, it stopped for the briefest moment, preened its feathers and looked at them out of bright beady eyes.

"That thing's alive," Min hissed at him.

Ethan nodded. "I didn't notice how strange this place was when we first came here. I was too busy looking at you."

A second later, out swept Adina from her office. Her hair was piled high in a beehive, and she had a pair of pink winged spectacles on. Her dress was a shimmering deep rose color—much like her peacock coat; where did she get that material?—and fitted close to her shapely frame. It was extremely difficult to gauge her age, Min decided. She could be in her late forties… or she could be hundreds of years old.

And that, in itself, told you something.

"Minerva, Ethan, so lovely to see you. Come and tell me all about the past few weeks."

When they were seated in her office, Ethan said, "It's been a very interesting time. We've fallen in love. Got engaged. Min, show her." He was blushing with pride. Min held up her hand with the emerald ring on it. "The airport deal fell through, but no matter, because Min will keep her bookshop. Which is really all that matters."

Adina beamed. "So the arrangement between you was a resounding success? If you ignore what you thought was *supposed* to happen."

"Absolutely," said Ethan.

"Marvelous." Adina looked smug. "I guess that's all you need from me, then?"

"Well, no, actually." Min sat forward in her chair eagerly. "There are a few loose ends that still need to be tied up. I mean, what *exactly* was us fake dating meant to achieve?"

Adina sat back in her chair, a tiny smile playing on her lips. "I'm not sure I understand your question, my dear."

"Well," Min said, "it seems to both of us now, that our

fake dating was always supposed to turn into real dating. I mean, we both knew, didn't we Ethan, in our hearts that day we first met, that we were fated to be together, and when you appeared at the Westerly, I had this sense... Almost like you knew me, and the bookshop, and... and what's more, Gingerbread really *liked* you."

Adina nodded. "Cats do tend to be drawn to me."

"No, no, it was more than that," Min said, rubbing her forehead in frustration. It occurred to her that Adina was behaving just like Gingerbread. Obfuscating. "Can I show you something? It's just a hunch, but I think you may be able to explain how my father came to have this book in his possession."

Carefully, Min took the book out of her bag and laid it on the desk.

Adina looked at the cover and smiled. "Ah, *Verigo te Muto Draconis*." She leaned forward and reverently stroked the cover, then turned the pages, her face thoughtful. "I always knew your father would find it in the end."

Min's glasses nearly fell off as her eyebrows lifted. "You knew my dad?"

Adina's smile broadened. "I did."

"How?"

Adina sat back in her chair. "Very well, now that you have found this, I'm willing to tell you the full story. But it must remain strictly between us. You understand me, my dears. Things are changing in Motham, but there are still malevolent eyes and ears that would like to bring us down."

"Bring who down?"

"LOMAH—the League of Monsters and Humans. Your father and I were founding members."

Min let out a little gasp and groped for Ethan's hand.

Adina continued, "I studied at university with your father, and when he came back to Motham I was instrumental in him getting the old building that now houses the Westerly. It was my first brokering job, an easy one, because of course the humans didn't want it, ugly tumbledown old thing that it was back then. After your sweet mom died, your father needed a cause to throw himself into, so we set up the league together."

"How come I never knew any of this?"

"It was very hush hush my dear. Very undercover. You were too young to understand, though your father's intention was to tell you one day. But once the wall came down, things started to change in Motham, and so we slowed down our activities."

"Do you mean, The Hole In The Wall?"

"Yes, The Hole In The Wall was LOMAH's first big project."

Min's jaw dropped. "You and Dad did that?"

"A group of dedicated activists, to be precise." Looking at their startled faces, Adina huffed a little laugh. "What? You think it just blew down? It took hours and hours of tunnelling under the foundations to make that part of the wall unstable enough for us to push it down one night." Adina turned her gaze on Ethan. "Your father Clifton provided funds on the quiet, but he distanced himself for fear of reprisals."

"Good gods," Ethan muttered.

"The League was powerful in those days, and funded by monsters with money and humans with a conscience. It's less active now the hole has opened up and there are more trading opportunities. Though believe me, we still have plenty of work to do. But getting back to your father, Min. His shame about his links to Colonel Westwind sent him on a quest. He had heard from a fortune teller that the Westwind family were once close consorts of dragons, and maybe even dragon's mates. Not surprisingly, he could not get that thought out of his head. It became something of an obsession for him."

"The day of his death, he contacted me to tell me he had an exciting lead. He'd been tipped off about a cave in the Wasteland where an old dragon had lived as a hermit for many years. She'd just died, and her stash was up for grabs. And that was the last I heard from him..." Adina's face momentarily clouded. "And then came the tragic news of his accident."

Min was frowning so hard she was getting a headache. "But... if you're such an old friend of my father, why have I never met you? You weren't even at the funeral..."

"I was at the funeral." Adina looked hurt. "I would not fail to send off such a dear old friend. But I was not detectable to human eyes. I couldn't afford anyone knowing about my double life." She added casually, "Besides, I knew you had Gingerbread to look after you."

"Gingerbread!" Damn it, Min *knew* that cat had a special bond with Adina.

"Yes. My familial. Or he was. I chose to free him from his duties after your mother died. I figured you and your father needed him more than I did. Seems I was right."

Min stared at her, round eyed. "Are you... a witch?"

Adina smiled beatifically, as though she'd been waiting for Min to work out the final piece of the puzzle. "I am. And a distant cousin of the warlock, Waldo Zabazin."

"Good gods," Ethan said with awe. "Waldo is Mom's new therapist. He's the best in Motham."

"Yes, indeed. I'm very proud of his achievements. I'm from the city of Selig, over the mountain ranges. The Thrimble witches fled from The Valley at the time Motham City was formed. We set up practices in Selig, but it was always decreed that a Thrimble would return to Motham one day to help reactivate the magic that was so badly damaged at the time of The Great War. So, when I met your father at university, I decided to return here and help him dig out the truth about the Westwinds' past."

Min sat back, rubbing her forehead. "This is all so overwhelming."

Ethan squeezed her hand. "It is. But so much of it makes

sense, especially finding out how we became twilight dragons."

Min sighed. "Why was Colonel Westwind so cruel to monsters, when the Westwinds were bonded so closely to dragon kind?"

Adina shook her head sadly. "Human folly. Greed. Wanting more than he could have. As I understand it, Colonel Westwind got involved with the Jordaks, and they are—and always have been—a nasty bunch. He betrayed the dragons that had been his family's allies for centuries for promises of land and coin. Handed over the magic of the Westwinds to the Jordak family. But it proved to be of no use to them. The magic refused to work for the Jordaks. My understanding is they were so enraged by that, they employed a dark mage to destroy the dragons' shifting powers. But obviously, he wasn't a very skilled mage because, well, look what happened."

"Twilight dragons," Ethan grunted.

"Exactly."

"But for some reason, my sweet ones, you have been gifted a moment in time for dragons to reconnect with their magical powers. I wish I could explain this more adequately to you both, but just because I can harness magic, doesn't mean I understand how it works. All I really know is that I was sent to bring you together, that was my role."

"Who sent you?"

"The whisper of the Westwinds, and your father's spirit, Min."

Min sat with her hand tightly held in Ethan's for long moments, trying to take it all in.

Ethan cleared his throat. "Does that mean... that my family could shift again?"

A shadow passed over Adina's face. "It will be not be possible for current dragons. I'm sorry, Ethan. The way you were born is not reversible. But for your offspring, with a Westwind as your mate, ah, well, it is feasible."

Min turned to the dragon she adored and hugged him hard. "I love you just the way you are."

He hugged her back. "Truthfully, I don't care for myself. But Mom will be disappointed."

"I'm sure with Waldo's help she can learn to accept herself as she is." Adina's smile was kind.

"But you're saying," Ethan was frowning now, his head scales rippling, "that there's a possibility that Min and I could have offspring... that can shift?"

"Potentially, yes. If the magic running through your love is strong enough."

"Love has magic running through it?" Min's eyes widened in awe.

Adina tinkled out a laugh. "Oh my dear, what do you think love is, if not magic?"

"So you did know?" Min said. "When you introduced us, that there was a... special bond that bound us?"

"I let my intuition guide me, as witches do. When Ethan contacted me needing a date, my intuition led me to the door of the Westerly Bookshop."

"And Gingerbread? He kept dropping whopping hints." Min laughed.

"Ah, of course. I did worry that Gingerbread's powers might have gotten rusty, but it seems not."

"He did a great job," Min said, stoutly defending her cat. Or was he Adina's? "He pushed me with his paw to call you, and once, he walked to my father's study door and just sat there, looking at me. Except, that's another strange thing—the book had been in a box in Dad's study since he died. Why didn't Gingerbread lead me there sooner?"

Adina smiled softly. "Because everything has its rightful time, my dear. Finding the book had to happen in the right stitch of time, and every stitch before that had to lead to the next one. Ethan making the first contact with my service, me coming to find you that day, at the same moment that nasty little Quentin fellow told you the bookshop was up for sale. It all had to happen in the right sequence. When love had grown between you and Ethan to exactly the right resonance, when Ethan and Beau had put aside their differences, and the Blade family had healed, then the portal could open. Imagine if you'd found that book before you'd met Ethan. It would probably have just sat on a shelf, gathering dust."

Adina had a point.

Min realized it wasn't just the past that had stopped her opening her father's study and going inside, it was the future, too—her future with Ethan, holding her back until the very right moment.

The perfect stitch in time.

She looked at Adina, her mouth forming an O of understanding.

Adina smiled back at her. "Gingerbread dropped hints, like little treat trails, but he never pushed you, Min. He was wise enough to let events unfold as they should. Seems I trained him well after all." Adina picked up the book and handed it back to Min. "And, voila, here you both are. Isn't magic wonderful?"

CHAPTER 29

An hour later, Ethan stood with Min outside on the sunny sidewalk.

It felt like many centuries had passed, and yet at the same time, not even the blink of an eye.

Which all made sense now, bearing in mind Adina's comments about time. So much had happened, so much made sense, suddenly, about his family's history, about him and Min.

But all that paled in comparison to the fact that right now, here he was, with the love of his life beside him, out in the sunny bustling street.

His eyes panned to The Hole In The Wall. It was hardly a surprise, he realized, that Adina's office was right next to the rubble.

Of course it was. She'd tugged bricks away with her own bare hands, along with Min's father.

Ethan really wished he'd gotten to meet the man, but the fact that his father was also involved in LOMAH—that meant a lot.

Magic. Yes, it sure was amazing, just as Adina said.

His chest puffed out; he was one proud dragon right now. At peace with himself, as though the missing parts of the puzzle had been slotted into place. And he was totally, madly in love with his Westwind woman.

He may be a strange hybrid of human and dragon, but so what if he'd never shift? He'd never own an airport on human land either, and hey, he was okay with that.

The future... it belonged to his younglings, to the ones that he and Min would have together, the life they would lead, to his family succeeding in ways he hadn't even imagined possible.

Excitement bubbled inside him.

No promises, Adina had said, but so many possibilities.

He held onto Min's hands and swung her around right there in the street in front of everyone, his wings arcing out behind him. "Let's fly home."

"Really?"

"Yep. You are a Westwind—for centuries your people flew on dragons' backs."

She looked at him, still a little hesitant. "But Ethan, the rules about flying... the keeping up appearances."

"Oh, sod that!" He laughed, then ripped off his jacket and dropped it on the street, earning him some strange looks. A young bear shifter walked past. "You're not throwing that away, are you?"

"Have it. Finest daisy moth silk and linen. The jacket's yours." He tied his shirt around his waist, then crouched down.

"Climb on," he told Min.

"Oh gosh, this isn't going to be very elegant." Min giggled. "Hope I don't lose my glasses up there."

"You'll be in the ley of my wings. It will be completely calm." How he knew that, he wasn't sure, but he did.

He felt her soft, warm little hands around his neck, and

then he unfurled his wings to their full width. It wasn't the easiest of take-offs in the middle of a busy weekday street, but his heart was already soaring. He could do this, with his mate on his back.

"Step to the side, please, dragon about to take flight," he bellowed at the crowd.

They stood aside, gaping. "Oh gawd, just look at that will you Millicent?" a centipede said to their ant mate.

And then they were off, soaring above the street, up, up to the roofs of buildings above the streetlamps, his arms circling back to hold Min tight as her arms wrapped equally tightly around his neck.

Into the sunshine and clouds they soared, dipping and diving, and when finally they reached the Blade mansion, the lawns looked so pristine, the gardens laid out so beautifully, he felt like in that moment, the world belonged to him and Min.

He came in to land gently and was quite certain it was his best landing ever, as if having Min on his back stabilized his wings.

She slid off him and when he turned to her, her eyes were glowing behind her glasses.

"How was that?"

"Amazing. Beautiful. I wasn't cold and I didn't lose my glasses."

He grinned and wrapped his tail around her waist.

"And now I'm going to take you upstairs, before Mom or Beau realizes we're home."

She laughed, gave a little salute. "Lead the way, my dragon."

Upstairs, they were barely through the bedroom door before they were kissing and shedding the rest of their clothes.

"Min, the perfection of our lovemaking, the way you fit with my body, and I fit with yours... Is that..."

"I don't know Ethan, I guess we'd have to have an eye

into the past to find out how dragons developed such perfect sexual pleasuring tools for humans." She giggled. "Maybe your beautiful cocks were part of the magic. They sure feel like it."

She kissed him long and deep and, as if in answer, he felt his two cock heads jostling for her attention.

He took her in his arms. "I am going to make love to you, my mate, my found true love, the one I've been waiting to make me complete for my whole life. Min," Ethan said, suddenly serious, "I'll never be perfect, I'll always be this mix of human and dragon traits, but inside, I am all dragon for you."

"And I am your Westwind." She smiled, then added, "And together we make magic."

She raised her lips to his and they kissed long and deep as she ran her hands across his chest and shoulders, flicked her fingers down his spine. "I love the way your scales prickle up as you get aroused," she sighed, "how they turn hard."

"There's another place you make me hard, baby. See?"

She palmed him, and he felt his cocks twitch in unison.

As he lay on the bed and she moved down his body, Ethan lay back with a sigh as she kissed him from his root to his tip, his groc hardened as her lips closed around it, lapping his moisture before she licked him like a lollipop, all the way up his ridges.

"It's too big to take in your mouth, babe."

"Just watch me."

He did, fascinated as she placed her lips around his groc, teasing it. She nibbled and sucked and licked the head of his groc, then opened her mouth wider and sucked his big cock deep into her throat.

It was so erotic—she still had her glasses on, but they were getting knocked sideways in the process.

"Maybe take these off, Min," he growled.

She squinted up at him and he removed them, then lay

back and let her have her way with him until he was nearly at bursting point.

But now it was his turn to tease her.

He sat up and flipped her over, then buried his head between her legs, his long tongue forging in and out of her until he felt her inner walls vibrating around him and he knew she was ready to take more.

She slid up his body and sat on him, and he positioned his groc right on the bud of her clit. She moaned and moved up and down his length, both of them finding their now-familiar rhythm.

Pleasure surged through Ethan in great waves. Nothing gave him more joy than watching Min riding his cocks, his primary cock being sucked inside her, bit by bit, as she rotated her clit on his groc, and her little body bouncing on top of him with those ripe beautiful tits in his palms.

It was all—almost—too much.

How incredible was the pleasure cascading right down his spine, drawing up his balls, making the scales stand up all over his body.

She looked into his eyes, and he knew by her hazy stare she was close. He rubbed her nipples with just a tiny hint of claw, the way he knew would turn her even more wild and wanton, and watched as those big brown eyes bloomed with her impending release.

"Oh gods, Ethannnnnn!"

Ethan's hips snapped hard into her pelvis as he thrust into her and she matched him, his beautiful dragon mate woman, until he felt her vibrating around him to the point of no return.

Ethan roared her name. The dragon in him came to the fore, his scales rippling, eyes sparking, accessing his ancient form.

And when a moment later, Min threw back her head, her copper hair glowing, her body arching above him as her orgasm crashed through her, Ethan was right behind her, chasing his release on the wings of pleasure.

As they fell together, he imagined they were tumbling through the sky, being carried by the Winds from the West for all of eternity.

EPILOGUE

Two years later.

It was a perfect Sunday afternoon. Dappled sunlight shone through the trees. A fountain gently splashed, and a rug had been spread out on the lawn in the garden of the Westerly Bookshop.

Min lazed against her husband's chest, which was naked and golden and green, and as soft as a pillow, as they enjoyed their afternoon.

"It's so lovely just us here on a Sunday." She sighed contentedly. By now they'd converted the top floor of the bookshop into an apartment that suited them both. It wasn't large, but Ethan said he didn't need all the pomp and grandeur of the Blade mansion anymore.

Besides, there had been the issue of Gingerbread, who had totally refused to move homes.

They'd left Cressida happily living in the mansion with Beau, who had taken over Ethan's apartment. Now that his gaming business had taken off, he liked having the extra space to work in.

So the Westerly, they'd decided, was where they wanted to bring up their dragonlings.

At least for now.

Maybe once they'd really got the plants growing on the perimeter road area, they'd build a house next door.

Who knew? They might need more space as their family grew. Min smiled to herself and touched her belly.

Theo had been born nine months ago. Not from an egg, that was a given. With her being human, conception had been tricky, with a fair bit of mage intervention. But, the surprise—not disappointment—the *surprise* was that Theo was definitely dragon. In fact, he was the most dragonish twilight dragon ever to be born—he had hardly any human characteristics at all. Which was very odd, considering Min was human.

Luckily, even Cressida hadn't been disappointed, and Ethan certainly wasn't. He adored every one of Theo's green and golden scales.

"Shall I go get some iced tea?" Ethan asked now.

"Sure, there's a pitcher in the fridge. I'll keep an eye on Theo." Min looked lovingly at their son playing on a rug nearby, his tiny tail swishing. He'd only just started to walk, waddling on his chubby dragon legs, aided by that tiny tail, and you really had to keep an eye on him. Soon he'd be flying.

The only part of him that resembled Min were his eyes. They were big and brown with a few golden flecks, just like hers, although they blinked from side to side.

Looking at Theo happily enthralled with a bouncy rubber dragon egg, Min went and picked out a weed. She couldn't help herself, if she saw one, she had to tug it out.

When Ethan emerged a few moments later with a tray of iced tea, his face paled.

"Where's Theo?"

Min's head swung around. "Oh, I—" She looked around, horrified. He was no longer on the rug.

From somewhere in the bushes there was a thud, then a scream.

"Oh Ethan, I think he's hurt himself."

They raced over, Ethan winging it, rather than using his legs.

"Where is he?" Min started searching frantically in the bushes, but there was no sign of Theo.

Then a cooing sound came from a patch of flowers a bit further away.

Min parted the leaves, and gasped.

There lay a chubby, soft-skinned pink baby. A fully *human* baby.

He lay gurgling in a patch of pansies, holding onto his toes and staring at them in awe.

"Theo," Min whispered. "Is that you? Are you in there?"

And then she realized, Theo wasn't in there, hiding. *This* was Theo. One side of Theo. Just as real as his baby dragon form. He'd shifted into fully human form.

He hadn't been born with twilight features for a reason.

Because he was always going to shift when the time was right.

He blinked out of huge, long-lashed brown eyes, his eyelids sweeping up. And down.

"Oh, my goddess, Ethan. Come quickly!" Min called.

Ethan was at her side in seconds. They both stared, rapt, speechless for long moments.

"Oh, goddess be blessed," Ethan finally rasped out.

At which their son gurgled and lifted his chubby little hands up.

"Min. He's shifted."

"Yes, I—I can't believe it."

"Will he—I mean, what now? Will he turn back to his dragon form again?"

"Yes, I guess so. At some stage."

"But when? how?"

"Ethan, I have no idea. This is new to both of us."

As she went to pick him up, Theo giggled. There was a flash of green light and he flitted out of the bushes in dragon form. He landed, then bounced along the lawn on his chubby green little butt, tail flying behind him.

They ran after him. "Heck, this is going to keep us on our toes," Ethan panted.

A matter of seconds later, Theo was rolling around holding his human toes, a chubby glistening little ball of human baby, crowing with delight at his own cleverness.

"I guess he probably can't maintain his human form for long, but he's playing with it." Min laughed, clapping her hands together.

"Heck, now what?" Ethan stood scratching his head scales.

"I guess we wing it," Min said. "This is the first time this has happened in… literally centuries, Ethan. There's no rule book."

"I guess we'll cope, the way all first-time parents cope."

"He's our baby boy and we'll love him however this works out," Min said firmly as she went to pick him up. Holding him in human form was just as wonderful as holding him in dragon form.

Ethan came and stroked his cheek in wonderment. "He's beautiful, just like you."

"Oh dear." Min handed him to Ethan, and he stuck a pudgy little fist in Ethan's eye, then squirmed so much that Ethan had to put him down. As they watched, he started to crawl. "Will you just look at that?" Ethan said proudly. "Though maybe with the work this one is about to give us, we should put off our plans for number two."

Min bit her lip and said nothing.

Ethan turned and looked at her. "Min. Already?"

Min nodded. She'd just found out this morning. "Yes, already."

"Oh my gods. That is wonderful—and so damn scary." Ethan put his wings around her and kissed her. "Min, what have we got ourselves into?"

"Parenthood," she giggled.

They both looked up to see Theo crawling determinedly toward the door of the Westerly.

"Quick, catch him, before he gets those little hands on the books." Min laughed.

And with that, the two overjoyed parents tore off after their perfect little shifter.

ALSO BY LILITH STONE

Thank you for reading Fake Dating The Dragon. If you enjoyed it, this author would be so happy if you left a review on Amazon and/or Goodreads.https://www.goodreads.com/book/show/205186771-fake-dating-the-dragon

Motham City Monsters series

Mail Order Minotaur

The Gargoyle Grinch

The Billionaire Orc

Coming mid 2024 - The Kraken Games

ABOUT THE AUTHOR

Lilith spent her childhood checking for monsters under the bed. Now she writes sweet and steamy romances for grown-ups who'd rather have a monster in their bed than under it.

    Lilith wrote and illustrated her first gothic novel at age 12 and hasn't really stopped since.

    English by birth, she now lives in Australia and keeps out of the sea where there are way too many real life monsters.

    Currently, she's too busy writing the next book to get her act together with a proper website but you can sign up for Lilith's Newsletter for a **FREE short story, Rescued by the Orc (A prequel to Motham City Monsters),** plus publishing updates and sneak peeks/free reads.